WORLD WITHOUT CHANCE

Borgo Press Books by JOHN RUSSELL FEARN

*1,000-Year Voyage: A Science Fiction Novel * Anjani the Mighty: A Lost Race Novel* (Anjani #2) * *Black Maria, M.A.: A Classic Crime Novel* (Black Maria #1) * *A Case for Brutus Lloyd * The Crimson Rambler: A Crime Novel * Death in Silhouette* (Black Maria #5) * *Don't Touch Me: A Crime Novel * Dynasty of the Small: Classic Science Fiction Stories * The Empty Coffins: A Mystery of Horror * The Fourth Door: A Mystery Novel * From Afar: A Science Fiction Mystery * Fugitive of Time: A Classic Science Fiction Novel * The G-Bomb: A Science Fiction Novel * The Genial Dinosaur* (Herbert the Dinosaur #2) * *The Gold of Akada: A Jungle Adventure Novel* (Anjani #1) * *Here and Now: A Science Fiction Novel * Into the Unknown: A Science Fiction Tale * Last Conflict: Classic Science Fiction Stories * Legacy from Sirius: A Classic Science Fiction Novel * The Man from Hell: Classic Science Fiction Stories * The Man Who Was Not: A Crime Novel * Manton's World: A Classic Science Fiction Novel * Moon Magic: A Novel of Romance* (as Elizabeth Rutland) * *The Murdered Schoolgirl: A Classic Crime Novel* (Black Maria #2) * *One Remained Seated: A Classic Crime Novel* (Black Maria #3) * *One Way Out: A Crime Novel* (with Philip Harbottle) * *Pattern of Murder: A Classic Crime Novel * Reflected Glory: A Dr. Castle Classic Crime Novel * Robbery Without Violence: Two Science Fiction Crime Stories * Rule of the Brains: Classic Science Fiction Stories * Shattering Glass: A Crime Novel * The Silvered Cage: A Scientific Murder Mystery * Slaves of Ijax: A Science Fiction Novel * Something from Mercury: Classic Science Fiction Stories * The Space Warp: A Science Fiction Novel * A Thing of the Past* (Herbert the Dinosaur #1) * *Thy Arm Alone: A Classic Crime Novel* (Black Maria #4) * *The Time Trap: A Science Fiction Novel * Vision Sinister: A Scientific Detective Thriller * Voice of the Conqueror: A Classic Science Fiction Novel * What Happened to Hammond? A Scientific Mystery * Within That Room!: A Classic Crime Novel * World Without Chance*

THE GOLDEN AMAZON SAGA

1. *World Beneath Ice* * 2. *Lord of Atlantis* * 3. *Triangle of Power* * 4. *The Amethyst City* * 5. *Daughter of the Amazon* * 6. *Quorne Returns* * 7. *The Central Intelligence* * 8. *The Cosmic Crusaders* * 9. *Parasite Planet* * 10. *World Out of Step* * 11. *The Shadow People* * 12. *Kingpin Planet* * 13. *World in Reverse* * 14. *Dwellers in Darkness* * 15. *World in Duplicate* * 16. *Lords of Creation* * 17. *Duel with Colossus* * 18. *Standstill Planet* * 19. *Ghost World* * 20. *Earth Divided* * 21. *Chameleon Planet* (with Philip Harbottle)

WORLD WITHOUT CHANCE

CLASSIC PULP SCIENCE
FICTION STORIES IN THE
VEIN OF STANLEY G.
WEINBAUM

JOHN RUSSELL FEARN

Edited by Philip Harbottle

THE BORGO PRESS

MMXIII

WORLD WITHOUT CHANCE

FIRST EDITION

Published by Wildside Press LLC

www.wildsidebooks.com

DEDICATION

To the memory of Stanley G. Weinbaum

CONTENTS

INTRODUCTION

by Philip Harbottle

The two best-known early science fiction magazine pseudonyms of English writer John Russell Fearn were 'Thornton
Ayre' and 'Polton Cross'. The perceived wisdom amongst SF
commentators is that both pseudonyms were conceived by
Fearn more or less simultaneously in 1937 in order to increase
his chances of selling to the American pulp magazines. And
further, that initially stories under these names were written in
an imitation of the style of the late Stanley G. Weinbaum. Then,
when the 'fad' for Weinbaum imitations began to die out in the
magazines—led by John W. Campbell at *Astounding*—Fearn
changed his style and thereafter wrote under both pseudonyms
in his own original style (or rather, two styles.)

Whilst such a summation is broadly correct, it is actually
grossly simplified, and barely hints at the full, quite complicated background story. The full story of Fearn's Weinbaum
imitations is rather fascinating, and has never been fully docu-
mented. The present two-volume Borgo Press original set,
World Without Chance and *Valley of Pretenders*, which collects
these stories for the first time, is the result of many years of
research. It uses primary sources that, collectively, are simply
unavailable to other commentators. Most valuably, I been able
to draw on information contained in Fearn's personal prewar
and early wartime letters to British SF magazine editor Walter
Gillings, and to his friend and fellow author William F. Temple.
Additionally, I have complete runs of the early magazines

during the period Fearn contributed to them, and I myself have conducted further correspondence with Fearn's agent at the time, the late Julius Schwartz, and with Geoffrey H. Medley. Medley, who lived near Fearn in Blackpool, was one of Fearn's closest prewar friends. In his letters to magazine editors, Fearn had claimed that 'Thornton Ayre' was actually one Frank Jones, who was initially resident in the same house as Medley!

In October 1952, some five years after the last Thornton Ayre story had appeared, Fearn gave a speech as Guest of Honour at a Manchester SF Convention. He was then questioned about his pseudonyms and asked directly as to whether he was 'Polton Cross' and 'Thornton Ayre'. He readily confirmed he was Cross, but had apparently replied that he was *not* Ayre, and that the name belonged to a friend of his, Frank Jones! His talk was reported in a couple of UK fanzines, the most detailed account appearing in *Camber* No. 1 (1953), written by attendee H. P. 'Sandy' Sanderson. Speaking about the Ayre byline, Sanderson wrote:

> "Reverting back to pen names, he does insist that Thornton Ayre is not one of his. Apparently it belongs to a friend of his, Frank Jones. Mr. Jones does a lot of travelling, and he leaves his MSS with JRF. Publisher's sending cheques to JRF's house must have assumed he was Thornton Ayre."

We can't know if Sanderson's account was entirely accurate, but the salient fact was certainly confirmed in a concurrent report in another fanzine by the Liverpool fan Group that stated: "Polton Cross is one of his pseudos, but Thornton Ayre, it seems, is not."

But if Fearn's remarks *were* correctly reported, it seems clear that he was speaking with his tongue very firmly in his cheek, and was just pulling the legs of his audience, for he most assuredly *was* Thornton Ayre! It would seem that Fearn could never quite get over the fact that his secret authorship could have been exposed when the Thornton Ayre byline *had* in fact been invented and used by someone else!

But who *was* this Frank Jones? Did he really exist? Hitherto, no SF historian or commentator has ever troubled to find out. The assumption has been that he did not exist.

In point of fact, Temple's correspondence in the late 1930s contained many letters actually signed 'Frank Jones', and claiming to be that separate person, By then Jones was no longer living at the same house as Geoff Medley, and the letters to Temple gave his address as that of Fearn—Jones was now allegedly *lodging at Fearn's home*!

Recalling these letters from Thornton Ayre (which he generously allowed me to copy), Temple told me: "...Jack kept trying to kid me he was really another person. I didn't believe it...but I played along with him for the fun of it."

In his first letter to Fearn's alter ego Frank Jones (Thornton Ayre) in December of 1939, Temple touched briefly on the personal side:

"Re you being Jack—Jack has told me you are not, and I'm quite willing to believe him. In fact, I'm sure that Thornton Ayre and JRF are too different personalities. I do not pursue inquiries as to whether Jack is schizophrenic or not; his business is his business and not mine, or anyone's. All I know is that he is a decent chap himself, generous and helpful to those who cannot be helpful to him; and an unfairly maligned author. I hope you won't think it is flattery if I say that your letter shows traces of this same unasked-for generosity too. To continue this psycho-analysis, I'd say that this generosity is not a weak point because you both have hard business heads (which I definitely have not) and have it well under control."

And to add to the mystery, Walter Gillings' earlier 1936-1938 editorial correspondence details separate story submissions from a Frank Jones, sent from a different address than Fearn's!

So how to reconcile the above with the fact that all of the published Thornton Ayre stories were all quite definitely written entirely by Fearn? My own careful analysis of the style of the Ayre stories—and much more significantly, the fact that years later Fearn would "mine" many of these stories and incorporate them, in adapted form, into his own novels, not to mention his reprinting several of them in the *British Science Fiction Magazine* in 1954-55, after he became its editor, have established Fearn's sole authorship beyond all reasonable doubt. And the only story actually published under the name Frank Jones ("Arctic God", *Amazing Stories*, May 1942) was also definitely 100% by Fearn. So...was there really anyone called Frank Jones? And what was his connection with 'Thornton Ayre'? I have now uncovered the answer to that question....

Around 1935, Fearn had become a member of the Blackpool Writers' Circle, one of the many regional writers' club support groups which flourished in England, and who were the target audience for Hutchinson's national monthly magazine *The Writer*, which gave them publicity and regularly printed the addresses of their Secretaries. The first Secretary and founder of the Blackpool group was Miss Margaret Dulling, who was later to become a very successful romantic novelist, writing as Margaret St. John Bathe. Two young sisters, Doris and Muriel Howe, also became prolific romantic novelists. Yet another successful romantic novelist to emerge from the Circle was Iris Weigh. Iris became a particularly close friend of Fearn's, and when he founded a rival Circle, the Fylde Writing Society, after the war, she moved to join him there.

Because of his rapid success in the American pulps, Fearn soon became a leading light in the Blackpool Circle, and he would have been friendly with one Frank Jones, who took over the Circle's Secretarial duties in January 1937. The evidence for this can be found in the contemporaneous issues of the magazine *The Writer*, which announced that Frank Jones was now the Secretary, and gave his address as 51 Cheltenham Road, Blackpool—totally separate from Fearn's address at 164 Abbey Road, Blackpool. So Frank Jones *was* a real person, *and* a writer.

On 7th September 1936 Gillings had informed Fearn that he had been secretly given the go-ahead by the World's Work publishers to prepare a trial issue of a new British science fiction magazine, *Tales of Wonder*. Secretly, because a rival publisher, Newnes, was also preparing a new SF magazine, *Fantasy*. Jones had then been encouraged by Fearn to try his hand at writing science fiction short stories, with Fearn subbing and revising his mss.

Frank Jones' first story was submitted to Gillings on 18th September 1936 on his behalf by Fearn. His covering letter to Gillings read:

> "Herewith is Frank Jones' 'Mr. Podmore Does It,' written under the name of 'Briggs Mendel'. I've read it through and made one or two minor pen corrections. Personally I don't think it half bad. If you can give him a break any way it will encourage him a lot. He has other Podmore stories, which he intends to work on. I feel, and maybe you will too after you've read it, that a series of this quaint little gentleman will interest British readers quite a lot. Enclosed also is one of mine which I came across. 'Planet X,' refused recently by *Thrilling Wonder Stories* as not quite convincing enough, but would, I feel make a good English one."

Gillings was told to reply to Jones direct concerning his story. Gillings, however, had very rigid editorial criteria—he was reluctant to use anything that was too imaginative or took SF tropes for granted, in the style of the US pulps, He rejected and returned Jones' first story.

On 27th January 1937, Fearn sent the following 'Flash' to Gillings:

"*Thrilling Wonder Stories* have accepted my 'Lords of 9016.' Frank Jones, whom you met in London, is writing science fiction under the name of 'Thornton Ayre' (and this name *only* must be used in publications, *not* his own.) Julie [Schwartz] thinks he has promise. He tells me that he's just done 'Little God', after his first, 'Composite Man', failed. Oddly enough, Julie believes he might click. Will send you his address when he gets it fixed. Like me he is in removal at the moment."

On 22nd February 1937, Fearn again told Gillings:

"Now here's something else. I spent Saturday evening with Frank Jones—or, as he calls himself for fiction—Thornton Ayre. So his name won't leak out and perhaps queer his pension for an accident of long ago, I suspect. Anyway, I do believe I had that guy all wrong! He *can* write SF! His latest story, 'Dark World', is in my opinion a corker with real thought-variant slants. Can it be that a rival grows on my own doorstep? Anyway, I've suggested that he write to you so perhaps he did so over the weekend. In any case— confidentially—though he seems a bit odd on the surface, he certainly knows how to slap words together. I'm very surprised to find he really knows his stuff. Unless I'm mistaken he will click before long."

On 4th March 1937 Gillings told Fearn that Frank Jones had indeed contacted him direct, and he was intending to give him a write-up in the next edition of his printed fanzine *Scientifiction*. Sure enough, there was an announcement in the magazine's second, April 1937 issue:

"Another newcomer to fantasy field is Thornton Ayre, Blackpool protégé of John Russell Fearn, who predicts he will burst into print shortly with thought variant, 'Dark World', following inevitable rejections of first efforts."

On 24th April 1937, Fearn told Gillings in another letter:

"Here's another secret—for you ALONE and not for any publication. Schwartz has suggested, in view of my turning out work so fast as Fearn, that I become somebody else with a totally different style, different typewriter, different paper and what not. So I have become Polton Cross (a village two miles out of Blackpool) and have turned out two yarns on the Weinbaum style, namely 'World Without Chance' (10,000 words) and 'Outpost' (6,000). If these yarns do click, I defy you to tell it's me, so totally new is the arrangement of the ideas. The idea being, of course, that Fearn and Cross can click simultaneously and double my chances all round.

"I've only told Frank Jones about World's Work—and your secret is safe with him. He wants to know if you'd like to see some of his work? Carbons, I suppose. Maybe he'll write you himself, but if not perhaps you'll tell me and I'll relay it. He's rather a dilatory letter writer. He's down in the mouth too because he hasn't clicked over the ocean so far."

In the ensuing months, from time to time, Jones tried Gillings again, but without success. In order to try and help his friend, Fearn's revisions to his mss. became more and more extensive, so much so that Gillings actually doubted whether Frank Jones actually existed; he suspected that the prolific Fearn (who was himself submitting stories unsuccessfully to Gillings under his own name) was using a pseudonym to increase his chances of success.

In this Gillings was initially quite mistaken. Frank Jones

was a member of the Blackpool Writers Circle. But the overly-suspicious Gillings remained intractable. He remained equally so when Fearn began to submit mss. by his other friends in the Blackpool Circle, Edgar Spencer and Geoffrey Medley.

On 26th May 1937 Fearn wrote Gillings again:

> "You'll find an MS herewith from Geoff Medley. He lives at the same house as Frank Jones, and, to my mind, has turned out a fairly decent English or *Amazing* type sf yarn. I suggested he might try you before *Amazing* and see if you could find room anywhere in a future edition of *Tales of Wonder* for him. I've enclosed a stamped envelope for him. Please write to him direct. Don't be too hard on the guy. He spent all his Whit Weekend typing on this machine (which he borrowed) in order to complete the yarn. If you think anything of it, OK. No business of mine."

But Gillings would reject this story, plus Medley's follow-up effort, "Carcinoma Menace".

On June 10th 1937 Fearn reported to Gillings:

> "Julie thinks that 'World Without Chance,' Cross' first effort, is a first class effort and remarkably like Weinbaum. Same applies to 'Chameleon Planet,' which I've just completed. If Cross should prove more of a hit than Fearn I'll be tickled to death!"

Fearn wrote to Gillings again on 19th June 1937:

> "I saw Frank Jones the other day and so far his yarns haven't clicked in the US, because they're too simple. I've read them through and I think they're pretty good for England. I'm attaching their synopses also. If you think them worthy I'll get him to send them on."

I managed to trace and contact Geoffrey Medley a number of years ago, and he told me how he had come to know Fearn:

"Fresh from school at the age of fourteen, I reported to 15, Birley Street, Blackpool, to take up the duties of junior office boy to the pompous Mr. John W. Roberts, Solicitor, Town Councillor and drunkard...."

Geoff went on to identify the other staff members, including the senior office boy, the common law clerk, the secretary and cashier. He continued:

"...During my five years at Birley Street (we moved from No.15 to No.16, across the road) other junior office boys came and went.... It was some time before I came to know the part-time typist. Full-time there was Marjorie Nixon, plus another girl whose name I forget. But this man was of another world. He showed no knowledge of law, no interest in the clients at the practice, and he seldom spoke to anybody. At irregular intervals he just was there, hawk-nosed, smouldering-eyed, apparently unaware of his surroundings. Usually a cigarette dangled from one corner of his mouth, and one eye was half-closed against its rising smoke, as two fingers of each hand pounded the keys of the big, brief-carriage typewriter, churning out abstracts of Title—long, rambling documents—faster than the girls could type with five fingers, and faster than I have ever heard a man type.

"This was John Francis Russell Fearn.

"Gradually 1 came to know that he did our typing jobs just to eke out, and that his main occupation was writing magazine stories. This was exciting news to a boy who had always been top of his classes in English and who vaguely felt that his own best hope of success was to be a writer. And when Jack learned this he was more than helpful. I came to know *Amazing Stories* and *Astounding Stories*, and his contributions to them....

"I went to his house and used his typewriter to rattle out my own attempts at science fiction stories, which he read through and said were in his opinion worthy of publication. The magazine editors never agreed. In retrospect 1 think the yarns were too juvenile. The only one I remember now *['Carcinoma Menace'—editor]* was about a cancer sufferer in whom the malignant cells, treated with radiation in an effort to kill them, reacted rather unexpectedly. The radiation triggered off mutations in the cells, and the chap finished up with an intelligent being—malignant, of course—inside him, and taking over. The science was suitably blinding, but the fiction, I fear, was rather lame." *[In point of fact, this plot seems to be an uncanny anticipation of one used by John Kippax (John Hynam) in his powerful short story "It" a full twenty years later in* Nebula, *November 1958 issue!—editor]*

"Sometimes we took a break from writing, largely at Jack's mother's instigation, and we all three played Bezique, watched by 'Benjie,' their wire-haired terrier."

By then Medley had joined the Blackpool Writers Circle, where he would also do a stint as Secretary later in 1938 (taking over from Fearn, who had succeeded the now departed Jones). Geoff recalled these days thusly:

"Coming back to the period when I was typing my MSS at the Fearn house, I recall that Jack was working on a 'straight' novel in the intervals between writing his science fiction potboilers. It was called *Little Winter*, and dealt with Blackpool seen from the resident's viewpoint. I don't remember his completing it."

{Fearn did *in fact complete this during the war, and entrusted it to a literary agency. Unfortunately it never sold, and the MSS was inadvertently destroyed following the death of his widow in 1982—editor}.*

"Jack and I were members of the Blackpool Writers' Circle, which met on one evening each week in Jenkinson's café, in Talbot Square. Jack was then the only full-time writer in the membership."

Other members whom Geoff recalled included Edgar Spencer and Arthur Waterhouse Painter ("whose legs were paralyzed". *[Painter became a particular friend of Fearn and his mother, and was a very successful writer of juvenile fiction after the war; he also appeared in the* Vargo Statten/British SF Magazine—*editor.]* Geoff continued his reminiscences:

"The Misses Howe were our most regular attendees. One sister, innocent of make-up, wrote for publications like *The Methodist Recorder*. The other, more smartly dressed and colourfully powdered, wrote for more romantic women's magazines.

"We all discussed and criticized the MS. of the evening, giving quite well-reasoned analyses, and being ever mindful of the criteria which the books on writing laid down. All except Jack. He listened gravely, but his own contributions to the criticism were not particularly well argued or explained. All Jack could do, really, was write—and make money by it. The rest of us seldom sold anything.

"I lost touch with Jack during the War, and I outgrew my boyhood interest in science fiction. The brown Bombardier who produced and acted in plays in the Orkney Islands was a different person from the wide-eyed youth who had concocted 'Carcinoma Menace'. Or nearly. Just once my old science fiction familiarity surfaced. It was on Salisbury Plain. One of our sergeants came back from the mess bubbling over with good news. 'You know them bombs, Geoff, that they used to bust them dams in Germany—they were over a ton apiece. Well, it's on the wireless over in the mess, we've got a bomb over a hundred times more powerful than them, and do yon know how big it is?'

"I froze. His lead-up could only be to an impressively *smaller* bomb.

"'Christ!' I said. 'Don't tell me they've already got some form of atomic power....'

"'That's what they said—atomic or something....'

"'Now,' I said, 'we're really in trouble.'

"'You don't understand, Geoff. We've got it—not them.'

"It took a science fiction man, then, to realize what trouble we were in."

In a letter dated 5ᵗʰ July 1937, the suspicious Gillings told Fearn:

"I'm afraid, as far as my anticipations go, 'Thornton Ayre' doesn't get much of a look in; nor, so far, does your friend Geoff Medley, whose 'Death From the Star' is much too advanced. Incidentally, these two write surprisingly complex stuff for amateurs at SF don't they? Particularly Frank Jones, whose style and ideas are remarkably reminiscent of your own. So much so that in 'Dark World' he gives almost word for word the same account of the destruction of Atlantis as you do in your 'Born of Atlantis' (which would be okay for England if it was more leisurely-written and more convincing in spots, by the way), and even chooses the same name—Izma—for the arch-villain scientist, also making the same acknowledgement to Manly P. Hall! Can you explain this, to satisfy my curiosity?

"I still don't realize who Frank Jones is. You say I met him in London. I recall meeting two of your friends; the tall one, who said little, and the other one who spoke so quietly, and who seemed to have invented such a lot of useful things. Is he the latter? I believe it was he who wrote the Podmore story you sent me before Sprigg closed down; if so, he's improved mightily since then.... How was it his yarns didn't click in the U.S.? They seem just cut out for *Thrilling Wonder* to me. Medley, however, wants a little more practice, though he certainly has ideas."

Fearn replied on 7th July 1937:

"Haven't seen Geoff or Frank, but I guess they'll both be a trifle cut up. No matter—the editor's decision is final. Jones is the tall one who spoke little; the other is Ed. Spencer. With regard to Jones' stories, probably the similarity of style is accounted for by the fact that I did piles of correction to his MSS to try and help him, and my own flavouring has crept in. I noticed it myself. The destruction of Atlantis accounts being similar is easily explained since they're both lifted piecemeal from the quotations of Manly P. Hall, hence the acknowledgement in both cases. Afraid I can't figure out how we both got Izma. Unless with his reading my 'Born of Atlantis' he unconsciously clicked on the same name. I didn't remember the name again when I read his, which shows my rotten memory for the things I write.

"Frank Jones' yarns didn't click for *Thrilling Wonder* because they were too tame and too unconvincing, I understand. Ah me!"

Fearn, meantime, had learned from Schwartz that "World Without Chance" by Polton Cross had been accepted by

Thrilling Wonder Stories in July 1937, but that publication was likely to be delayed for some little time, because the magazine was overstocked, At this point, it would appear that Frank Jones more or less gave up any hope of making it as a SF writer. Fearn may have told him that since he was now writing stories as Fearn *and* Cross, he was unable to extensively rewrite his mss. as he had been doing. It is not known what became of Jones, but it is possible that the clinching reason why he gave up SF writing was that he may have left Blackpool altogether. Fearn had stated that his regular profession was that of a commercial traveller.

However, Frank Jones would have been grateful to Fearn for the help he had given him, and so, whilst dropping out of writing himself, he must have agreed that Fearn could appropriate his— as yet unpublished—pseudonym 'Thornton Ayre', And Geoff Medley agreed to let Fearn continue to use his (Medley's) home address on his 'Thornton Ayre' mss.

For the astute Fearn had scented a golden opportunity, and hatched a cunning scheme. Whilst his agent Schwartz knew that Fearn was Polton Cross, and would keep this a secret for commercial purposes, Schwartz also believed that 'Thornton Ayre' was another person entirely—Frank Jones. As indeed he then actually was! But what if *Fearn* was to now begin secretly writing stories *himself* as Thornton Ayre, also in the Weinbaum style? With Schwartz believing he was still Frank Jones (the Weinbaum imitation technique would effectively disguise the fact that Fearn and not Jones was now writing the stories), Fearn reasoned that his chances of regular sales under all three names, Fearn, Cross, and Ayre, would be immeasurably increased.

How right Fearn was would soon be proved when the January 1938 *Astounding Stories* would carry stories under *all three* names—"Red Heritage" by Fearn, "Whispering Satellite" by Ayre, and "The Mental Ultimate" by Cross! (He would repeat the same trick in the May 1942 *Amazing Stories*, even adding a *fourth* story—as by Frank Jones!)

When I wrote to Julius Schwartz in 1983 (after I had discovered in *The Writer* that Frank Jones had been a real person), and asked him if he had known Fearn was Thornton Ayre when he began selling his stories, he confessed:

> "I didn't deduce that Thornton Ayre was Polton Cross till *much* later! Same goes for the SF Editors!"

John W. Campbell was certainly one of the editors to be fooled. The January 1938 issue of Gillings' fanzine *Scientifiction* ran a real scoop article, "Campbell's Plans for *Astounding*", quoting from a postal interview with Campbell himself.:

> "Included in the January (1938) issue will be stories by Warner Van Lorne, Clifton B. Kruse, John Russell Fearn, Thornton Ayre (the English Author, whom Campbell describes as 'one of the best of the newer writers'), and Don A. Stuart, otherwise Campbell himself."

On November 25th 1937 Fearn had told Gillings:

> "Frank seems to be doing all right for himself. I understand that Julie highly praised his recently sold 'Whispering Satellite' as one of the best things he'd read. I did think it was tops myself, though confidentially how he ever manages to have such a swell slant on the Weinbaum angle will be an eternal mystery to me. His latest efforts, 'The Minitors' and 'Sanctuary', are both real pips. Certainly he no longer needs me to help him!"

Thereafter, all of Fearn's Thornton Ayre stories would be first directed to America, and all of them would eventually sell there.

So there we have it. Frank Jones had indeed been a real person, and, coached by Fearn, he had tried writing SF in 1936 (as Briggs Mendel) and continued into 1937 (as Thornton Ayre). Then he had given up and handed his Thornton Ayre pseudonym to Fearn, who had already created his own pseudonym of Polton Cross, initially writing in the style of Weinbaum. And when Fearn began writing *Ayre* stories, even more blatantly in the style of Weinbaum, he was initially very successful, selling his first two stories to *Astounding Stories*. For his 'Cross' efforts, Fearn abandoned the Weinbaum slant, and instead developed a third quite distinct style of "scientific nemesis" stories, beginning with "The Mental Ultimate" (*Astounding Stories*, January 1938).

What happened next is best illustrated in an article Fearn wrote (as Thornton Ayre) that was published in the March 1939 first issue of Ted Carnell's fanzine *New Worlds*, entitled "Concerning Webwork":

> "Some little time ago a much esteemed mutual friend Julius Schwartz paid me the compliment of calling me a webwork writer. Since then the words have stuck in my mind—and since English readers will be as much in the dark as 1 was I might as well explain that 'webwork' means a complicated mystery wherein all the strands are drawn together in the last chapter to form the complete whole. By accident I stumbled upon this mystic formula in 'Locked City' and repeated it in 'The Secret of the Ring' (originally called 'The Circle of Life.')
>
> "Now all of this brings me to something. If webwork mystery is a new slant to science fiction—and presumably it is—what a colossal field it opens up for other writers as well. I don't mean in webwork (I stick to that now as my personal angle) but in other slants. Consider a moment—what has SF been like up to now? I am virtually new to the game but I've read tons of it since being a boy.

"Here's my reaction. It's all been *adventure*. The pages of past SF reek with curly headed heroes and smooth hipped heroines. Villains have been monstrosities of other worlds. Rarely if ever was the formula altered, save for a few gems from Campbell, Smith, Keller or Taine. Yet even they—though their characters were life-like—pandered to the eternal hackwork *adventure* formula.

"Yes, and even Weinbaum. What are all his stories but adventure? True, they are magnificent adventure with living people—but they remain the same.

"For myself, I copied his style in my yarns 'Penal World' and 'Whispering Satellite' because, in the words of the old song, 'It seemed the right and proper thing to do.' Then it occurred to me, after a series of rejections, that something had gone wrong. I needed a new technique—I tried a complicated mystery ingredient *added* to adventure. It worked!"

These sidelights on Fearn's writing as Ayre were further clarified when Fearn wrote an "About the Author" article to accompany his Thornton Ayre story "Face in the Sky" in the September 1939 *Amazing Stories*:

"...It all started about two years ago when I was getting pretty fed up with poor returns from occasional articles and short straight yarns in England. You see, the trouble over here is they don't like anything sensational, or off the beaten track. At least, they didn't *then*! But times are changed.

"As I was saying, I was getting fed up when my closest friend, the redoubtable dynamo known as Fearn, slanted my ideas towards science fiction. I'd read several odd tons of the stuff and I must confess it had appealed to me quite a lot. I thought there was nothing to lose by having a shot at it—but oh! Those first efforts were pretty awful, My brains, what there are of them, revolved around queer asteroids, men down in the sea, talking protoplasm, and other things usually associated with over-indulgence in opium or heavy cheese late at night.

"About that time Stanley G. Weinbaum was at his peak. Everybody was nuts about his particular slant and so, being a trier, I imitated his style and produced Jo, the ammonia man of the planet Jupiter. This was in the yarn 'Penal World' published in *Astounding*, in 1937. Shortly afterwards I followed it up with a similar type of yarn called 'Whispering Satellite,' also in *Astounding*. On that point my activities with *Astounding* terminated because everybody was going like Weinbaum and the Editor was plenty sick. Campbell wrote me an explanatory letter and suggested changes of style.

"I chewed things over. The science fiction business was getting a hold on me, and imitation would not do any longer. Why not try the other extreme and find out what had *not* been done? I felt I had got something there. Well, what hadn't been done? *Mystery!*

"Mystery! Of course! So far as I could figure out all the yarns were more or less straight experiments, adventures, theories—or, very rarely—a detective sort of problem. But what about a real juicy mystery woven round with science? Something to explain Mars, for instance, as it had never been explained before?

"So I launched on a style which, I have since found, was unique. I unwittingly brought webwork plots into science fiction with my initial yarn in a new style— 'Locked City.' The praise for that one made me all of a benevolent glow and produced 'Secret of the Ring' (which I shall always privately regard as the best yarn I've written so far)."

Fearn's initial stratagem to write stories as Polton Cross in imitation of Weinbaum (who had died in December 1935) would almost certainly have been suggested to him by his U.S. agent, Julius Schwartz. So when shortly thereafter 'Thornton Ayre' followed suit, Schwartz would have been quite happy about it.

Schwartz, in fact, had been Weinbaum's agent, and in 1937 he was also representing many of the most prolific and successful American authors. It was surely no coincidence that many of those in his stable all began to write Weinbaum imitations at about the same time.

In his introduction, "The Wonder of Weinbaum" in the landmark Weinbaum collection, *A Martian Odyssey* (Lancer, 1962) the leading SF historian Sam Moskowitz outlined just how celebrated and influential Weinbaum's short career (1934-35, with posthumous stories in the next few years) had been:

> "Many devotees of science fiction sincerely believe that the true beginning of modern science fiction with it emphasis on polished writing, otherworldly psychology, philosophy and stronger characterization began with Stanley G. Weinbaum. Certainly few authors in this branch of literature have exercised a more obvious and persuasive influence on the attitudes of his contemporaries and through them on the states of the readers....
>
> "...what cannot be argued away are the strong influences of Weinbaum to be found in the work of authors as outstanding in science fiction as Henry Kuttner, Eric Frank Russell, Philip Jose Farmer and Clifford D. Simak specifically."

The full roll call of other authors following in his footsteps is even longer, including, amongst others, Arthur K. Barnes, Eando Binder, Moskowitz himself, and not least John Russell Fearn.

Their borrowings involved not just the stories themselves, but Weinbaum's astronomical backcloth to his stories. This useful framework was astutely identified by Isaac Asimov in his brilliant introduction to *The Best of Stanley G. Weinbaum* (Del Rey, 1974):

> "Weinbaum had a consistent picture of the solar system (his stories never went beyond Pluto) that was astronomically correct in terms of the knowledge of the mid-1930s. He could not be wiser than his time, however, so he gave Venus a day-side and a night-side, and Mars an only moderately thin atmosphere and canals. He also took the chance (though the theory was already pretty well knocked out at the time) of making the outer planets hot rather than cold so that the satellites of Jupiter and Saturn could be habitable.
>
> "On each of the worlds he deals with, then, he allows for the astronomic difference and creates a world of life adapted to the circumstances of that world."

These two new Fearn collections present all of the Weinbaum pastiches that Fearn published—a dozen in total. And, as a bonus, the second volume also contains a thirteenth story, "Locked City" by Thornton Ayre, his first story marking the radical new direction Fearn was to take when he *abandoned* the Weinbaum slant. Each story is annotated with further sidelights, setting the stories in the context of the science fiction magazine scene in the late 1930s and early 1940s, one of its most interesting and dynamic periods.

I hope you will enjoy reading these stories as much as I did compiling them...and that they may intrigue you enough to want to seek out Weinbaum's own stories if you have not already encountered them.

—Philip Harbottle,
Wallsend, England, July 2012

PENAL WORLD
BY THORNTON AYRE

FROM *Astounding Stories*, September 1937

That Fearn—and not Frank Jones—was the author of this, the first Ayre story to be published—is proven by the fact that a dozen years later, he incorporated whole swathes of it into his own 'Golden Amazon' novel, *Lord of Jupiter* (1949).

As the Amazon series progressed, the superwoman had been planet-hopping, and in this novel she adventures on the tempest-lashed hell planet of Jupiter, where she meets Relka, a true Jovian. Relka is one of Fearn's most fascinating alien characters, and he was entirely based on Jo, the 'Joherc' Jovian character in "Penal World."

Stanley G. Weinbaum was universally acknowledged by his peers as the creator of the first really memorable alien in science fiction. The noted SF historian Sam Moskowitz has written in *Explorers of the Infinite* (1963) that:

> "It was Weinbaum's creative brilliance in making strange creatures seem as real as the characters in David Copperfield that impressed readers most. Tweel, the intelligent Martian, an ostrich-like alien with useful manipular appendages—obviously heir of an advanced technology—is certainly one of the most memorable aliens in science fiction. The author placed great emphasis on the possibility that so alien a being

would think differently from a human being and therefore perform actions which would seem paradoxical or completely senseless to us."

Whilst Fearn's Joherc is not quite in the same league, he is not so far below it.

On rereading "Penal World", Fearn had realized that, suitably adapted, much of it could nicely be incorporated into his novel, including his vivid descriptions of the conditions on Jupiter's surface:

> "They afforded him a little shelter from the tycane—technical name for the two-hundred-and-fifty-mile-per-hour wind forever raging from pole to pole of the giant world. Yet by reason of the enormous gravity the effect of the wind on a human being was about equal to a gale of one hundred miles per hour." ("Penal World")
>
> "...as they emerged from beyond the protection of the dome's bulk the full fury of the eternal hurricane of Jove smote them. They both staggered beneath its onslaught, but did not lose their balance. Mightily though it blew they could still make slow, laborious progress, the reason being that the wind, held by the vast gravity, only equalled the pressure of an earthly gale at perhaps ninety miles an hour." (*Lord of Jupiter*)

> "With lackluster eyes he peered into the shadows beneath the Fishnet Trees. In every direction about their boles sprouted the weird below-zero Jovian plants, bearing not the vaguest relation to Earthly vegetation, but patterned in some incomprehensible surrealist style, full of bars, cubes, oblongs and angles, more crystal than vegetational in form. Flowers there were none. Jovian vegetation, in the main, reproduced

itself by fission and lived in the slow, creeping style of the unicell." ("Penal World")

"...the trees of the crystalline jungle sprouted branches of much the same pattern as newly woven cobwebs, rings of interlace, glittering crystal, the outermost edges of the rings being octagonal in shape. Here there was weird, fantastic beauty, every atom of it composed of ammonium base. Even the 'grass' was composed of fantastic spears of glass-like substance, which cracked to powder as the pair advanced.

"Ever and again, as they stumbled more deeply into the preposterous wilderness, below-zero forms—living by dividing upon themselves in the fission style of a unicell—scudded into safety, looking rather like spiked glass marbles shot through with veins of superb colour." (*Lord of Jupiter*)

"Still they watched as the joherc came into complete view—a biped, only two feet tall, with two legs nearly as thick as a man's body and almost fantastically muscled. Further support was provided by the broad, kangaroo-like tail on which it sat ever and again. Its remaining anatomy was made up of a pear-shaped body, stumpy arms, enormous pectoral muscles and chest—in which, according to description and reconstruction at the settlement bureau, there beat three powerful hearts to create a normal circulation in the enormous drag. On the mighty shoulders was the strange, triple-jointed neck, semi-human face with wide, half-grinning mouth and scaly head. A pure product of ammonia, living in a climate ideally suited to it—a living, thinking creature of superhuman strength and swiftness, mentally active, yet humanly childlike in manner—a veritable cosmic paradox." ("Penal World")

"He found himself gazing at an incredible creature. He had the contour of a man standing three feet in height and probably every inch as broad. Short, blocky legs were very powerful. His arms, too, were short and corded with muscles. To this was added a great barrel of a chest, a neck like a pillar and a perfectly round head. He had yellow eyes, broad nose and a fanged mouth. He had neither hair nor raiment, his entire body seeming to be covered in crystalline scales." (*Lord of Jupiter*)

Relka also shares the joherc's passion for consuming crystalline ammonia salts. And like him he has no ears, and is telepathic ("nature's provision to prevent us being deafened by the vibrations in this heavy atmosphere") and is highly intelligent. However, Fearn added some new qualities for the purposes of the novel—Relka has a decided sense of humour, and a unique philosophy: "...we are a lazy race. We don't want to progress. We understand most scientific things but are not interested enough to develop them. Our theory is that the more refined you become the less happiness you have."

Fearn clearly had great fun with this amazing character, and he provides much light relief, as well as figuring in some key plot developments. He was to feature to even greater advantage in later novels, electing to join forces with the Amazon out of his own, queer sense of loyalty.

"Penal World" by "Thornton Ayre" was submitted to *Astounding Stories* and accepted by its editor Orlin Tremaine on 23 July 1937. Thus encouraged, Fearn went on to produce more stories in the same vein.

PENAL WORLD

Mad, idiotic world! Air of absolute poison—trees basically ammonium carbonate—creatures living in a temperature of a hundred and twenty degrees below zero centigrade—

James Cardew, former American citizen, was on Jupiter through no fault of his own. He was in no way to blame for the fact that he now stood inside his enormously reinforced spacesuit gazing out on a landscape incredibly vast and rugged, stretching to a colossal distance, bounded at remoteness by the boiling horror of the seven-thousand-mile-wide Great Red Spot.

Jupiter was the penal world of the system, last working place of the criminals of Earth, Mars, and Venus. And for a very good reason! Once a space machine landed on Jupiter it was common knowledge that, in the case of the huge convict machines at least, it could never leave. The titanic gravity of the planet claimed large-sized ships absolutely.

James Cardew had been framed by certain jealous officials of the space ways—shipped to Jupiter because he knew too much of graft and corruption in high places. For two years he had worked among the bitter-hearted men at the settlement—a vast underground abode of itanium metal, Periodic No. 187, vastly heavy, and the only known metal capable of withstanding, for six continuous months, the unbelievable pressure of Jupiter's atmosphere and down-drag. By the time the six months were up, this highly radioactive metal began to collapse—

The convicts' entire life, therefore, consisted of building up the very walls that hemmed them in, And twenty miles away, where the walls were likewise always being repaired by good behavior men, was the underground residence of Governor Mason and his family, voluntarily marooned on this colossal world.

Despite the fact that within the governor's abode and the settlement there were machines which nullified the crushing gravitation, men did go berserk at times—warders and prisoners alike. Some went to the exterior—a freely permitted act—quite unprotected, to die instantly in an atmosphere of pure ammoniated hydrogen at a frigid temperature of a hundred and twenty degrees below zero centigrade.

Others were smarter. They frisked itanium spacesuits and furtively escaped in them—but they were never heard of again. Either way it was suicide.

James Cardew had done pretty much the same thing. Suicide had been in his mind for months; he'd been on the verge of walking unprotected to the exterior. Then, from the external reflectors in the main machine room, he had seen a spaceship of the private variety—small and easy to handle—fall like a brilliant comet in the dense atmosphere, dropping finally about two hundred miles due east. If he could reach that ship he might, by very reason of its smallness, break the effect of Jupiter's drag and get back to Earth, square his wrongful conviction.

It was pretty obvious that the vessel had been accidentally caught in the giant world's enormous attractive field; maybe the pilot had been an amateur, unauthorized by the space flying committees. Whatever it was, James Cardew realized that he had to reach that ship within three weeks before the violent atmosphere and pressure made an end of it.

Three weeks—two hundred miles across Jupiter's terrible terrain. To escape the prison had not been difficult. It was now that the difficulties began.

Cardew's gray eyes were grim behind the six-inch, unbreakable glass of his helmet; his lean, powerful face was set in grimly determined lines, the lines of a man accustomed, by now, to bearing inexorable strain. For every step he took he was forced to raise a weight about three times in excess of normal, including his densely heavy spacesuit, so designed as to exclude external and maintain internal pressures.

Even so, being a one hundred and sixty eight-pound man, he

weighed four hundred and forty-eight pounds on Jupiter, with his space suit and heavy equipment added to it. It made of his body a vastly heavy, aching machine.

He took stock of his position from behind the protection of two upjutting rocks of tremendously dense material. They afforded him a little shelter from the *tycane*—technical name for the vast two hundred and fifty mile-per-hour wind forever raging from pole to pole of the giant world. Yet by reason of the enormous gravity the effect of the wind on a human being was about equal to a gale of one hundred miles per hour. Around the Great Red Spot, the one remaining portion of Jupiter still un-solidified, despite the frigid cold of the rest of the surface, the *tycane* had been known to reach the incredible velocity of over four hundred miles per hour—but then the Spot was recognized by all experts as the fester spot of Jove, seven thousand miles of bubbling, densely heavy materials—

Cardew, moving his arms with enormous effort, studied his compass inside its protective *itanium* case, and took stock of his direction. His route would lead him to the Fishnet Jungle, through a cleft of the Seven Peak Mountains, and after that along the shores of the Turquoise Ocean. The points were fairly familiar in his mind, but the jungle was the main thing that worried him—how he was going to pick his way through its weird mass.

Finally he pushed his compass back in place on his back and swiftly checked over his heavily shielded equipment—first-aid pack, down to a common container of smelling salts, tabloid provisions, and an oxygen-jet pistol, the only practicable weapon of destruction in an atmosphere containing vast preponderances of hydrogen and ammonia. Not much equipment, but enough in a world where every scrap of weight added to an already crushing burden.

Cardew braced himself and emerged from his protection into the full blast of the eternal wind. Since dawn had arrived about an hour ago, he had about eight clear hours in which to make further progress; with a bit of luck he might reach the Fishnet

Jungle in that time. That it was already quite visible to him in the weak daylight filtering through the writhing clouds signified nothing. There were always the *tycane* and the constant down-drag to be reckoned with. He moved with labored effort, the strain bathing him in perspiration inside his hot, heavy suit.

To the rear, now far distant, gleamed the sunken dome of the penal settlement, and farther away still the governor's habitation. To left and right there was naught but hard red ground. Once it had all been like the Red Spot; now it had cooled to produce an effect as dreary as anything that could be imagined.

Only the Fishnet Jungle, with its blunted trees and weird tracery branches—from which the fanciful name was derived—provided any relief in the otherwise crushed monotony. Even the highest summit of the distant Seven Peak Mountains only reached a thousand feet in height, held down by the mighty gravitation.

Cardew struggled on, forcing his weight-anguished body into the teeth of the *tycane*. He found it hard to believe that the wind outside his helmet was absolute poison, that the trees of the distant jungle were basically ammonium carbonate, living in a temperature of a hundred and twenty degrees below centigrade zero....

Mad, idiotic world! It was populated, too, by creatures as mad as their environment. Cardew had heard of them—mighty strong things with a fairly high scientific intelligence—known as the *joherc*, derived from Jovian Hercules. Where they abided, however, was something of a mystery; since they were rarely seen on the surface.

Grunting with effort. Cardew went on slowly, slipping and sliding on ground of enormous hardness, one wary eye fixed on the distant, quivering upspoutings of molten matter from the Great Red Spot. No telling when it might decide to erupt. It had a nasty habit now and again of covering thousands of square miles of Jupiter with molten chemicals. That, in a landscape normally bitterly cold, produced effects almost too cataclysmic for imagination—certainly death for a lone traveler.

Occasionally the fitful gleams of sunlight through the dense scurrying clouds made the scene even more desolate, painted it with weak, washy colors, like some redstone plane of Earth at twilight. Gloom, depression, and barrenness—mighty Jove had all these attributes.

Cardew stopped only once, to nourish himself, on his journey toward the jungle. He moved a switch on his helmet and a spring, releasing itself, dropped into his open mouth a vitamin pellet, following it with a rejuvenating drink-essence tablet. Neither of them were more than quarter of a centimeter in size, but so potent in effect that he felt renewed strength surge into his aching limbs.

He rose up again from the rock against which he had been lounging and staggered on—onward all through the drab afternoon, battling the eternal wind, muttering threats, in good American, upon Jupiter and all it contained.

As he had calculated, he reached the outskirts of the Fishnet at dusk. The twilight was brief, dimmed from murky drabness into night, relieved only slightly by the clouded glow of the attendant moons.

With lackluster eyes he peered into the shadows beneath the Fishnet trees. In every direction about their boles sprouted the weird, below-zero forms of Jovian plants, bearing not the vaguest relation to Earthly vegetation, but patterned in some incomprehensible surrealist style, full of bars, cubes, oblongs, and angles, more crystal than vegetational in form. Flowers there were none. Jovian vegetation, in the main, reproduced itself by fission and lived in the slow, creeping style of the unicell. There was something almost disgusting about the way the growths occasionally popped noisily and became two, growing with extreme slowness thereafter toward maturity and further reproduction. Cardew heard them bisect quite distinctly through his sensitive external helmet detector as he plodded onward—

Until he gained a Fishnet tree with branches lower than the rest— To scramble into them, though they were only six feet from the ground, demanded enormous effort—took thirty minutes of muscle-wrenching strain. But once he was in their firmly spread, bed-like mass he relaxed with a sigh, satisfied that he was safe from the weird ammoniacal crawlers.

Beyond a wish that he could get out of his space suit and have a real breath of honest fresh air, he had no regrets. So far, so good. His eyes closed with leaden weariness; the tree branch moved up and down in the grip of the *tycane* slowly, ceaselessly—

As he half dozed, the detector phones brought in a medley of vaguely familiar noises above the wind's whine, chief amongst which were the weird, half-human twittering of the *ostriloath*—strange, birdlike creature crossed vaguely between ostrich and sloth—and the deep bass grunting of the feather-sphere, the porcupine of Jove, rolling everywhere at terrible speed like a heavily flaked cannon ball. Familiar sounds all—

Then, suddenly, Cardew jolted violently upright, wide awake, his heart slamming painfully with the sudden intensity of his effort, his ears still ringing with what had definitely been a human shout of fear!

"Damned delusions!" he breathed quickly, staring round and below at the crazy jungle. "Couldn't have been—"

He frowned in bewilderment. A scream from inside a helmet would be carried to the amplifier on the helmet exterior; even the slightest cry from anybody would be instantly enormously amplified by the dense atmosphere. But nobody else could be in such a cockeyed spot, surely—

Cardew broke off in his quick reflections and stared with amazed eyes through the clear patch between the nearest Fishnet trees. The light of Europa shone down through cloud breaks upon a space-suited figure lying flat on the ground, struggling against the gravity to tug out an oxygen pistol. A little distance away a hideous little-headed *sican*, violently strong, sheathed in an armor plating of frozen scales, fixed his intended prey with enormous glassy eyes. It was the largest of all Jovian animals, measuring five feet in length and nearly the same in width. Then it began to advance slowly on its six immensely powerful legs.

Almost as quickly as the danger registered in Cardew's mind, he had dropped violently to the ground and tugged out his own oxygen pistol. With ponderously dragging feet, the ghastly pull of a nightmare's dragging chains, he tried to run forward—fired his gun as he went.

Immediately a vicious stream of devastating flame spouted through the moonlight, momentarily lighted the mad glade with bluish-yellow fire. The force of the jet struck the *sican* clean in the center of its body, sent it rearing upward in a sudden paroxysm of searing pain.

Maddened, it twirled round and jumped dangerously near the sprawling, motionless figure. Then, at another vicious cut across its hideous face, it twisted round and traveled at high speed on its enormously strong legs into the jungle fastness.

Cardew felt the sweat of relief suddenly start to pour down his face. He replaced his gun and clumped slowly forward against the raging wind, turned over the prostrate figure with considerable effort. Jerking out his torch, he flashed the beam through the dense face glass, then started back in astonishment at beholding the perspiration-dewed face of a girl, eyes closed, hair raven-dark, lips pale with unconsciousness.

"Where in Heaven's name did you drop from?" he said in bewilderment. Then he turned industriously to his first-aid kit and set to work with her helmet trappings. Swiftly he uncapped the triple valve socket connected to her respirator, screwed the heavy metal tube to the top of his smelling-salt container.

Immediately the powerful aromatic ammonia fumes surged into her helmet, set her lips moving with sudden revulsion, forced her clear, dark eyes to open in sudden alarm.

"Better?" Cardew whispered into her external receiver, as he recapped her respirator and laid the salts container beside him.

She nodded weakly. "Yes—I think so. I—I don't know where you've come from, but it certainly was opportune." She spoke rather shakily in a voice that was pleasantly mellow. "I thought I was going to make a perfect target for the *sican*!"

"Not with my oxygen pistol in good order." He smiled. Then,

locking his arms round her metal-clad waist he heaved her to her feet. Her face was clearly relieved and grateful in Europa's murky light.

"I guess that was good of you," she said warmly. "You risked your life. Probably you're thinking I'm an awful fool to pass out like that? Suppose we call it plain fright?"

He ignored her apologies. "American?" he questioned eagerly.

She nodded. "By inheritance, yes—but born on this ghastly planet through no fault of my own. I'm Claire Mason, daughter of Hubert Mason, the settlement governor."

He stared at her in amazement; her gaze, too, was one of polite inquiry.

"I've heard of you, of course." He hesitated. "Like the rest of the people on this ghastly world, you're its prisoner. But that doesn't explain what you're doing here all the same."

She laughed shortly. "That's easy! If you'd been born here because your father and mother's social position demanded that they give up all thought of Earthly life and devote their lives to this planet, what would you do on seeing a private, small-sized space machine fall two hundred miles to the east? You'd head for it, of course! Well, that's what I'm doing. I reckon about three weeks before pressure wipes it out. Naturally, there are no small ships at the settlement—only the useless, heavy prison machines, and they're about crushed to powder."

She paused and regarded him rather naively. "I know you can't be Dr. Livingstone," she said demurely. "But just the same, I suppose you have a name?"

"I did have a number," he growled; then, more sociably, "James Cardew's my name—escaped prisoner trying to get back to Earth to prove my innocence. I'm heading the same way as you are."

"Really?" Her voice seemed a little cool. She seemed to sense there was something not quite right about hobnobbing with an escaped prisoner.

"I suppose, since the governor's place is twenty miles from the settlement, you took a wider route to this jungle?" he asked.

"Obviously," she said calmly. Then, tossing aside her uncertain manner, she went on earnestly, "I want to see the world I belong to, feel natural instead of artificial gravity, breathe fresh air, see fields and great cities—New York in particular. It must be wonderful!"

"Not bad," he admitted reflectively.

"To get back to Earth—or, rather, to visit it for the first time—I'm prepared to risk Jupiter drag in the spaceship. That is, if it's still spaceworthy."

"It'll probably mean death," he said.

But she only shrugged inside her huge suit. "Supposing it does? Better than Jupiter. In fact, I—"

She stopped short and gave a little cry, made a clumsy movement backward into Cardew's protecting right arm.

"What—what is it?" she gasped in alarm, pointing. "Look!"

He tugged out his gun again. "Take it easy," he murmured. "A *joherc*, or I miss my guess!"

They stood motionless, watching the fantastic creature that had suddenly appeared in the clearing, plainly visible in the now combined lights of unclouded Europa and Ganymede. It moved cautiously, with a certain oddly childlike nervousness quite incongruous for such a tremendously powerful body.

"A *joherc*, all right," Cardew affirmed. "Heard of 'em many a time, and heard their description, but never saw one. They're pretty good scientists in their way—maybe a bit dangerous, though."

Still they watched as the *joherc* came into complete view—a biped, only two feet tall, with two legs nearly as thick as a man's body and almost fantastically muscled. Further support was provided by the broad, kangaroo-like tail. on which it sat ever and again. Its remaining anatomy was made up of a pear-shaped body, stumpy arms, enormous pectoral muscles and chest—in which, according to description and reconstruction at the settlement bureau, there beat three powerful hearts to create a normal circulation in the eternal drag. On the mighty shoulders was the strange, triple-jointed neck, semi-human face with wide, half-grinning mouth and scaly head.

A pure product of ammonia, living in a climate ideally suited to it—a living, thinking creature of superhuman strength and swiftness, mentally active, yet humanly childlike in manner—a veritable cosmic paradox.

The two remained motionless as the creature advanced. His broad nostrils were quivering oddly, scenting something. The deeply-set, many-layered eyes stared penetratingly round the coldly lighted clearing—then suddenly espied Cardew's smelling-salt container! That was enough! The *joherc* dived like a flash of gray and seized the container in a powerful hand, picking out the already half-pressure-crushed crystals with the blunt fingers of the other, tossing them into his huge mouth,

Cardew came to life at that and let out a yell. "Hey, you! That belongs to my kit! Get out of it! Get going!"

He flung himself forward strainedly and snatched up the container with a gloved hand, slammed the cap back on top of it. The *joherc* sat on its broad tail, licking its lips complacently. Obviously, with its usual phenomenal sense of smell, it had detected the crystals from a distance. Such a treasure trove, though sheer poison to an Earthling, was evidently too much to resist.

"On your way, *joherc*!" Cardew snapped, returning the container to the hook on his belt. "No crystals going free!"

The *joherc* made no move, but his keen eyes followed Cardew's every move as he returned to the relieved girl, replacing his pistol in its holster.

"Obviously not hostile," was her comment.

He grinned behind his face glass, "Not while I have these crystals, anyhow." He chuckled. "Try to imagine a guy wandering around with a bag of priceless gems, not caring much whether he had them or not. If you were naturally decent, would you be hostile? No, sir! You'd just stick around on the chance of getting some—"

He stopped and looked about him. "What do we do?" he asked. "Stop for the night or carry on?"

She surveyed the jungle's menacing depths. "Might as well carry on, since every moment counts. We've got to find our way through this tangle somehow and reach the Seven Peaks. Let's be going."

"Suits me!" He fell into clumsy step beside her as they began their laborious struggle forward into the Europa-and-Ganymede-lighted madness of the Jovian forest—

And behind them, sniffing the ammoniated breeze, shooting against the enormous gravity with the ease of an Earthly kangaroo, came the *joherc*, odd face almost like that of an anxious child, as its unmoving gaze watched the bobbing smelling-salt container on Cardew's waist belt—

The forest became sparser as the two progressed, but its life teemed as furiously as of yore. Here and there a deadly lance-stem, fastest growing thing in the wilderness, stabbed outward with an unbearably cold, dagger-like frond, able at close quarters to penetrate the thick armor of the spacesuits.

Somehow the two avoided the horrors, only to find themselves constantly dodging whizzing feather-spheres and jabbering *ostriloaths*. Ever and again they found themselves hurled to the ground as the cannon-ball hardness and speed of the feather-spheres knocked their legs from under them. Nor were their feelings improved at finding the *joherc* not far behind in the moonlight.

"I wish you'd go away, Jo!" Cardew snorted in discomfiture, and his voice boomed through his microphone on the creature's tiny ears. "Go play tag with the cannon balls! In plain words, scram!"

Jo sat on his tail and waited, cast a thoughtful pair of eyes toward the now vaguely dawn-lighted sky.

"No go," Cardew growled to the girl, shrugging. "I guess he'll follow until we reach the spaceship."

They struggled on again. Then, in the increasing light, they suddenly saw ahead that lance-stems and Fishnets were smashing and splintering violently under the force of enormous feet. Exactly as they had expected, a huge specimen of the *sican* genus came blundering into view.

Cardew's fingers tensed on his oxygen pistol; but long before he could take aim, something shot past him in a blur of motion, stumpy arms and hands flung wide, block-like legs tensing into bulgings of muscle at each terrific spring.

"Jo!" the girl cried in amazement. "Of all the foolhardy things—"

"Don't be too sure!" Cardew interrupted her tensely. "These Jovian blighters, especially the bipeds, have got strength beyond imagination. Look!"

He pointed quickly. The *joherc* had already seized the powerful *sican* by the throat, was crushing, with every scrap of his enormous, concentrated, tight-packed strength, into that leathery neck, performing his actions at such a terrific rate it was hardly possible to follow him. Working against a gravity two and a half times more powerful than Earth's, his actions correspondingly increased in like ratio.

He was obviously lighter than his antagonist, and by far the more intelligent. The *sican* finally retreated, thin, aqueous humor freezing solid on its thick neck as fast as it appeared.

"Bet the air smells even more pungent than usual outside," Claire said reflectively as she watched the brute retreat in the now full daylight. "Imagine bursting a bladder of pure ammonia in an atmosphere already thick with it!"

"I can imagine!" Cardew murmured. Then he turned quickly as Jo came springing back, grinning hugely. "Nice going, Jo!" he exclaimed in gratitude, swinging round his smelling-salt container. "Here are some crystals for services rendered!"

The Jovian's powerful tail sent him thumping to Cardew's side. The greedy, scaled fingers scooped out a dozen of the crystals before the pressure had a chance to crush them, transferring them to his wide mouth with astonishing avidity.

"Ammonia, so you say," he said suddenly in a hoarse voice—and the two stared at him blankly. "Your poison. Good to me. Block salt extra good. Cliffs of it—way there!" He swung his blocky arm vaguely.

"That covers a lot of territory," Claire murmured.

"Yeah, about two hundred and sixty-five thousand miles of it," Cardew agreed dryly. Then he looked at the Jovian in puzzlement. "So you talk, eh?"

"Read mind," Jo explained briefly. "Not very clear—only damn smatterings. Not sure of position of words but meaning get. Read minds easily."

"You're ammonia, aren't you? Formed by pressure and below zero temperature?"

"For years numbering hundreds," Jo agreed affably. "Eat white salt. Water, you call it. Peroxides, too. Plenty of those. And crystals—like I saved your life for. You got them."

"Hm-m-m," Cardew murmured, frowning. "Strikes me as queer to find a fellow like you hopping about on a mad world like this, and yet you can read thoughts. High mental development, eh?"

"Very high," Jo agreed modestly. "I am clever. I have oriental, too. No, not oriental—orientation!"

"What's that?" Claire asked in puzzlement.

"Sort—sort of homing instinct common in pigeons," Cardew explained. "And you've got it, Jo?"

"You're right I have! And I smell, too!"

Cardew grinned. "You're telling us! But I suppose you mean you have a strong sense of smell? Well, thanks for the help, anyway. We've got to be getting along."

"You can't do without my clever ideas," Jo remarked flatly. "I'm coming like hell with you."

Cardew winced as he caught sight of the girl coolly smiling at him.

"Seems to be reading your language quite well, doesn't he?" she asked sweetly.

He looked anxiously. "Just what I'm afraid of! If he happens on the language I used at the settlement, he'll set the atmosphere on fire."

He caught her by the arm, and they pushed on again, followed constantly by the tireless Jo, occasionally directing their path.

He stopped only now and again to break off pieces of unclassifiable crystallized bark and jam it in his mouth. Then, with that same look of asinine foolishness on his face, he sprang on behind them.

By another nightfall they had cleared the jungle—but away to the west, under the lowering sky, there beat scarlet tremblings and pulsings.

"Guess we ought to rest, but I don't like risking it with that going on," Cardew muttered wearily.

"The Great Red Spot, eh?" Claire mused.

"Correct. And from the look of things, it's in a state of eruption. It may mean a thousand-mile flood of destruction. Coming our way, too! Eh, Jo?"

The *joherc* fixed his odd eyes on the disturbance. "Better step on hurry," he suggested anxiously. "Give yourselves gas, I imagine. The way is straight; I know it."

"What way?" Cardew demanded irritably. "For Heaven's sake, pick your words straight, Jo! Can we rest, or is the danger too great?"

"I'll say!" Jo responded surprisingly. "Straight is the way to Seven Peaks, and then to Turquoise Sea and oxygen block cliffs—out to spaceship. That's where you head?"

"Sure, but how did you know?" Cardew shrugged wearily. "Oh, I'd forgotten your thought reading for the moment. If you know the way, why didn't you say so in the first place?"

Jo didn't answer the question. Instead, he said slyly, "Way guided for crystals only. Like hell I want them now. Step on it!"

Cardew grimaced and handed him some more from the container.

"There you are. Now lead on."

Jo needed no second bidding. He leaped forward with astounding energy, leading the way across the barren red plain in the direction of the main giant cleft in the Seven Peak range. Weary, unutterably leaden, the two jogged after him. Then, suddenly, Claire, exhausted beyond measure, could stand it no longer. She sank weakly to the ground. "It's no good; I can't make it!" she panted, her face pale and strained in the Europa light.

Cardew braced himself against the screaming wind and looked down at her in perplexity. Certainly he could not carry her; his own weight was severe enough. He glanced anxiously to the rear and beheld visible streams of redness crawling through the night—searing overflows from the erupting Spot. Once through the cleft there would be safety, but here— To wait until dawn meant certain death.

"Only another few miles, Claire!" he implored desperately. "We've got to make it! It's the difference between life and death—"

She did not answer—only lay flat and relaxed.

Then Jo descended from the gloom. "No dice?" he questioned anxiously. "Claire lie down?"

"It's the damned gravity," Cardew growled. "We're not used to it."

Jo did not respond. Without a moment's hesitation he bent down and hauled the girl, spacesuit and all, onto his broad left shoulder; then, before Cardew could grasp the situation, he was treated likewise on the other shoulder. The next thing he knew he was flying through the air with dizzying speed, heart and lungs strained to the uttermost by the upward pulls against the gravity.

"Trifles mere!" Jo tossed out enthusiastically, vaulting mightily with legs and tail. "I have clever brain and big legs. Strength in large size. Get you safe, or else—"

Cardew couldn't reply; he was too strained for that. But the apparent marvel of Jo's activity soon vanished from his mind. The odd creature, gifted by Nature with a complex brain in which there ran a decided streak of generosity, was deliberately risking his own life to save two people of another world—unless it was for love of the smelling salts. The extraordinary nature of his giant strength became more and more evident as time passed. He seemed to regard the weight on his shoulders with no more concern than a man would trouble over a couple of canaries.

And he kept it up, mixing American slang with observations of considerable scientific significance ever and again—until at last the mountain cleft was reached and all possible danger from the overflowing Red Spot was far behind.

Ahead, in the light of the moons, lay the amazing Turquoise Ocean, greenish blue in the pale light—enormous in extent, pure ammonia; its heavy, turgid waves thundering ear-splittingly on a beach that was red rock, backed to the rear with crawling cliffs of white, frozen oxygen.

Here Jo stopped and dropped his burdens rather violently on the shore. Like a gray streak, he headed toward the cliffs and began tearing at their frozen hardness, until, at last, he wrested free a jagged, splintering square.

By the time Cardew and the girl had sat up, he was eating the stuff hungrily. When at last he finished, he came forward rather sheepishly.

"The eats," he explained.

Cardew nodded as he and Claire allowed tabloids to drop into their own mouths. "Not surprised, old man. Guess I'd never get used to your diet any more than you'd get used to mine. Incidentally, how much further shall we have to go after staying the night?"

"No further. Spaceship right here."

"Here!" Cardew looked round in puzzlement. He only saw the bleak desolation of that ammoniated shore. "Think again, Jo!" he said. "I reckon we've another hundred and fifty miles to cover at least."

"Get wise to yourself!" Jo suggested calmly. Then he motioned, with his thick arm, toward the cliffs.

Fatigued though they were, the two got to their feet and followed him, stopping finally before the argent masses. Jo pointed to the red ground and grinned gleefully.

Cardew started and the girl gave a little cry as they beheld a mighty circle of metal, apparently similar to *itanium*, sunken into the redness—a colossal manhole cover.

"We live below," Jo explained calmly. "Rarely come up except for special reason. Two reasons this time. We have many instruments. They showed us spaceship fall and two people leaving prison settlement. I was told to get the lot—you and spaceship."

Cardew felt something clutch at his heart. "You—you damned traitorous little horror!" he burst out. "You mean you've kept up with us all this time so you could turn us into your rotten underworld? Why, you—"

"Keep on shirt!" Jo interrupted quickly. "No captives. I could easily lose you. Our leader wants you, sure—but I don't. Prefer to help. Very clever and generous; that's me."

"You mean you'll let us go?" Claire asked anxiously.

"You betcha!"

"But how can we—without a spaceship?" Cardew yelped. "You say you were told to capture it—"

"I did; it's down below—but only in the first gallery. I can get it. Now you know how came I on the surface to meet you. Obeying orders."

"That's clear enough." Cardew nodded tensely. "But about the ship. You say it's below. Did you drive it here?'"

"I can do anything. I carried it."

"Carried it?" Cardew's voice was faint with amazement.

"Sure. Damned easy! I'll show you."

The two stood aside and watched, in bewilderment, as he locked his hand in the manhole's ring and pulled with all his power. By degrees the great valve rose upward under his enormous strength until it was vertical. Then he jumped down into a cavernous pit.

For nearly five minutes the two waited; then they both gasped in surprise as the familiar, blunted nose of a small private space flier began to appear. Little by little the whole ship began to emerge, thrust up the long pit incline by Jo's tremendous muscles. When at last it was on the flat ground he looked at them anxiously.

"Down below it was safe from pressure for much longer time than up," he explained. "Better go quick, scram. Very light to me—almost vacuum."

Cardew quickly looked the ship over. It was only dented from its earlier fall. He turned to Jo. "Did you manage to find out who it belonged to?"

"Sure. Two people like you—Pluto travelers. Caught in drag and crashed—necks broken. I read their brains before I threw them outside. Darned smart of me, and then some!"

Cardew looked; at him gratefully. "You're a great scout, Jo," he said warmly. "I only wish I could repay your generosity. Your orientation was right, by the way. How the devil you knew your way to these cliffs from the Fishnet is more than I can figure."

Jo's huge mouth grinned expansively.

"Oriental sense first class," he agreed modestly. "You carbohydrates—me ammonia, but we think regular, Darned good race mine. Wish I could come with you, but your world would let my compressed body blow apart. No dice and deep regrets offered right now."

"There must be *something* we can do!" the girl insisted, turning toward the spaceship's airlock.

"Perhaps—crystals?" Jo said almost shyly.

Laughing, Cardew unhooked the container from his belt and tossed it over. Then, with a final farewell, he and the girl passed inside the vessel and screwed up the airlock.

Once their stifling suits were removed, Cardew fired the rocket tubes. With a grinding roar, the ship tore furiously against the gravity; the terrific drag of Jupiter made itself evident instantly, a drag mounting with every second that the ship boomed and exploded upward from that titanic world.

In eight minutes both Claire and Cardew were unconscious, robot machinery alone firing the tubes. Then, little by little, as the distance increased and the gravity correspondingly lessened, they came out of insensibility, to find Jupiter a vast, banded disk behind them. Ahead was the void with the single green star of Earth plainly visible in the firmament.

"We made it!" Cardew breathed thankfully. "We actually made it!"

"Thanks to Jo," the girl put in quietly. "I shall never see smelling salts again but what I'll think of him."

Cardew did not answer, but he was smiling.

WHISPERING SATELLITE
BY THORNTON AYRE

FROM *ASTOUNDING STORIES*, FEBRUARY 1938

In September 1937, John W. Campbell became the new editor at *Astounding*, succeeding Orlin Tremaine. It was Campbell who accepted the next Ayre story, "The Whispering Satellite" on 22 October 1937 (along with Fearn's "Red Heritage").

The story was heavily influenced by Weinbaum, and had a controversial reception because of this. Most readers praised it, one rating it one of the best ten stories of the year. Writing in the May 1938 issue reader Patricia Evans summed things up:

> "It seems that whenever a reader dislikes a story that tries to be humorous he immediately states in his Brass Tacks:
> "'Was—trying to imitate Stanley Weinbaum?'
> "I fully realize the exalted place Stanley G. Weinbaum occupies in the hearts of science fictioneeers and that this phrase is meant as a flattering comparison, but how does the author feel about it? If he writes a new story, someone is sure to say—'Reminiscent of Weinbaum'. Compliment though it is intended, I don't imagine the writer enjoys being compared with a rival. Just because his story was 'different.' Now it is ridiculous to suppose that Stanley G. Weinbaum holds first rights to every type of plot in existence that is in

any way entertaining. But one gathers that impression from the letters published.

"Last issue, Thornton Ayre's 'Whispering Satellite' was pounced upon by the back-biters. Before that it was 'Surgical Error' which was hallelujahed as a 'gift from Weinbaum.' This issue, I imagine, John Victor Peterson will squirm when he reads that his 'Martyrs Don't Mind Dying' is grand reading, superbly written, clever and—'reminiscent of Weinbaum'."

Although Cambell had dryly headed the letter: "Are all time-travelers 'imitating H. G. Wells?' he had in fact already made up his mind. He wrote to 'Ayre' personally, and explained that, as a matter of editorial policy, he had decided not to run any more such stories in the magazine. Accordingly, he rejected the story's sequel, "Domain of Zero". Simply too many authors were imitating Weinbaum, and Campbell was not happy at the trend. He did, however, invite him to continue writing for *Astounding*—but with a change of style.

WHISPERING SATELLITE

The System's finest basso more than proves his worth—
Discovered—the finest basso in the System!

"Rocked in the cradle of the deep, I lay me down in peace to sleep—"

The flawless, basso-profundo voice ceased. Clark Mitchell stopped humming the tune that had prompted those notes, and looked up across the crude table toward the great, heavy-stemmed flower standing in the Saturnshine streaming through the window.

Sometimes he rather regretted the time two earth-years before when he had taught this particular product of Titan's Whispering Forest to sing. He knew it did it by air suction through its broad yellow face, vibrating in turn on hair-like vocal cords, but he'd never quite gotten over the uncanny effect of it.

Two years on Titan had done much to orient Clark into the strangeness of this little satellite flying round its primary in fifteen days, twenty-two odd hours—a little desert island of a world, bathed in the torrid heat of Saturn 770,000 miles distant. Unlike Jupiter, the ringed world has cooled less swiftly and pours its warmth on its whole retinue of moons.

Of course, Clark hadn't come to Titan for pleasure. He'd been fleeing Earth when the thing had happened—a jammed recoil tube, a dizzy spin, then Titan—with his machine wrecked beyond repair. Fleeing Earth because a girl looked likely for putting him in a spot for a murder he'd never committed.

He smiled bitterly now as he thought of her—Nan Henshaw. He wondered how he'd ever come to love her in the first place; why, even still loved her.

And now? Well, like any other marooned traveler out of the line of the regular space ways he'd done a Robinson Crusoe act and fixed himself up as best he could. He had such food as the jungle provided; his spaceship water equipment gave him water from the atmosphere. It was just a case of waiting—waiting for the day when he might possibly be rescued from this steamy, saturating wilderness with its thick, murmuring jungle and varying moonlight, primary-light, and distant sunlight.

Of coarse, there were *vilictus* deposits somewhere to the north of the satellite—metallic compound of enormous value to Earth chemists in the making of explosives. Clark's ship detectors had revealed the presence of the deposits, but all his searching had been futile. And the stuff was worth three thousand a gram! If outsiders ever heard of it, there'd be a second Klondike on Titan.

At least, he wasn't lonely. Basso, the singing plant, was company for one thing, and so were its weird, sub-intelligent, singing contemporaries in the Whispering Forest outside. Then there was Snakehips, a true Titanian, actually an upright mass of quivering, darting gristle—entirely invertebrate—pretty intelligent so far as he went. His own race had their abode to the south of the little world, but mainly because Clark had once saved him from death at the hands of the blue biters, he'd elected to stay with him ever after that.

Clark roused himself from his reflective mood as he thought of these things, ran a troubled hand through his crudely cut black hair. He glanced at the calendar on the wooden wall—20th July 2614.

"Wonder how many more Julys are going to come and go on the earth-scale before I get out of this blasted hole?" he muttered. Moodily he studied the sky.

To the west, halved by the horizon, magnificent Saturn was slowly turning on his ten-hour revolution, the shadow of his rings, even to the bright streak of Cassini's Division, curving in a gray, arcing penumbra across his banded disk. In the east the ridiculous sun, shedding but one three-hundredth of the light normal on Earth, was nearly at the zenith. In other directions, at varied distances, Iapetus, Tethys, and Hyperion were shedding their differing light-strengths according to their particular albedos.

He glanced toward the fantastic Whispering Forest and listened for a while to the weird, senseless chanting of the talking plants. Behind him, Basso began to wail the bass aria from Isis and Osiris—Clark twisted round in nervy exasperation.

"Oh shut up!" he screamed furiously. "Basso! Shut up, I tell you!"

Silence fell instantly. Basso's blossoms closed up timidly. Its sensitive organism responded instantly to human emotions. The forest, too, was suddenly subdued. As Clark turned to re-enter the hut, there came something else that made him halt. It was something apart from the notes of the forest—a deep, husky voice, unmistakably that of a human being!

"I tell you, Nan, that this is ridiculous! We're heading the wrong way entirely—"

The voice broke off. Two figures emerged from the jungle in the mixture of blue and green lights, one a slim girl and the other a rotund man of middle age. They were both attired in what had once been white, tropical clothes.

Seeing Clark, they stopped dead. He stared back at them with sagging jaw. It just didn't make sense! Nan Henshaw—here? And her father, too, the drunken old rascal—

"Clark!" the girl screamed suddenly. She raced joyfully across the clearing—too joyfully indeed. She overlooked the lesser gravity and fell sprawling in Clark's outthrust arms. Rather mechanically he steadied her, then dropped his arms slackly, surveying her pretty face with the dark hair peeping damply under the white hat.

"Of course this is a dream," he said hopelessly. "You just can't be real because—"

"Who isn't real?" snorted Henshaw, coming up and then leaning back so that his ample stomach protruded. He mopped his shiny brow vigorously. "I'd have you know, young man, that Nan has been searching space for you for two years! We tried everywhere, and Saturn's moons were the last hope. We saw your hut from the ship and landed over by a crazy-looking mountain range. Then we came through this forest." He looked back at it disgustedly. "Sure makes you plenty thirsty," he finished reflectively.

"You sound real enough anyway," Clark said dryly. He looked from one to the other of them. It was real enough all right, but the murder frame-up— His lips tightened a little.

"Better come inside," he invited briefly. It felt good to speak to human beings again. "If we stop out here too long, we're likely to attract the blue biters, and that means a whole lot of trouble. Their migratory period is about due."

He preceded them into the hut and kicked forward crude chairs.

"Sorry I've no highballs," he remarked, lifting a bottle of red fluid from his jumbled equipment. "Try this—it's *sephma* juice. Not bad, but highly intoxicating; roughly 50% alcohol basis."

The girl ignored the drink, but her father rubbed his hands complacently, sank down with a deep "Ah!" and mopped his face. The cork popped—

Quietly Nan took Clark's hands, looked at him seriously.

"Listen, Clark, I know what you're thinking—that I was responsible for you getting into that murder mess back home. But I wasn't! Honest, I wasn't! The minute I knew you'd left to wander around in space, I had father build a private machine and cruise around to find you. I thought long ago you'd met with disaster or something. Then as we studied Titan—" She stopped and her dark eyes were suddenly intense. "Clark, you *do* believe me, don't you?"

"You mean you were framed as much as me? That we were poisoned toward each other by idle gossip?"

"Just that," she nodded seriously. "The real murderer was found long ago. If I didn't love you, why otherwise would I search space for you?"

That was logical enough. Clark rubbed his roughly clipped hair ruefully, "Guess I've been a sucker, Nan—but somehow I never could quite figure how you turned out like that—"

He broke off and turned as Snakehips came quietly in. The girl drew back quickly. Her father lowered the bottle of *sephma*, looked at it doubtfully, then back to Snakehips— The Titanian came forward on his rubbery feet—a nine-foot, upright worm, incredibly flexible, surprisingly human in main contours, with big, serious green eyes and a flapping mouth.

"*Blue biters* coming," he announced phlegmatically.

Clark started. "Then we've got to get away from here quick!" He turned to the girl. "Where exactly is your ship?"

"Beyond that funny mountain range that looks like"—she thought swiftly—"like knife blades!"

He nodded briefly and said: "Piano Key Range, eh? That's eight miles to the north—"

Henshaw interrupted him. "Just a minute! What the hell are these *blue biters*? And Piano Key Range?"

Clark grinned faintly. "I forgot you don't know the local geography. Piano Key Range is merely called that because of its resemblance to a keyboard. The *blue biters* is a name of my own for the technically classified *sapphiritus termite*, or blue ants of Titan. Damned deadly things," he went on seriously. "The white ants of Earth have nothing on them. They fly like locusts and eat every darn thing in sight. Periodically they migrate and eat all wood and flesh in their path; metals they leave alone."

"Mind if I take this *sephma*?" Henshaw ventured. "Good stuff to drink in case—"

"I'm drinking—drinking—drinking—" rumbled Basso from the window.

Henshaw leaped up in sudden fright, then he shook himself unbelievingly at the sight of the humming plant. Clark gripped his arm.

"Come on, sir, we haven't a moment to waste— Listen!"

They fell into quiet. Above the murmurings of the forest, there was a dull buzzing note, rising and falling in beating cadences, the whir of a million wings. The oblong of Saturn-and-Hyperion-light in the doorway began to dim.

"The *biters*!" Clark muttered tensely. "Clouds of 'em, blotting out the light— We may make it yet! Snakehips, give us a hand!"

The Titanian sprang across the room in a little bound, but the only thing he did was to grip Basso, complete with pot.

"What the hell—?" Clark demanded impatiently.

"Help," the Titanian said ambiguously, and Clark gave it up. Snakehips' ideas were beyond him.

Cautiously, they all moved to the doorway—and met a humming barrier of flying, viciously biting shapes, half ant and half grasshopper in appearance, each about three inches long.

The heavy moist air was thick with the things; they crawled on the sloppy ground, smothered the walls and roof of the hut, were black in numberless myriads against the wild sky.

"Here's my gun, Clark," the girl said briefly, jerking it out of her pocket. "Five charges in it."

He took it from her, tossed his awkward provision pack further round his shoulders, then plunged forward. The girl and her father, he clutching his *sephma* bottle, floundered behind him. Both of them staggered in the weak gravity; Henshaw in fact was half intoxicated.

Immediately, all three of them were smothered in the little horrors. Teeth bit into every portion of exposed flesh, tore clothing to ribbons. Clark found his hands mottled with drawn blood-specks.

"Run like hell!" he cried hoarsely. "They'll thin down in the forest because the flowers'll get 'em—"

Henshaw and the girl plunged beside him as he flayed round with a blast from the ray-gun. Behind him in the clouded light he saw his hut already smothered with *biters* as thickly as flypaper in midsummer. A thousand of the things vanished at the slash of the gun, but ten thousand refilled the gap.

Snakehips came slithering up, still holding Basso. "Basso help!" he cried in triumph. "Watch!"

He charged fearlessly through the thick of the flying mass, and for the first time Clark saw the idea, wondered why it had escaped him before. The singing flowers possessed lethal properties, a natural protection of nature against the frightful blue termite scourge. As an Earthly plant absorbs carbon dioxide and chemically alters it to its own uses, so the more intelligent plants of Titan utilized similar methods, but for protection—simply another facet of nature's endless adaptability.

Basso drew in a tremendous draft of the heavy atmosphere that set his vocal cord stem and face bulging—then he suddenly exhaled an evil-smelling vapor, the oxygen converted into a different molecular construction and highly poisonous. It was so strong it made both Clark and Snakehips stagger dizzily. But the scheme was successful. The *biters* fell quickly away from that mephitic area.

Again and again Basso inhaled and exhaled, and little by little the bitten, aching party staggered into the forest's depths. Here the attack fell away; the air was heavy with the stench of fetid vapors from the countless hundreds of singing flowers, all of them emulating Basso's methods.

They sank down breathlessly on the curious, spongy

amalgam that was the ground. The vapors were less mephitic—their heads began to clear. Clark studied the innumerable blood spots on his bare skin.

"Poisonous?" the girl questioned, surveying her own bites.

He shook his head. "Fortunately, no. The termites overcome their prey by biting it in pieces; it's their only method. No venom. They scarcely need it," he added bitterly.

"Nice place to come to!" growled Henshaw argumentatively. "I've seen *zinrota* on Ganymede and *johercs* on Jupiter, but this lot's got 'em beat." He braced his nerves with a further draft of *sephma* juice, then peered hazily round the clearing. Finally he looked at the sinking sun. "Say, whadda we do when it gets dark?"

"It's never dark," Clark answered him. "One moon or the other is always over the horizon, so is some part of Saturn. We'll have light enough—and I think you'd better lay off that juice!" he went on seriously. "You're getting tight!"

"S' what? At leasht I'm happy," Henshaw grunted, and took another drink. Then he put the cork back in the bottle and closed one eye speculatively. He looked up again as Snakehips began to reveal signs of uneasiness.

He flexed his absurd body into all manner of positions in an effort to convey his alarm.

"What is it?" Clark asked sharply. He knew the Titanian's quick, natural ability to detect the unusual on his own planet.

"Ground-shift," he said awkwardly, stumbling over the unaccustomed words. "Ground-shift—"

"Ye're not foolin' me," Henshaw said complacently, half asleep. "It's another of—hup!—your funny names!"

Clark shook his head worriedly. He began to speak, then paused as Basso, standing in his pot near by, suddenly raised his beautiful petalled face and began to sing:

"Sailor beware, sailor take care—danger is near so beware, beware— Many brave hearts are asleep in the deep—"

Clark looked round him quickly, the girl with him. Basso wasn't singing that famous song for the sake of it; something had inspired it. Danger, obviously. Where? Clark looked at the other singing blossoms on every side. Their petalled faces were dosing up in readiness for something unpleasant. Basso did likewise when he'd rumbled a final. "Be—ware!"

Snakehips pranced frantically up and down. "Ground-shift!" he nearly screamed—then at a sudden quaking along the very floor of the jungle it dawned on Clark what was implied, Ground-shift! Earthquake! They were common on this insubstantial little moon with its plasmic upper crust and almost eternally shifting and changing under-stratum.

He was on his feet in an instant, briefly explained. The girl clutched his arm in dumb terror as a low rumbling growled under their feet and the huge blossoms of the singing plants began to quiver perceptibly.

"'What *is* this—?" Henshaw demanded in irritation, getting to his feet—but his sentence was cut short as the ground suddenly pitched mightily and hurled him, *sephma* bottle and all, nearly twenty yards away in the weak gravity.

Clark clutched the girl and reeled helplessly away with her. They narrowly missed a falling section of singing plants, and got shakily to their feet in the midst of dense undergrowth.

Again and again the ground heaved. It was impossible to keep upright. In normal times the gravity was tricky enough; in a quake one was utterly at its mercy. Helplessly, clutching each other frantically, they spun round and round, came up hard against a natural tree and then whirled on again, caught now in the grip of a surging, super-heated wind.

"What about father?" the girl cried huskily, bracing herself for a moment. She raised her voice and screamed: "Father!"

There was no response from the lashing, collapsing vegetation. A row of singing plants went down with a twang like badly played harps. Of Henshaw, Basso, or Snakehips there was no sign.

Clark began to speak to the distressed girl, but he was interrupted by yet another convulsion. The ground rippled again. Slipping and sliding, they escaped the very edges of a suddenly parting, newborn fifty-foot chasm. There, ground and air heaved and twisted in a million insane furies. Half jumping, half falling, Clark and the girl blundered into the crumbling jungle's remoter depths—

Then suddenly—so suddenly it was almost a shock—everything was still. Broken branches creaked. The wind ceased, the concussions stopped. Half uprooted plants drooped sadly, others toppled over with dull tinkling sounds as their roots snapped—

Nan sobbed unashamedly. "Oh, Clark, do you think that father was—?" She couldn't finish. She buried her head on his chest.

Megaphoning his palms, he yelled at the top of his voice. As before, there was no answer—but his eyes saw something over the more distant, remaining trees that he kept to himself. A flock of *blue biters* were buzzing in a solid cloud over a solitary spot.

The flowers there had died in the quake—and the termites had nothing to oppose them. If Henshaw had survived the quake—which seemed unlikely from his silence—the *blue biters* would get him anyhow. Nor was it possible to get across that fifty-foot chasm in time to save him.

Clark successfully concealed a shudder as he turned to the girl, raised her tear-stained face. "We've got to face it, Nan," he said gently. "Come on—chin up!"

Her lips quivered in a futile effort to smile. In silence she walked along beside him. Fifteen minutes later they left the remains of Whispering Forest and came out onto the Saturn-lit plain leading to the coldly white, perfectly even mountain range so fantastically named the Piano Keys.

Clark came to a halt and silently studied the stars, checking his direction for due north. As he had expected, the path lay through the Cleft of the Scissors—but when he came to look for it in the varied lights it wasn't there.

He stared intently, sudden fear at his heart. If the forked cleft was blocked, it meant climbing the Piano Keys, and that wasn't possible without equipment. Else circumnavigating Titan itself, which was as difficult.

Laying a hand on the girl's arm he said worriedly, "You're quite sure you brought your ship down beyond the Range?"

She nodded miserably. "Of course. We came through the Cleft—"

"That's just the trouble; I believe the quake's blocked it up. Come on."

The distance to the Piano Keys was probably five miles; the varied lights and changing shadows precluded any sureness, Clark judged that they reached the base of the lofty, upflung heights an hour later. Stopping, he looked round him in utter amazement.

The whole topography had changed. The Cleft of the Scissors had gone, yes, but in its stead was a gulf going down to an unknown depth, its floor lost in abysmal dark. To get through the range meant descending into that abyss and then traversing its floor.

Clark looked at the girl quickly. She was dry-eyed now; something of the sadness had gone from her face with the need to face this new problem.

"Down there?" she questioned, and he nodded gravely.

"Only way, I'm afraid. I'll go first. Watch your step. With a depth like this, despite the slight gravity, you could easily break your neck. Here goes!"

He eased himself cautiously over the edge to the first ledge and assisted the girl down. The entire great escarpment was fortunately on a slight incline; otherwise descending it would have been an impossibility. Even as it was, every move called for infinite caution. For one thing, the innumerable rocks that formed the ledges were by no means stable; for another, the constantly conflicting light rendered judgment deceptive.

Two hundred feet down the descent, the slanting light of the moons and Saturn ceased. The two were obliged to stumble downward through a cold gloom, so cold it was biting in intensity through their thin, torn clothes, Clearly, the wind was blowing from some internal point of the satellite's cold interior—a contradiction only made possible by external warmth and internal cold.

After an apparent age of struggling, the girl suddenly stopped and pointed below.

"Look. Clark! What's that?"

He looked in puzzlement at a long line gleaming and sparkling faintly in the brilliance of the overhead stars. It almost resembled ice-facets, yet he knew that couldn't be. The air, though cold, was not down to freezing point. Besides, there was no water worth mentioning at this depth. What there was lay on the surface.

"No idea," he confessed at last, and resumed the descent.

It took them another slipping, fumbling thirty minutes to reach the chasm bottom. In silence they stood looking up at the lofty wall beside them, its upper half painted by the Saturnshine, then they moved to that long line of brightness.

The moment they reached it, Clark only glanced at it, then let out a yell that echoed and re-echoed between the towering walls.

"It's *vilictus*! A whole vein of it!"

"And?" Nan asked, unimpressed.

"And it's worth three thousand dollars a gram!" he said in rapture. "Oh, boy, think of it! Untold wealth! Just what I need to put me right when I get back to Earth. It took every penny I had to hire that spaceship of mine—I knew this darned stuff was northward somewhere, but I could never find it. Obviously below surface, and the quake revealed it."

He tugged out the ray gun from his pocket and fired. Great chunks of the brittle, diamond-like substance sailed through the air. The noise of the explosion boomed and rumbled to the heights above.

Clark began to jam his pockets with the stuff. The girl did likewise, filling the provision packs as well. By the time they had finished, they couldn't possibly estimate the worth of what they had, and by interplanetary law it was all theirs, though the vein itself would belong to America, since that was Clark's birthplace.

They went on again at length along the ever-rising chasm floor, stopping only once to rest and eat. Then forward once more until at length they reached the level plain beyond the Piano Keys. Not very far away stood the deserted space machine.

"We made it," Clark said very quietly,

Nan agreed in a low voice; he knew what she was thinking— Then he looked up sharply as a fairly large pebble dropped from the heights and struck him a glancing blow on the shoulder. In the slight gravitation it was trivial, but—

"Great heavens, look!" he shouted desperately, pointing upward.

The girl only glanced, but immediately she screamed. An avalanche was beginning! Part of those lofty mountain heights, evidently shifted by the recent quake, was breaking free. Stones, boulders, and dust were falling with apparent slowness—but by the time they reached the ground they would be traveling at dangerous velocity.

"Back! Back down the chasm!" Clark yelled. He clutched the girl's arm as he spoke and they hurled themselves at top speed down the incline up which they'd come.

Even as they ran, the first stones thudded and hammered around them. One hit the girl on the back and sent her sprawling on her face, but she was up again almost instantly, running as never before, until at last sheer lack of breath brought her to a gasping halt. Panting, Clark stopped beside her.

They looked back just in time to see numberless tons of white, powdered rock come crashing down at the far end of the incline, rocking the very floor with the concussion, spreading a vast choking haze of dust that set them coughing furiously. Then with the minutes, the disturbance began to settle.

"Gosh, that was close!" Clark breathed, his face tense and dusty in the reflected starshine. "Good job it didn't block the chasm opening. Only fallen to one side of it."

"Think the ship will be all right?" the girl questioned anxiously.

"No reason why not. It was a good distance from the line of fall."

They turned to return up the slope, then they paused in complete bewilderment. Clearly to their ears came singing—clear cut and profoundly deep, echoing against the walls!

"—and all day long the precious draft I'm drinking—drinking—drinking—"

"Basso!" Nan gulped in amazed relief. Then she frowned. "But how did he get this far? He can't walk—"

"Unless Snakehips—" Clark began, but he paused as an undeniable human voice, congested with liquor and much fainter, tried to take up the same refrain and failed miserably.

"It's father!" the girl screamed hysterically. "It's father! He's alive!" She shouted hoarsely, "Father, is that you?"

A reply floated out of the darknesses of the chasm, far down the long incline.

"Course itsh me, girlie. An' why shouldn't it be, I'd like to know? Aw, c'm on now, letsh have it again—I'm drinking, drinking, drink—" He finished in a throaty gurgle.

"What in Heaven—?" Nan started in bewilderment, then at that moment a figure came reeling into view, a figure in soiled white, hat on the back of his head, shiny face faintly visible. In one hand he clutched the now empty bottle of *sephma* juice, and in the other the pot containing the deeply singing Basso. Something else merged up like green grease paint. It was the faithful Snakehips.

Snakehips came forward eagerly. "Heard shot. Came," he said briefly from his great height.

Clark frowned. "Shot? Oh, you mean the ray gun when I cut off those *vilictus* chunks? It guided you here?"

Snakehips nodded. Nan went over to her father and shook him violently. "Father, listen to me! Are you hurt?"

"Snot a bit," he confided in a whisper, and she jerked her face away at the garlicky reek. "Never felt better—hup!—in my life!" He waved an arm to prove it and nearly overbalanced. Clark caught him tightly.

"Listen, Mr. Henshaw; how'd you escape the *blue biters*?"

Henshaw chuckled thickly. "I fooled 'em! Easy! They bit me an'—an' left me alone—" His eye closed significantly.

"Left you alone!" Clark cried. "That's impossible!"

"Oh, so you call me a liar, huh? Wanna fight—"

"Forget it," Clark said briefly, and signaled to the girl. Between them they marched the arguing Henshaw up the incline, still clutching pot and bottle tenaciously. Once they circled the remains of the avalanche, they stopped again.

"Come to think of it," the girl said, "we'd have missed father if this avalanche hadn't turned us back. And then we mightn't have known but for the range of Basso's voice— Why Clark, whatever's the matter?"

He was grinning amusedly. "Just been thinking about your dad's escape from the *biters*. Sure they'd leave him alone! He's drunk so much *sephma* juice his blood stream is charged with alcohol. Alcohol is utter poison to them, even in the minutest quantity. Like—like bathing insect bites with beer back on Earth," he finished reflectively. "Gosh, it was lucky he got drunk. It saved his life."

"And Snakehips led him?" the girl said eagerly.

"Snakehips did," the Titanian acknowledged. "Man here was asleep when—when you called. I carry him down chasm in jungle. Not deep, but wide. Carried him most times down wall here—" Snakehips' huge eyes saddened momentarily. "Miss you," he said simply, then suddenly turned and went off into the gloom of the lower incline, heading back undoubtedly for his own distant people.

"Well, swat we waiting for?" Henshaw asked disagreeably. "I wanna sleep—"

He slept all right—slept until the ship had pulled well clear of Titan and was on the earthward run. But he spent the greater part of the journey trying to pitch his voice as phenomenally low as Basso.

DOMAIN OF ZERO
BY THORNTON AYRE

FROM *PLANET STORIES*, FALL 1940

"Domain of Zero" was a direct sequel to "Whispering Satellite", and was submitted to *Astounding*. However, it was rejected by Campbell, who had made a sudden decision not to feature any further Weinbaum-inspired stories. The ms. was returned to his agent. Meanwhile, in the UK a number of possible UK markets began to emerge, and here Fearn represented himself. To this end he retyped fresh copies of some his recently rejected American stories to have on hand for possible UK sales.

John Carnell was soliciting stories for a new English SF magazine to be called *New Worlds*. At the beginning of 1940, Fearn submitted and placed with Carnell at least five stories, "Domain of Zero," "Memory Unlimited," "Knowledge Without Learning," "Lunar Concession," and "Solar Assignment." Had *New Worlds* been established at that time, Fearn (who was then the *only* full-time SF writer in Britain) would undoubtedly have become its leading contributor under his own name and various aliases.

In its early planning stages, *New Worlds* was 'big news' for American sf fans, and news of the sale of three of these stories was printed in the leading U.S. fan newspaper, *Fantasy News*, edited by James W. Taurasi. The March 24, 1940 issue announced:

PROMINENT FAN HEADS ENGLAND'S NEW PRO SCIENCE FICTION MAGAZINE!

A new professional science fiction magazine will hit the stands soon in England. It will take its name from the now defunct but very well-known British SF fan mag. *New Worlds*. Stories already accepted for publication are John Russell Fearn's "Memory Unlimited", and Thornton Ayre's "Domain of Zero" and "Lunar Concession." *Fantasy News* is not at liberty to reveal the name of the prominent English fan who will edit the mag and is withholding this information until actual publication by special request of the fan in question. Suffice it to say that he is probably England's outstanding fan and author of many fan articles in American fan magazines. Full details will be published soon in *Fantasy News*.

Disappointingly, the next announcement concerning *New Worlds* in the April 24, 1940 issue dashed everyone's hopes:

PLANS COLLAPSE FOR BRITISH *NEW WORLDS*

According to advice received by telegram and letter from our England informants, Ted Carnell's proposed science-fiction magazine *New Worlds* has collapsed. According to a news report printed in *John Bull* for March 16, 1940, the man behind World Says, Ltd., publishers of the magazine, has been exposed as a swindler.

It transpired that Alfred Greig, the London-based Canadian publisher, was a conman. He specialized in tricking would-be editors and writers to invest money in his planned magazines.

John Carnell had invested £50 (about ten weeks' salary in 1940 terms) on the promise of a salaried editorial position with the company.

Greig's racket was revealed in an investigative article in the leading British weekly magazine *John Bull*, headed HE IS GRAND—BUT SHADY! John Carnell was shocked to read the article, just over a week before he was supposed to take up his editorial position. As he later told me:

> "By then I was too late. The company had closed down. Mr. Greig had folded his prospectus along with his tent and departed for his native Canada and the pieces of the proposed magazine were filed away in my desk to await another day. I was richer by a vast amount of experience and poorer by £50 (most of which had been borrowed) but...the experience and the expense were worthwhile."

Meanwhile in America Fearn's agent Julius Schwartz still held separate copies of the mss. Fearn had sent to Carnell. Two of them were eventually placed with the emergence of new magazines: "Domain of Zero" appeared in the Fall 1940 issue of *Planet Stories*, whilst "Lunar Concession" copped the cover for the September 1941 *Science Fiction*. More about "Lunar Concession" can be found in my companion collection *Valley of Pretenders*, in which this story has been included.

Like its predecessor, "Domain of Zero" was heavily indebted to Weinbaum, specifically in regard to the alien life forms on Callisto. The 'balloon bird' in the story are clearly based on Weibnaum's 'Bladder Birds' in "Redemption Cairn", and the malevolent germ-creatures have resonance with the 'Slinkers' in "The Mad Moon", whilst 'Zero', the icy salient, has even clearer resonance with Weinbaum's vegetable intelligences in "The Lotus Eaters". Notwithstanding, Fearn rehashed these elements in an amusing and entertaining fashion, and "Domain of Zero", which *Planet* termed a "swift-paced short story" was popular with the magazine's readers. It paved the way for Fearn to sell new Ayre stories to the same magazine

DOMAIN OF ZERO

Spacemen gave tiny, far-flung Callisto a wide berth. For it was the domain of the shrunken, ice-skinned brain who called himself "Zero"

I.

Clark Mitchell stirred uneasily in his bunk. His space-trained mind and body could detect a change in the direction of the private space flyer; there was a distinct leftward pull, the drag of an unaccountable gravity field.

Sitting up abruptly, he switched on the safety light. Reaching across, he shook the white shoulder of the girl fast asleep in the neighboring bunk. She uncoiled drowsily amid the sheets, blinked at him from her dark eyes.

"Wassamarra?" she slurred, yawning.

"That's what I'm wondering," he said anxiously. "Plenty's the matter by the feel of things."

He threw on a dressing gown, stumbled over to the port window, and shook the tousled hair from his eyes. In an instant all sleep was dashed from his mind.

"Suffering cats!" he yelped. "We're headed toward Callisto! What in the name of—?" He twirled round swiftly, jerked a thumb to his wife as she stretched languidly.

"Come on, Nan, you'd better come with me. You've more influence over your old man than I have. He must have gotten tight again, or something. This is what comes of leaving a souse at the controls!"

Clark stalked savagely from the bed-cabin and into the adjoining control room. In the doorway he stopped, staring blankly. Jathan Henshaw, millionaire *magnite* manufacturer, father of Nan, was slumped in the control chair, half asleep, his protruding midriff rising and falling steadily, double chin on his chest. On the bench close beside him a half-emptied bottle of *teticol* stimulant stood in significant isolation.

Clark's jaw set. Muttering under his breath he leaned over the sleeping man and slammed the controls into position. It was useless now to try and drag away from Callisto; the vessel was too close. Only thing was to land there and then make a fresh start. Another hour would finish it.

"Why, father!" Nan cried, coming in, silk gown molding her shapely young form. "What's the matter?" She shook him gently with a slender hand.

"Canned—naturally!" Clark said impatiently, and the girl glanced at him indignantly.

"Oh, Clark, how can you say that! You know he has to take this stimulant to keep his heart in order. Otherwise—"

"Bunk!" Clark snorted. "I don't forget the way he filled up with alcohol when we were on Titan. You remember, when he tried to match his voice up with those bass singing flowers? Boy, was he plastered!" he whistled reminiscently.

"Who's plastered?" demanded Henshaw suddenly, jerking up and flattening hair he didn't possess. "Whatja mean, Clark? Or is it a fight you want?" he finished, bunching flabby fists.

Clark turned deliberately. "That's a sure sign you've been tippling; you'd never want to fight otherwise." He drew a deep breath, then asked sharply, "How'd the ship come to get off the course for Saturn? We were heading back to Titan to make a study of Piano Key Range, and now this has to happen. What did you do?"

"You've got me there," Henshaw muttered. He closed one eye and meditated; then he said, "I guess it must have been Jupiter's gravity field that did it. It sort of swung the ship round and— hup! Pardon me—I found Callisto coming toward me. Then— then I do believe I fainted," he finished with dignity, licking his lips,

Clark sniffed. "Fainted! O.K., I get it. You mean you got so tight you didn't know what you were doing, forgot to put the robot controls in action, and then passed out. Well, we'll be delayed in getting to Titan, that's all. Darned good job I woke up or we might have crashed into Callisto...." He frowned through the main window. "Pity it has to be Callisto," he murmured. "I don't know as much about it as I'd like. The other trading moons are all right, but Callisto's a bit of an outpost well over a million miles from Jupiter. Frozen world, by night anyhow. Least albedo of all the moons."

Henshaw got unsteadily to his feet. "S-sorry, Clark," he apologized, laying a hand on his shoulder. "I guess I do sort of mix things up, don't I? But I never"—he strangled an incipient belch—"never did know how to control one of these things." He looked across at the stimulant, picked it up reverently. "My heart," he explained anxiously. "I—I think I'll just lie down."

Clark nodded bitterly and said nothing, watched Henshaw unsteadily depart. Then he turned as the girl took his arm. Her face was serious in its soft mantle of dark hair.

"Honest, Clark, I don't think he meant any harm," she said anxiously. "He's—he's weak, you know."

Clark grinned slowly. "Weak! Weak enough to build up a fortune from *magnite* explosive. And that heart business is a lot of applesauce, too.... Still, I guess you wouldn't be anything of a daughter if you didn't back him up," he sighed. "After all, but for his generosity a year ago I would never have been rescued from Titan, or found those *vilictus* deposits that provided the fortune to make this trip possible."

Pausing, he glanced through the window again.

"You'd better get dressed, Nan, then you can take the controls while I scramble into some duds. We'll land in about an hour."

"Right!" She moved lithely to the inter-door, paused. "Shall I wake dad?"

"No need. We'll only stop long enough to level out, then we'll push away against the gravity field and head for Titan. We can't straighten out from this position. Too much momentum...."

The passing of the hour brought the 3200-mile globe of

Callisto to a point where it filled all heaven—a curious outpost of a world, a million miles further out from frozen Jupiter than the other satellites of Io, Europa, and Ganymede. Possessing the lowest albedo of all, a density that bespoke the possible presence of hydrogen, and maybe oxygen in scarcer quantities, the moon was rarely visited save in an emergency. Nobody knew much about it: those who did pronounced it pretty much like Earth's Arctic Circle, save that the Arctic Circle is warm and cozy by comparison.

"I don't like this a bit," Clark muttered, staring fixedly ahead. "We're moving toward the dark side of the moon as misfortune has it. Makes it difficult to see; the other moons and Jupiter don't give such a vast amount of light at this distance."

Nan strained her neck over his shoulder. "Looks like mountains to me," she commented. Then suddenly, "But I thought Callisto revolved in relation to the Sun? What do you mean by dark side?"

"Sorry—I meant night side. Callisto does revolve in the solar sense, of course—about once a fortnight. Always turns the same face to Jove, though."

Clark took hold of the controls firmly and watched earnestly as the vessel began to drop, shooting downward toward a dark mass of mountain range and valley. Ridges of bluish-white rose up at frightening speed. The light of Jove and the moons vanished as the ship hurtled under the overhanging shadow of the vast range. "Look out!" Nan yelled suddenly, pointing. "Look! That cliff—!"

Clark saw it a second later—a titanic wall, a diagonal extension of the mountain range spread straight across the flier's path, towering to an incredible height. Savagely he blasted the rocket tubes, ripped the vessel round in a circle, dipped—helplessly plunged and tore through a huge mass of apparent powdered ice and snow.

In seconds it was all over. The ship came to rest at a weird angle, surrounded by piled bluish-whitnesses that had crept half way up the observation windows. Through what clear space there was, was a vision of that enormous cliff—a long icy slope—and far overhead, the ebony, star-strewn sky. Down here, Jupiter and the moons were completely hidden.

"Correct me if I'm wrong," Nan murmured, straightening up, "but I think we've arrived."

"But only for a moment," Clark answered. "This is where we leave. The gravity pull will be squared against us now. The under-jets will see to the rest."

Confidently he released the blast switches, then instantly sprang them back into non-contact as a vicious aura of flame zipped around the ship from end to end. White sheets of fire stabbed savagely outside the windows, momentarily illuminating the drear, wild landscape.

"What in—?" Clark stopped in bewilderment, staring at the girl. "Say, I nearly incinerated the ship!" He swung round and depressed the switch on the external registers. "What sort of an atmosphere have we got in this dump, anyway?"

He stared with the girl at the registers. "Hydrogen—and another gas that looks like argon," he said, wincing. "Ouch! Then— Let me think. Hydrogen freezes at -264° C, and it would float to upper levels like this. Oxygen, if any, would drop below, freezing at -212° C. This stuff outside must be it...."

He snapped the lever on the sampler and it released a portion of the exterior substance down a chute into a vacuum trap. The two stared through the thick glass partition.

"Frozen oxygen crystals right enough," Nan murmured, gazing at the bluish shining powder. "That makes the external temperature somewhere around -200° C. Nitrogen, if any, must also be frozen; it seizes up around the same degree as oxygen, but it's pretty heavy. Probably at lower levels than this. Can't be much of it around or it would have doused that fire you nearly started.... Argon wouldn't do much," she went on, musing. "It's unsociable stuff—if argon it really is. Looks to me like some other unknown element. Assuming it is argon, it doesn't like mingling with other gases...."

"Let's see now. Frozen oxygen, hydrogen gas, traces of water vapor in the oxygen and also in the blast tubes due to condensation in change from blast-heating in space to sudden cold here.... Gosh! This is no spot to try out a flame, Clark. And it isn't a place for a deckchair, either...."

Clark sat down and rubbed his tousled black head.

"Right enough.... But how the devil do we get out of here, anyway? The jets are the only way."

The girl shrugged. "I have the idea that we're just going to park around until the dawn comes, then this stuff may congeal into normal, though thin, atmosphere. If there's any nitrogen around and it mingles up, we'll be all right. If not—"

She broke off suddenly. The ship had noticeably jerked a little, slid a slight distance. The curious squeegeeing noise of grinding crystals echoed ominously through the walls.

"Hell, we're slipping!" Clark gasped hoarsely, leaping up. "Moving down the slope— Look down there!" he finished with a yell, pointing through the window.

Nan caught her breath. She could see now in the starshine that the ship was perilously poised on a long, sloping shelf of frozen oxygen, extending downward for perhaps a mile and a half. After that there was a sheer drop into— They knew not what. Probably a chasm.

Clark swung around. "Come on, we've got to get out! Get the space suits. Wake up dad—"

"No need to wake me," growled Henshaw, coming in. "Where the heck are we? I thought you were a good pilot, Clark— Whew, have I got a hangover?" he finished, shutting his eyes tight.

Holding his forehead he lurched toward the window, and his very action set the ship sliding again. Frantically Clark pulled him back.

"Look here, Clark, what is this—?"

"It's the balance," Clark panted. "When we move we set the thing sliding. Your weight, dad, is—"

"And what's the matter with my weight?" Henshaw demanded fiercely. "Two hundred and forty pounds of muscle—that's me! Strong as a horse, except for my heart, of course. Now, ever since I was a boy—"

"Cut the history, father, and get into this," interrupted Nan practically, hurrying forward with an outsize spacesuit. "We've got to get out of this ship—at least until dawn comes."

Grumbling, Henshaw stepped into the suit, lurched and heaved wildly as Nan fastened it up. He was still protesting as the helmet clamped over his bald head.

"What about a drink first?" he yelled, but instead of a drink he found three ray guns thrust in his arms by Clark.

"Hang onto these, dad," he ordered quickly. "But don't use 'em until we come to some nitrogen or something, otherwise we'll go up like *magnite* powder. And put these rubbers over your boots. The slightest friction sparks may have disastrous results.... Nan and I will bring along the food and stuff."

Henshaw grunted and struggled into the massive goloshes, then he stood waiting as Clark and the girl scrambled into their own suits. Finally, equipment strapped on their backs, Clark led the way with gingery steps to the airlock and began to unscrew it. He snapped a length of cord to his belt, linked it to the girl and her father, then stepped outside.

The ship slithered a little. The girl came out, ankle deep in the blue crystals. Henshaw was at no pains to be careful. Being naturally big and still slightly intoxicated he visibly staggered, reeled clumsily through the opening outside.... That did it!

The rocking action started the sliding ship into a real slither. With a sudden grinding of crystals it commenced moving off down the slope with its port lights brightly gleaming.

"To one side!" Clark screamed—noiselessly, for the helmet transmitters were not linked up. Frantically he dragged the girl and Henshaw aside, just in time to avoid the bulging center of the vessel as it slipped invincibly past them.

Dazed, wide-eyed, they watched it travel up the end of the slope and there, visibly half over the edge of the chasm, it came to a standstill, supported by the congealed oxygen it had plowed before it.

Clark got up and flicked on his communicator. "Gosh, that's

done it!" came his voice. "Even if we wanted, we wouldn't dare get inside it. It'd be over like a shot."

"And when the dawn comes the thaw will drop it down instead," Nan muttered hopelessly. "Suppose we go down and see how far it will have to drop? Come on, dad...."

"Damned silly business altogether," Henshaw grumbled, getting up and stumbling after the two down the slope. "What with a third normal gravity, these ice crystals or whatever they are, and my heart—I'd give my fortune for a drink."

"You've got water tablets in your helmet trap," Clark grunted, "Why not use 'em?"

"Water!" Henshaw echoed in horror; then he unaccountably said no more. A sudden thought seemed to have struck him. He released his helmet switch and allowed a tabloid to automatically drop into his mouth.

"G-great stuff!" he mumbled, staggering along like a baby elephant. "Solidified *teticol* tablets! I remember now—I put them in my helmet in place of the water tablets; and there's a spare tin of them on my belt here. Easy enough, since my suit's the biggest, neither of you would get it by mistake. Dammit, no man can live on water!"

Clark sighed. "O.K,, dad, you win. I'll bet you'd find your beloved *teticol* in the middle of outer space. Only please don't get tight! We need our wits about us. And don't forget those things have a pretty strong potassium basis. Too many of them will send you to sleep."

"Yeah; but before I get that far I find—hup!—bliss," Henshaw observed wisely, and he licked his lips in satisfaction in the cold starlight....

II.

In ten minutes the three had gained the edge of the long slope. Carefully Clark lay down on his face and peered into the abyss below. It was wreathed in either dense mist or frozen air; he couldn't determine which in the faint light. Either way it was a terrific drop, would be certain to smash the spaceship when the thaw allowed it to fall.

He stood up again, his serious face faintly visible inside his helmet.

"Only one thing for it," he said worriedly. "At the first signs of sunrise we'll come back here, take a chance on getting inside the ship. Then when the congealed oxygen in front of it breaks up, we'll let the ship take a natural chute into the air of this valley. By snapping on the under-jets we'll perhaps save ourselves from dropping down. Gravity's pretty weak here, so we might manage it. It's the only chance.... Down there will perhaps be nitrogen too. If there isn't—? Well, I guess we'll go up like shooting stars. That's all in the cards."

"And in the meantime?" Nan quietly asked.

Clark glanced toward the frowning mass of the cliff along the slope edge. Dimly visible dark holes were distinguishable on its main ledge.

"Might as well try that," he shrugged.

"Be able to shelter in one of those caves and watch for sunrise at the same time. It won't be so very long according to my calculations.... Come on."

They began to return up the slope. Henshaw was chanting to himself, entirely oblivious to his surroundings, to the possible danger, to the possibility indeed that split seconds lay between life and death when the dawn-thaw came at the rise of the far distant Sun. Far distant, yet sufficient to raise the temperature during the fourteen-hour day to create an admixture of oxygen, hydrogen and argon—and it was to be hoped, nitrogen....

Overhead, the stars loomed with steely glitter against a backdrop of misty nebulae and cosmic dust. Against this the upper mountain heights, the base of which formed the immense cliff, were etched out like the teeth of a monstrous saw.... Cold—merciless cold—is the lot of the Callistian night.

As they gained the long, frozen ledge leading to the caves, Clark turned.

"Better hand out the guns, dad. We never know. If anything

attacks us we'll have to chance starting a fire. Not so much water vapor around here as on the ship jets, so it might be O.K. The guns will make their own firing mixture, of course."

"Huh?" Henshaw's huge, bloated figure came to a stop. "Guns? What guns?"

"What guns!" Clark yelled. "The ones I gave you on the ship, of course—" He broke off, staring fixedly as Henshaw drearily raised his arms. He was not carrying anything in them.

"I—I dropped them," he hesitated. "When you threw me aside from the ship. I remember they fell in the crystals. You see I—"

"And you were so darned interested in those *teticol* tablets you forgot to pick them up!" Clark groaned. "Lordy, what a sweet mess you've made of things! We can never find them now; they'll be buried in the oxygen.... Even if we knew where to look," he wound up unhappily.

"I'm sorry....," Henshaw mumbled. "Darned careless of me, I guess. Don't see why we need them, anyhow," he finished irritably. "No life can be on this hell-fired planet, anyway."

Clark smiled bitterly. "Think not? My conclusions after trips around space are that life can exist anywhere. It exists on Jupiter, with nearly absolute space temperature—same on Io. And it lives in the steamy heat of Titan. So why not here...? But what's the use?" he growled. "We'll have to take a chance. Come on."

The journey along the ledge resumed. Henshaw, realizing he was in disgrace, clumped at a little distance behind, hanging onto the connecting cord. Another *teticol* tablet relieved his contrition somewhat; he felt his head swim pleasantly. With a supreme effort he fought down a desire to yodel.

Then suddenly Nan stopped, pointing. Clark bumped into her and stared blankly as he followed her finger. A cluster of objects like children's toy balloons were gathered on the acclivity— perhaps twenty of them in all. One or two of them went floating away into the starry dark, suddenly distending their bodies to accomplish the feat.

"What do you know about that!" Clark whistled, staring at

their bulging, bladder-like bodies and scrawny, silly necks. He turned and cried. "Here you are, dad! Life already! Birds!"

"Some place to have an aviary," Henshaw grunted, stopping. "More of them there. Look."

Further along the ledge a veritable flock of the things were collected, remarkably like long necked Sun-fish when inflated; little better than a cast-out inner tube when deflated.

"So they fill themselves with hydrogen and float around with it inside them," Clark mused, watching closely. "No wings at all; they just rise and fall by inflating or deflating. Nice going!"

"But how?" Nan questioned, frowning. "How do they manage to separate the hydrogen from the argon—presuming it is argon?"

He shrugged. "How does a plant break down inorganic compounds? Nobody really knows; nobody can predict the exact nature of chlorophyll in plants. We have the same thing here: some internal chemistry on the part of these birds makes them able to separate hydrogen from argon. That shouldn't be difficult, since argon doesn't mix freely with hydrogen.... Since hydrogen is the lighter gas, these things float— Well, not entirely on that account," he amended, thinking. "A balloon only rises because of the heavier air pushing from beneath it. Same thing here, I suppose, and inflation or deflation raises or lowers them."

"Wonder what they do when the air becomes normal at dawn?" Nan mused.

"Ever hear of a butterfly that lives only for a day?" Clark asked dryly. "Well, it may be something like that. Birds of the night, to be born, spawn, and die in the space of the Callistian dark, leaving behind them eggs, which will hatch with the dawn. Maybe somewhere right at the top of this range, way up where the warmth will never have much effect, where hydrogen and argon are eternal."

Nan shook her head. "Poetic, but not very convincing. In that case they would probably retreat up to the heights at dawn and wouldn't die at all.... Or even, dawn may not have any thaw effect at all up here."

That was too startling a speculation. Clark took the girl's arm and the climb resumed. In the main the hydrogen birds seemed quite docile; only a few scattered away as the trio clumped through their midst. Then in another ten minutes they had reached the nearest cave and crawled gratefully into it, sat down heavily where they could look out over the cold, relentless frozen slope toward the sunward horizon—when the luminary rose.

Clark snapped off the cord and rolled it up, lowered his pack of provisions and small instruments. Nan did likewise. Henshaw swallowed another tablet and hiccupped solemnly.

"Still sorry about those guns," he muttered. "Darned stupid of me. You forgive me?"

"Of course, dad—" Nan began cheerfully, then she broke off in bewilderment as a hard, cracked voice cut across hers, distinctly audible in each helmet receiver.

"Implements of destruction! Foolish things! Disseminators of incredible violence, the outcome of bellicose yearnings.... So atavistic! So incomprehensible!"

III.

The three jerked erect and stared at each other in the dim starlight.

"Say," Clark whispered, "who slung those jaw crackers around?" He looked suspiciously at Henshaw. "Was it you, dad?"

Henshaw gulped. "Heaven—hup!—forbid! Elocution and grammar soured om me years ago."

"You, then?" Clark twisted to Nan, but her head shook. She was too startled to speak.

Clark got anxiously to his feet and switched on his torch. The beam penetrated clean to the back of the cave, framing an object that nearly dropped him to his knees in astonishment.

"Sweet Heaven, what is it?" he gasped helplessly. "Or am I nuts?"

"Or am I drunk?" whispered Henshaw, staring through his one soundly focused eye.

"Cla-Clark, let's go," Nan breathed nervously, scrambling up and clutching his arm. "It's—it's alive!"

"We are all alive. Life is variform—flux and confluence, yet it continues. In the void, in the air, in the planets—even in the stars."

"Gosh!" Clark whistled, and still stared in confusion.

The object might have been a man, only it was mummified beyond all comparison with a normal being. Perhaps it had once been Earthly, but now it was all skin and bone—a curious skin, with a dry, leathery aspect. The arms were of matchstick consistency; the legs were crossed and as thin as tapers. The skinny chest heaved up and down spasmodically with the effort of breathing—breathing hydrogen and argon at that!

There was a tiny chin, cracked, scar-like mouth, hooked nose, and beady, almost hidden eyes, the entire face swelling out into a preponderant, mighty bald dome on which the skin was stretched as tight as a carnival bladder. An utterly fantastic presence—a brain with a decrepit, featherweight body.

"Animal, vegetable, or mineral?" hazarded Henshaw. "Or have I got 'em at long last?"

Cautiously, Nan clinging to his arm,

Clark inched his way forward. Henshaw came up unsteadily behind them.

The object closed its eyes in the glare. Clark lowered the beam to the floor so the reflection alone served to illuminate the Thing.

"Who—who are you?" he ventured.

"I have no name," the Thing answered. "What is a name? Only an appellation or patronymic by which certain bipeds, and at times quadrupeds, to say nothing of other ramifications of life, are known or distinguished."

"If only he'd compile a dictionary!" Henshaw said regretfully.

"But how did you get here?" asked Nan, gaining courage.

"What are you doing?"

"I have always been here—I shall always be here. Maybe it is centuries since I was born. Maybe only yesterday. Who can say?"

"From the look of you it sure wasn't yesterday," Clark observed dryly. "Just what are you doing?"

"I brood. Sometimes I think actively—such as now, when I read your minds to ascertain your language, which you all speak so atrociously.... But most of the time I brood. And brood."

"He broods," Clark told the girl wisely, and she nodded and said,

"You're telling me! But what do you brood about?" she asked.

"My body. My existence. Why things are."

"Who doesn't?" Clark sighed; then seriously, "But how do you come to be here breathing pure hydrogen—or is it hydrogen and argon?"

"It is not argon; it is unknown to you. It has practically no freezing point. I do not breathe it. I breathe hydrogen. Why should I not breathe hydrogen?"

"Oh, no reason—only it seems kind of funny. You've got an Earthly body, and we breathe oxygen, hydrogen, nitrogen, and an admixture of various other things."

"But you are of Earth—I am of...of Callisto, as you call it. Therein lies the difference. I am the last...last man of Callisto. The end of my race. When I go, intellectual Callistian mankind will have gone too. My body only happens to resemble yours. I have never been to Earth."

"But listen," Nan put in quickly; "doesn't it get rather cold in here—just brooding? I mean, it's cold enough to freeze oxygen and nitrogen, yet you sit here with nothing—er— Well, unclothed!" She coughed demurely.

"Here it is always cold. It never alters. But it is only cold to you. The atmosphere does not mingle any higher than the edge of the slope where you left your spatial projectile."

"What!" Clark gasped in alarm. "There's never a thaw around here? Good Lord, then the ship—"

"I am not cold," the decrepit voice interrupted him. "I have not flesh and blood, but a mixture of hydrogen, oxygen, and water at a low temperature, kept from absolute solidity by a skin which is proof against external conditions, just as your skins are proof against some cosmic radiations. If you were to touch me with a bare hand, the cold would turn your fingers to powder. Only liquid air can compare with my exterior skin."

"I don't get this at all," Clark muttered. "How did you get this way, anyhow?"

"Evolution," said the creature impassively.

"For how long?"

"Maybe untold ages. Once Callisto was hot, when it left the primary. That was the time when our life flourished. We were an active race; then, as our world and the primary cooled, we used our bodies less and less. Nature, ever adaptable, gave us bodies that we're able to deal with the changing conditions, until there came the final species of hydrogen breathers, like me. I am the last. Intelligence of surpassing power—but physical ability nearly gone. Held in place only until I master it."

"You want to die?" Clark demanded,

"One day. I shall stay here and brood until the time when I detach mind from body, limb by limb, organ by organ. That may mean ages; it may be tomorrow."

"Limb by limb!" cried Nan aghast. "How—how horrible! And painful!"

"Pain is unknown; pain is begotten of ignorance. The arm or the leg does not think for itself. Detach the mind from the limb or organ in question and it ceases to be of interest. In time I shall detach my mind from my body; limb by limb I shall fade away. The hardest task of all will be to leave behind my brain."

"There may be something in it," the girl acknowledged, thinking; then glancing at Clark, "You know! Like the devotees who hold a hand up until it loses all feeling, or the guys who lie on a bed of nails and face the east.... Or is it west? Anyway, mind over matter."

There was silence for a moment. The intellectual monstrosity was so coldly logical about everything there could be no room for doubt.

"You evolved rather rapidly to an intelligent state like this?" Clark asked presently.

"Why not? Pressure here is slight. Pressure hinders the circulation of blood, or my own particular fluid, to the brain. Where there is slight gravity and low air pressure the brain is well fed, develops accordingly. Therefore I am intelligent."

There was another silence and the three stood looking at each other. They were each thinking the same thing—the possibility of Earthly life perhaps ending in such a creature as this—hideous, incredibly intelligent, impartial, brooding alone in a forgotten cave amid sub-zero cold. There was something terrifying about the thought. The pooling of endless ages of knowledge and culture into the brain pan of a gargoyle.

Henshaw broke the silence with a comment. "What d'you say we call him 'Zero'?" he suggested, grinning. "A step removed from Nero, who fiddled instead of brooding. Huh?"

"Good name, but this is no time for levity," Clark answered seriously. "Zero here brings home pretty forcibly the pointlessness of Earthly struggle—of anybody's struggle, for that matter. And besides—" He broke off and twisted round at a sudden noise. He stared unbelievingly at the cave entrance, seeing for the first time that it was blocked with stunted, hideous creatures, all mouth and ears, on blocky legs with short bodies. Wicked little eyes glinted in the torchlight. Every head was totally bald.

"Magnified germs, so help me!" Henshaw gasped—and his simile was oddly accurate. The things certainly looked like the real thing from a preventative advertisement.

"The others of my race—de-evolved," stated Zero placidly. "There must ever be two sectors—worker and intellectual. You have but to study your Earthly ant life to determine that. If the brain deteriorates, the body gains control and becomes a weapon of evil; in the opposite direction intelligence gains, and you have such as me."

"Are they dangerous?" Clark demanded.

"To me, no. To you, very."

Nan gasped in terror. "Oh, dad, if only you'd brought along those guns—! We might have stood a chance!"

She fell silent, clinging to her father and Clark, backing into the cave between them as the chattering, mouthing monstrosities came slowly forward, obviously intent on only one thing—destruction. Possibly their cave was being invaded; that might explain their presence. Clearly they were beyond reason.... Clark was more concerned for the fact that their sharp claw-fingers would rip the spacesuits. That meant instant, painful death.

Zero took no part in the proceedings. He sat on in impartial silence, still cross-legged, still brooding.

The three backed further into the cave until at last they were brought up sharp against the rear wall.

"Zero, do something!" Clark implored frantically. "Turn these things away! You've got the intelligence; we haven't."

"Only the fittest may survive in the course of evolution," Zero droned back. "Extinguishment—victory—survival—procreation— What are they? The evanescent, transitory movements of a race—"

"Oh, nuts!" Clark interrupted, and looked round him desperately. The creatures had stopped for the moment, as though deciding on a scheme of attack. Their vast mouths were still wide open, grinning caverns; their terrible clawed hands were extended.

"I'll bet they feed on either hydrogen birds or oxygen crystals," muttered Nan, trying to be brave.

"One rip from those things and we'll be playing harps," her father observed. "Guess I need a stimulant...." His helmet clicked faintly as he dropped a *teticol* tablet in his mouth.

"Clark, can't you—?" Nan began shakily; then he cut her short and twirled round, clutched the surprised Henshaw by the shoulder.

"Quick, dad—you said something about an extra supply of those tablets of yours. Where are they?"

"Huh?" The old man stared in the torchlight, then slapped his equipment belt. "Right here. But say, about my heart—"

"You won't have a heart to worry about if this doesn't work," Clark panted, ripping the container from the belt. "This is a chance—and a mighty slim one...."

He fumbled clumsily with his gloves, snapped the container open. The creatures had begun to advance again now. Nan gave a little cry and squeezed herself behind Clark's bulky form. Henshaw stood his ground, swaying a little. In his present mood of semi-intoxication he didn't care much what happened.

"Here goes!" Clark breathed, and scooping up a gloveful of tablets he tossed them unerringly into the mouth of the foremost grinning monstrosity. Then he crouched back, waiting agonizedly.

He hadn't long to wait. Suddenly the torchlight gloom of the cave was illumined by a blinding, sputtering glare of livid flame. The foremost creature gave one mighty yell, and that was all: the next instant flame spouted from his wide mouth; his whole body transformed in a flash into a blinding mass that sputtered and span wildly, consuming quantities of oxygen crystal from the floor.

Blinded with the light, the three jerked their faces away, flung up protecting hands. Zero still sat on with closed eyes. The remaining creatures twisted wildly and fell over themselves in their frantic efforts to get outside.... Smoke, slowly evaporating, took the place of the flame. The former shadowy, torch-lit gloom returned.

Carefully, Clark looked round, spots of color swimming before his gaze.

"It worked!" he breathed thankfully. "It actually worked!"

"Yeah; but what happened?" Henshaw demanded. "Those pills cost—hup!—money, and I haven't so many left. I—"

"It was the quantity of potassium in their basis that I relied upon," Clark explained, as they started to edge to the cave opening. "I took the chance that those creatures were composed of the same stuff as Zero—oxygen, hydrogen, and water vapor. You know what happens when potassium gets mixed up with water?"

"I'm no chemist," Henshaw growled. "What?"

"It drives the hydrogen out of the water at express speed, so violently and with such a release of heat that the hydrogen, mingling with the oxygen, catches fire. That's what happened, luckily for us. The germ turned into a glorified Roman candle."

"How many did you give him?" Nan asked breathlessly.

"Thirty! No wonder he blew up.... The whole tin full."

"We'd better get out of here before they come back," Henshaw said uneasily; then he glanced back at Zero from the cave opening and waved his arm. "So long, Zero. Hope you make it!"

"Though generations shall pass I will master the final problems of life and death," came the droning answer—then the three were outside on the ledge again.

IV.

Nan glanced around her at the starlit sky, at the sloping ledge at the end of which, far distant, lay the spaceship.

"No sign of dawn yet," she remarked seriously; "and from what Zero told us it won't have much effect even when it does come. Not up here, anyhow—"

"Take a look!" Clark interrupted her, and nodded his head along the ledge.

Not five hundred yards away the monstrosities, their first fright overcome, were returning, intent this time on vengeance, beyond doubt.

"Uh-uh!" exclaimed Henshaw hastily, and started off at a blundering run. His own dizziness, the slippery ledge, and the lesser gravity made him a ludicrous figure; almost laughable had the danger not been so great. Finally he fell over and collapsed in the midst of the startled hydrogen birds further down the slope.

"Hey! Come back!" Clark yelled. "I've got to fix the rope to your belt...." Clutching Nan, he set off after him.

"We'll never make it," Nan panted huskily. "They're gaining

on us. We'd be safe enough on that slope below, but it's too far to jump. Following this ledge it will take us half an hour at least, and by that time—"

"Look!" Clark yelled, stopping momentarily. "What the devil's dad doing?"

That was a problem. Instead of scrambling to his feet, Henshaw was rising as though dragged, tightly clutching a quartet of hydrogen birds in his huge gloved hands. In an instant he was off the ledge, floating away over the frozen slope below.

"Dad!" Nan screamed wildly. "Dad, what's happened?" And her voice thundered in echoes over the dreary reaches.

"Dunno," Henshaw's receding voice echoed back. "Clutched their necks.... See you later.... I hope!" He drifted out of earshot, floating toward the distant spaceship.

"I get it!" Clark whistled. "He must have grabbed a neckful of the things as he got up. They were inflating and lifted him right into the air. Actually they're strangled, but can't release their hydrogen gas—so they're a sort of balloon. Weight here doesn't amount to much. Four of those things could lift dad with ease— It's an idea," he went on hurriedly, resuming the scrambling run. "One way of getting off this ledge."

He cast another look around at the approaching Callistians, then at Henshaw's far off drifting figure.

"Why the blazes doesn't he release hold of them one by one?" he said anxiously. "He'd drop, then— Gosh! He's gone right over the edge of the slope toward the chasm. Disappeared! Come on!"

They redoubled their efforts, only slowed down as they approached the swelling and deflating hydrogen birds. One or two flew off; the others jerked their ridiculous heads round on their scrawny necks.

"Grab!" Clark ordered. "Four!"

He dived simultaneously with the girl as eight of the birds started to inflate. They caught them at the peak of their inhalation. The things struggled wildly as they found it impossible to exhale.... Clark found himself lifted from the ledge, carried upwards swiftly with the smooth ease of a balloon, buoyed up by the heavier argon-x, as he mentally named the unknown gas.

Behind him, clutching her own four birds tenaciously, Nan came. Back on the ledge the monstrosities arrived too late, were screaming and cursing threats in an unknown language.

"Hang on!" Clark shouted. "We've got to find your dad. Keep hold until I tell you otherwise."

The girl's helmet nodded. The drifting took them over the solitary, blocked spaceship to the yawning misty chasm beyond it. Nan closed her eyes at the frightful drop below, then opened them again at a cry from Clark.

"The Sun! Look!"

She stared across the misty wrappings, beheld the absurd far distant disk that was the Sun. Already at the touch of its slight but noticeable warmth the valley mists below began to stir curiously like cotton wool with a draft under it.

"Drop!" Clark ordered. "Let go of your birds one at a time."

He set the example and she followed suit. Each time they released a bird they fell lower, until by the time they possessed only one bird each they were falling almost sheer into the midst of the stirrings and shifting of reforming, congealed atmosphere.

Suddenly the clear, thin clarity of everything changed. They were in semi-gloom, blanketed under clouds. A sloping mass, presumably the foothills of the titanic cliff at the top of which rested the spaceship, rose up to meet them.

"Drop!" Clark yelled, and released the last bird. Instantly he and Nan ceased their drifting and fell vertically, slowly owing to the lesser gravity, dropped to the ground and rolled over and over, sat up amidst billowing gusts of wind as the irregularly warmed atmosphere took on balance.

They joined each other, stood up, surveying the towering height of cliff, clouds whirling savagely in the wind drifts at half way up its height.

"Well, we made it," Clark muttered, "but I don't know what good it's done us. Take a look at that cliff—it's unclimbable without proper tackle, and we haven't got any. Ice and snow ridges near the top, too—normal congealment." He stopped and stared round the desolation. Here and there the Sun was starting to peep through the twisting, warming air.

"There's nitrogen present down here, anyhow," he said thankfully, regarding the gauge on his belt. "Not that it does us much good with the ship way up there...." He put the instrument back and yelled, "Dad! Dad! Can you hear me?"

His amplifier at full strength his shout penetrated deafeningly, echoed from the cliff sides.

"Dad!" he bawled again, and for a long time there was only the echoes of his voice. He prepared to shout again, then stopped abruptly at a distinct sound not very far away.

"Yo-ho liety! Iddio—ladiay! Ooooo-yoohooo...."

Nan laughed in sudden relief. "Clark, it's dad all right. He's—he's yodeling!"

"Huh?" Clark gulped. "What the hell for?"

"He's always wanted to," she said fondly. "Good old dad!"

They stood waiting, calling at intervals. The yodeling went on, echoing weirdly. The tugging and puffing of the wind began to diminish, but far up the heights were curious rumblings and bumping as warmth surged upwards toward that forgotten waste, charging it with the lightning and thundering of heat and cold.

Then suddenly old Henshaw appeared, reeling gracefully, a deflated hydrogen bird in his hand like a Christmas turkey.

"Illi-idio!" he warbled, coming .up on clumsy feet. "I—hup!—guess I always wanted to—hic—yodel. It's the Swish—the Swiss in me.... Gosh, that was hard to say!"

"Thank Heaven you didn't break your neck," Clark panted, seizing him tightly.

"Mebbe you wanted me to, huh?" Henshaw demanded arrogantly. "Jus' so's you could inherit my money through Nan, huh? Nothin'—hup!—doin'! An, why shouldn't I fall easily, and near here? I came down on the same wind drift, didn't I?"

Clark agreed, then said ominously, "Dad, you've been parking away too doggone many of those tablets. You're tight again!"

"Sure—an' I like it!" Henshaw thrust out his chin behind his helmet. "S'what?" he demanded. "Without those *teticol* tablets you'd have been in a pretty—pardon me—fine mess back with those germ men, wouldn't you?"

He reeled round and stared up at the heights. The air had cleared a lot now. The weak sunshine revealed the basic rock soaring for a thousand feet and more, ending then in sheer snow and ice, pinnacles and buttresses of it joining the oxygen crystal plain. Somewhere up there, on the edge, reposed the spaceship.

"Say!" he yelped, wheeling. "How the heck do we get back?"

"I'm not good at riddles!" Clark sat down glumly on the black rock, stared moodily at the idiotic Sun, across the barrenness of the valley floor to the very near horizon.

"Y'mean, we can't—" Henshaw gasped, stumbling back. "But, Clark, we've got to! We can't jush stop here.... It—it isn't done."

"Lots of things aren't done, but this one is," Clark retorted. "If you hadn't have floated so far we wouldn't be in this mess. If it comes to that, you're responsible for the whole darn business!"

"Yes...." Henshaw closed a rueful eye and sat down. His face was so utterly woebegone behind the glass that Nan could not help but smile a little. She patted his gloved hand.

"Never mind, dad, we'll find a way to the top somehow," she said brightly. "There's always a way up mountains and cliffs."

"With tackle, yes—not otherwise," Clark told her gloomily. "You needn't fool yourself, Nan. We couldn't possibly scale those ice peaks at the summit. Our only chance is to rig up some kind of signal in the hopes of being seen by the regular Jove line space traffic. Mighty slim hope down here with the mountain range hiding things, but we might make it."

Henshaw twisted his head back and stared up at the snowy height.

"Funny," he muttered. "Funny to think we waited for the thaw and didn't know it never thaws up there. In that case we might have risked getting into the ship.... And down here there's the nitrogen we need.... Some things are mighty queer...."

Clark's sour look silenced him. He beat his gloves together unconcernedly and started to yodel again, His ringing cries went beating against the cliff side.

"Li-tiddly-oh-te-oh—! Gosh, is that a hot one! Listen, Nan. *Yiddley*!"

"Oh, shut up!" Clark yelled exasperatedly. "Things are bad enough without you bursting our receivers. Lay off!"

Henshaw shrugged, then suddenly his aggrieved expression changed slightly. He looked less stupefied. Swiftly he altered his sound transmitter to maximum output.

"What's the idea?" Clark demanded, watching.

"Ha!" Henshaw waggled a huge finger. "Idea, m'lad.... Lishen!" And he burst forth again with a streaming cacophony of most unlovely noises, yodeling that would have struck a Swiss mountaineer stone dead.

"For Pete's sake—!" Clark howled imploringly, clapping a hand over his receiver. "What the hell are you trying to do? Deafen us?"

"Nope—jush get ush out o' this mess...."

Henshaw stood up, yodeled again and again with the most shattering din, sent the thundering cries rolling down the valley... then suddenly he twisted round sharply and stared upwards. The constant muttering of the storm-ridden heights had changed to a deeper note—the growling, crumbling thunder of sliding matter.

"Avalanche!" Clark gulped abruptly, jumping up and clutching the startled Nan. "Yes—look!" He pointed upward. Already mighty boulders of frozen snow, oxygen, nitrogen, and other nameless elements were detaching themselves, moving downwards in a vast, overpowering flood.

"It worked!" Henshaw yelled in delight, dancing clumsily. "I knew it—! My yodeling— Come on!"

Sobered with the intensity of the moment he led the way. As fast as they could go they went blundering away across the stones, toward the steeply overhung level of the cliff itself. Directly underneath it they would probably escape the full force of the downfall.

Not a second too soon they floundered into the welcome shelter. Behind them titanic masses of white banged and powdered and exploded with terrifying power—some were frozen air, bursting apart under the sudden warmth. Others were actual rocks.

"You—you started this, dad," Clark panted. "Your damned yodeling voice vibrations shifted the upper ice and snow peaks."

"That's what I wanted," Henshaw answered complacently. "I saw it happen somewhere once—Alps, I think. A guy hollered an' a mountain fell down. Sound waves and that. I figured the ship would fall down too. Won't be hurt much with snow and lesser gravity to cushion it."

"He's right, Clark!" Nan cried breathlessly. "It might work at that. The ship *was* on the edge—"

She broke off and stared anxiously at the curtain of white hailing down outside. Clouds of white foggy dust came drifting into the retreat.... When at last the concussions were over, they were facing a hill of white with barely room enough to scramble over the top.

Clark began to claw his way through, held down a hand to the girl and her father. Standing knee-deep in snow they stared around them, amazed at the quantity of snow and ice that had dislodged.

"There!" screamed Nan suddenly. "Isn't that it? That black thing poking up?"

She didn't wait to be answered; she went floundering forward, waist deep in snow, until she gained the black protuberance nearly two hundred yards away. In a moment Henshaw and Clark were at her side.

"It's it all right," Clark acknowledged thankfully. "Came down with the snow. Saved it from damage.... We'll soon have this snow away." He turned quickly to Henshaw. "Nice going, dad! The moment we get this snow clear and into space you can yodel to your heart's content...."

"I don't want to yodel," 'Henshaw mused, scooping the snow away in his gloves."

"No? What then?"

"All I want is a darned good drink, mixed up with these makeshift tablets...."

THE DEGENERATES
BY POLTON CROSS

FROM *ASTOUNDING STORIES*, FEBRUARY 1938

This was to be the last 'Weinbaum flavour' story that Fearn would send to Schwartz under his 'personal' pseudonym of Polton Cross. It was also one that was only indebted to Weinbaum for its Saturnian moon setting (including especially Weinbaum's 'bladder birds'). The plot was more or less original to Fearn, and the story's main strength is its characterization and human interactions, not its borrowed alien ecology or SF tropes. It appealed sufficiently to Campbell for him to accept the story on 29 October 1937. But it was to be the last Fearn story appearing in *Astounding*.

Successive commentators have assumed that Fearn simply couldn't meet Cambell's 'higher standards' and was ruthlessly discarded. But that simply wasn't true,

Canpbell fully intended to continue to use Fearn in his new *Astounding*, and wrote to him following his acceptance of "Red Heritage". Fearn referred to Campbell's contacting him in his letter to Walter Gillings dated 9th January 1938:

"'Dark Eternity' (which Fearn had sold earlier to Tremaine in September 1937) marked the last thought variant story I ever intend to write. Come to think of it, it was a fitting closing story to a long run of crazy scientific expositions. 'Red Heritage' marks the birth of the new Fearn, with a new style story. Campbell has written me expressing his liking for this yarn and urges all future yarns be written in the same vein. Further (in confidence) he tells me that the readers are swinging from the heavy science thought-variant type of yarn to more interesting characters and lighter science. So I've changed my methods utterly. 'Red Heritage' was the start of the new method, and henceforth I shall change unrecognizably into the (in confidence) Polton Cross type of yarn. My latest yarn for *Astounding*, 'Debt of Honor' is almost straight fiction, but I think it'll click. I hope so."

Clearly, Fearn had every intention—and expectation—of continuing to write for *Astounding*. He had also received a second letter from Campbell at the same time, addressed to 'Thornton Ayre.' Whilst he had accepted "Whispering Satellite," Campbell gave notice that it was the last such story he was prepared to use. Apparently too many authors were "going like Weinbaum" and the editor was sick of it. He suggested that Ayre should write for him under a different style.

Then, early in February 1938, news reached Fearn via his agent that Teck Publications had sold the ailing *Amazing Stories* to the established Ziff-Davis chain. Payment was to be doubled, and paid on acceptance. The new editor in charge was Ray Palmer—who also happened to be a good friend of Julius Schwartz!

Palmer was horrified at the parlous state of the *Amazing* inventory he had inherited. He quickly decided that nearly all of it was unusable: "...half-baked ideas, screwy science, and pedantic, unprofessional writing...(a) dung heap of gadgets, theories, and interplanetary travelogues. There wasn't a living breathing character, emotion (or) adventure in the whole lot," he later recalled. In desperation, he appealed to his friend Schwartz for help, in his capacity as a literary agent specializing in SF. Amongst the mss. he offered Palmer were the stories that Fearn had written especially for Campbell, including "Debt of Honor" as Fearn, and "Locked City" as Ayre. Campbell never got to see them: they were instead diverted straight to Palmer. He eagerly snapped them up, with a request for more.

On learning of this, Fearn told Gillings on 14th March 1938:

> "It came as a surprise to know my 'Debt of Honor' has landed at *Amazing*. I figured it was for *Astounding*, but evidently Julie thinks differently."

Any misgivings Fearn may have had about his agent's action in bypassing Campbell were soon swept aside. On 25th March 1938 he wrote again to Gillings:

> "Learned this morning that as well as 'Debt of Honor' (to be re-titled 'A Summons from Mars') *Amazing* have bought Polton Cross' 'Eternal Sleepers' (to be re-titled 'Master of the Golden City') for publication in the same issue. Nice going, particularly as it's 17,000 words long. Two long novelettes in No. 1! Oh, boy, oh-boy! Got the check this morning, a comforting little total of well over fifty quid."

THE DEGENERATES

Adventure in the forgotten city of a lost race—steaming in the other-world jungle—

Lost in a forgotten jungle—a remnant of a greater civilization than Man's—in the hands of the Degenerates.

I.

Have you ever met a man whom you felt like hitting in the jaw? Such a desire rose in me when I first met Ludwig Reid,

He was so smooth, so polite about everything he said and did that—to me anyhow—he was instantly stamped as a man to be wary of.

I met him first when Captain Brook—the middle-aged millionaire owner of the Brook Spacesuit Co.—called me over to his palatial place on Long Island. I was just resting from my job as astrogator to Trans-Plutonian Explorers, and therefore open for any commission. Knowing Brook so well, I scented something good and presented myself at his home on the evening of November 10, 2119.

As usual, he was full of enthusiasm. Tall and gray-haired, he had the keen eyes and hard-lipped mouth of a commercial giant and fighter. But Ludwig Reid, our sole companion in the library, was of totally different make-up—short in stature, with a remarkably square face, untidy black hair, and steady, pale-gray eyes that never left your face while he talked. All this—combined with a moon-whiteness of skin, long thin nose, and cruel, inflexible mouth—gave him all the attributes of a man of iron ambition, centered only on one thing—himself.

He was cordial enough to me at first, even though I felt like hitting him in the eye there and then. Brook introduced us in his swift, clipped fashion.

"Meet Dick Cambridge, Reid. The best freelance astrogator in the business. With him as expedition pilot there'll not be a thing to fear."

Reid looked me over calmly. Evidently my six feet of space-hardened frame suited him, for he nodded slowly. When I shook hands with him I gave an extra powerful squeeze to express my dislike—but he didn't even wince. His sweetly odorous Titan-flower cigarette continued to smolder seductively.

"Delighted," he murmured coolly, releasing his hand. "I have invariably found that black-headed, dark-skinned pilots like yourself are better able to stand the free ultraviolet radiations of space. I think you'll do, Cambridge."

I nodded stiffly, but it was for old Brook that I did it. I'd do anything for him—and his daughter Ada. I glanced across at

Brook.

"What's all this about, sir?"

"An expedition, Dick—to Io; Reid here has discovered a natural form of *ilution*—which as you know is at present used in an artificial form for spacesuits. But Reid believes there are plants in the Ionian jungles containing the stuff as natural sap, and—well!" He laughed in his affluent fashion. "Reid and I will pick up multi-millions—and you won't exactly be left with a couple of cents if you see the thing through."

I looked at Reid quickly. "This on the level?" I asked him sharply. "I know most of Io, but it's the first time I ever heard of natural *ilution* trees in its jungles."

From his pocket he took two rolled pieces of substance like rubber and laid them on the library table. Both looked identical.

"Apparently no difference, is there?" he asked slowly. "And yet watch!" Fishing in his pocket once more he pulled out a nasty-looking knife that snapped open into a small dagger. With a swift stroke he drove the blade through the left-hand piece of rubber, and of course it instantly ripped.

"Ordinary *ilution*—the stuff we use now," he explained; "Now watch this—" He brought the knife down quickly on the second piece. The blade simply bounced off it and failed to make the least impression.

Wonderingly, I picked the stuff up and pulled and tugged at it. It was absolutely untearable. Although identical to its torn twin on the table, it was clearly a hundred times as tough. The possibilities of such a substance—something the hard rock or the vicious surfaces of other worlds couldn't tear—dawned on me immediately. I didn't like admitting Reid was right, but I had to.

"I've had the stuff tested at my laboratories and it is absolutely unbreakable," Brook exclaimed eagerly. "You see the possibilities, surely?"

"Actually I got to know all about it by accident," Reid remarked, putting the knife back in his pocket. "An Ionian native named Kiol stowed away on the *Wanderlust* last trip up and brought some of this stuff with him. I've been to Io before and he remembered me. In fact, he gave my name when he was apprehended by the spaceport authorities and I had to bail him out. I'm glad I did! The moment I saw the stuff, I saw the opportunity it meant for Brook and so got in touch with him right away. The site of these *ilution* trees is known only to Kiol as yet—but I do know the situation of the jungle clearing leading to them. It will take a skilled pilot to lower into it, and that's why we sent for you. Understand?"

"When do you plan to start, sir?" I asked Brook.

"In two days. I've had a special spaceship equipped for the purpose, complete with maps, detectors, and all the usual stuff. Reid has had carte blanche to order what he needed— You'll take it, won't you, Dick?" he finished anxiously. "It means everything to me!"

I nodded a rather slow assent. I had an odd idea at the back of my mind that Reid was up to something. Everything seemed logical enough and yet— Well, I didn't trust the man. Good scientist and explorer he might be, but otherwise—

I was just leaving the great residence when light, tripping footsteps came swiftly toward me along the broad gravel drive. Ada Brook came quickly into the stream of light from the doorway, a slim, dainty figure in her speed-auto togs. The scarlet muffler round her throat offset the healthy pink of her cheeks and merry blue of her eyes. She tugged off her neat little wool beret and shook free a mass of golden brown hair,

"If it isn't Dick Cambridge!" she cried impulsively, wringing my hand. "Remember me? I'm Ada! You piloted the F-18 that time when Dad and went over to Mars to study their lost civilizations."

"Of course I remember," I smiled.

In truth I had never forgotten this impish bit of femininity. She has that art of doing something to a guy.

"I suppose you're taking this Io expedition along?" she went on eagerly. "Dad told me he was going to commission you. It'll be such fun! Did—did you accept?"

I nodded. "But I didn't know you were coming," I said quietly. "I'm mighty glad to hear it!" It would make all the difference to me—probably save me building up what were no doubt foolish suspicions about Ludwig Reid.

"Course I'm coming!" she pouted. "How do you think Dad would remember to take his vita pills without me around him?" She glanced quickly toward the house, then shook my hand again. "I'll see you again, Dick. I'm late already and Lud's expecting me—"

"You mean Reid?" I asked grimly, and she nodded a trifle glumly.

"'Fraid so. You see—we're engaged. It's a sort of business deal, really. Since he and Dad are to be partners, I— Well, you know!"

I nodded bitterly and watched her go up the steps. Her, with her twenty-two years of freshness, engaged to that space-cold creature— Now I was certain I didn't like him!

II.

We took off right on time two days later, and it was certainly a joy to be the chief astrogator of the *Stardust*. She was a pip— the sort of vessel only a multimillionaire can build, and a space hog can dream about.

Apart from Ada, her father, and Reid, we had my close friend Nick Charteris as second astrogator; a Chinese cook by the name of Hu Ling, and Kiol, the Ionian. Like any other native of the hot little Jovian moon he was very tall—seven-feet-four—with a very nearly naked, blue-skinned body, hairless head, large eyes to cope with mainly varying lights, and a rather absurd little mouth.

He kept mostly to himself, timid as all Ionian natives are— afraid of harsh words, yet on occasions mercilessly vindictive in avenging a fancied wrong. Poor old Kiol! He took to the vessel's rocket belly and stayed there in the gloom, only emerging for his special meals. Besides, the terrible strain of Earth gravitation had pretty well exhausted him.

Until at last Io emerged from the nine-moon tangle around Jove. Here the real work began. Jupiter reaches out a terrific field of attraction for nearly 5,000,000 miles, and since Io is only 300,000 miles from his center, it demands a good deal of juggling with the jets to land square on any of his moons. Mainly for this reason Io, Ganymede, and Europa are trading satellites used for their production of minerals and special plants. Callisto—being much farther away from the primary— is a frozen waste. Except for refueling purposes on the main Pluto run, all the moons are out of the main tracks.

We accomplished our purpose by firing our right forward blasts against Jove to break his influence, then we gradually moved inward until at last the gages showed the faint pull of Io was holding us. Faint indeed—for Io is only 2,320 miles in diameter. Once we got below his occasional clouds, things were easier.

The landscape was a fairly familiar green tangle, bathed through the cloud rifts in the multiple lights of Jupiter, Europa, Ganymede, and the distant, disclike sun. Since Io also revolves in forty-two hours, the light effect is even more complicated on his surface.

We crossed the main Sawback Range, near the imaginary equator of Io and separating the unexplored jungle side from the *Ithtick* rock quarries. Deep in the quarries were the small huts of the guardsmen—only controllers and law-givers of this god-forsaken penal settlement where criminals rot out their bones in a temperature rarely dropping below 120° F.

Beyond the quarries again, seeming small and squat, reposed the Io fueling center from which most Earth-Pluto vessels get their supplies before starting on their long journeys. Obviously Kiol, in stowing aboard the *Wanderlust*, had done so from that very place.

Reid had me fly in a great circle over the jungle while he studied it intently through binoculars. He stood at the main spacescape window with his powerful legs spread wide to brace himself against the ship's circular motion. Beside him stood Ada and her father, gazing eagerly down.

"There!" Reid cried suddenly. "According to Kiol that's the spot. That T-shaped clearing—"

I looked down, too, and frowned. A T-shaped clearing was distinctly visible, with the dim silvery gleam of a river passing across one end of it. The rest was dense, mysterious jungle.

"Can you lower into that clearing?" Reid asked curtly, half turning.

"I think so," I said, and set to work with the underjets, signaling instructions to Nick as he kept a counter-check in the rocket-control room below.

Because Io's attraction is only a third of Earth's, the landing wasn't half so difficult as I'd expected, but most of it was done blind. The lower we sank, the less we saw, because of the blast shooting down below. Its terrific heat incinerated everything beneath us and made that clearing twice as big in about forty seconds.

Little by little we sank, wobbling ever so slightly from side to side, but never once falling into a fatal drop-spin—that is, when the jets strike obliquely instead of direct. The float-level stopped on even keel, and at last the gentle thud quivering through the vessel announced our arrival.

I cut the jets and looked round. Brook smiled his silent congratulations. Reid said nothing. He stood gazing out on the vision of lacing jungle bordering every part of the clearing, the river now crossing its center, so widely had we enlarged the area.

In silence I turned to the compressors and switched them on, their function being to adapt the ship's atmosphere to the exact density of that outside. The gravity plates, too, were slowly weakened. In all, the process took two hours and produced plenty of sick bouts—but at the end of the time we were all outside, gazing round.

It was saturatingly hot—steamy, fever-ridden, lit by a variety of shifting lights. The sky was now dark-blue to purple, visible in the clear patches where the fantastic shaving-brush trees thinned out a little. These ridiculous growths shoot up to four hundred feet and more, thriving in a third less gravity than Earth and a dank, hot air. Our clearing was nearly circular now—thanks to the blasting of the under-jets—and the swift river coursing into the jungle's depths went right across the middle.

Reid stood regarding it for a while, then turned. "We'll have to pitch camp on the other side of the river. Somewhere in the jungles over there are the trees we're looking for. That right, Kiol?"

The Ionian nodded his shiny head. When he spoke it was in the broken English he'd learned from the traders and penal warders.

"Remains twelve miles south, maybe," he jerked out flutily. "Soon make it."

"You'd better get the tents and equipment out," Reid ordered in a clipped voice. "You too, Ling. We'll be too cramped in the ship."

The Chinaman and Ionian entered the ship's airlock, keeping well away from one another. It needed no imagination to see they were anything but friends.

I turned to Reid sharply. "What was that remark Kiol made about 'remains'?" I demanded.

"Poor English, I imagine." He shrugged indifferently. "Why?"

Since I didn't answer he turned and looked at Ada, "Well, my dear, how do you like Io?"

"I don't," she answered, fanning herself languidly. "It's about the most ghastly place I've ever encountered."

He smiled rather coldly. "You'll get used to it in a week or two—that is, if you don't get moon fever."

I trembled to hit him. He said it as though he really wished she would get fever. The remark left her untroubled, but it sent her father inside the ship to find quinine and *galpha* tablets.

In two hours the ship was unloaded.

* * * * * *

Our camp, when pegged out, comprised six tents, including an extra large one to serve as a dining and general room. All—with the exception of Hu Ling and Kiol, and Nick and me—had tents to themselves. I doubted the wisdom of putting the Chinaman and Ionian together—if anything, it would only serve to increase their dislike for each other.

Once our first meal was over, Reid strolled some little distance from the camp with old man Brook, and they stood talking and looking down the swift river as it coursed into the fantastic jungle. I made it the opportunity to take a walk with Ada and show her the wonders of the Ionian sky and landscape.

To me, the sight from a nearby kopje was not new, but it brought a cry of amazed awe from Ada's lips as we came to the top of the rise. On every side of us stretched that wild jungle with its dominating shaving-brush trees. Here and there the queer rocket-birds were in view, hurtling up like bullets against the light gravitation. Then when they reached the shallow air 800 feet above ground they opened a membranous umbrella and dropped softly down again. Their prey, in the main, consists of hurtling insects.

In various other directions were the treacherous calcium areas—some of them inert, but others bathed in lambent, flickering fires as the calcium united with ammonia gas from rifts in the ground and produced the swift light of calcium ammonium. Io is particularly rich in calcium.

The sky, though, was the main thing that held our attention. Jupiter hung directly above us—huge, yellow, overpowering, with the oval of his Red Spot moving slowly as his enormous bulk turned. Close to him gleamed brilliant little Ganymede and Europa. Farther away still—disc-like and absurd—moved the Sun. Added to this were the hosts upon hosts of stars spewed in a myriad glittering dusts across the dark-purple heaven. It was superb—engrossing.

Ada talked of nothing else on the way back, when the trees

hid most of the sky from sight—and, as she was talking, something happened. Something puffed in front of our faces with dangerous closeness, so close indeed that Ada jerked her head back and then stared in alarmed wonder at the pineapple-like bole of the shaving-brush tree close beside us. Immediately I went up to it.

To my utter amazement I saw that the missile had been a dart! I tugged it out and stared at it in bewilderment, trying to figure how the devil such a primitive thing had even gotten into this wilderness—even more so who had fired it. Twisting round, I stared into the moon-and-primary-light, but nothing was visible. The lower tickle-brush grasses waved silently in the hot, sickly wind.

Ada gazed at the dart with alarmed eyes, then as she reached out her hand toward it, I slapped her fingers sharply.

"May be poisoned!" I warned her quickly. "Take it easy!"

Slowly I turned it over, and in doing so I saw something I could hardly believe. The tip of the dart was tempered *jilian* steel! Actually *tempered*. Yet Earth chemists can't get the stuff to melt under 8,000 degrees C. I happened to know they'd been trying it ever since the stuff was first discovered in ore form deep in the Martian deserts. The rest of the dart was ordinary shaving-brush wood stubbed with rocket-bird feathers.

"What's—what's the matter, Dick?" Ada asked anxiously, seeing my startled expression.

"Let's get back to camp!" was my abrupt answer. I was feeling decidedly worried.

* * * * * * *

In ten minutes we were back, but the rest of our party had retired to their tents. Reid was still up, however. I could see his shadow on the tent canvas cast by the portable gas-glow light on his table. I left Ada and went in to him.

"Reid, I want a word with you," I said brusquely.

He straightened from a survey of a map on the table and

looked at me coolly. The desk light made his eyes look like colorless marbles.

"As many as you wish," he assented easily. "Sit down." He lighted one of his Titan-flower cigarettes and watched me through the smoke. Without any trimmings I shot the whole story to him and finished up by flinging the dart on the table.

"I demand that we all be supplied with flame guns!" I finished grimly. "It obviously isn't safe to go wandering around unarmed in this place—much less so with things like this flying about. We've got enemies! And how the devil did that dart get a *jilian* steel tip? I thought that particular ore belonged solely to Mars. Do you realize that Miss Brook or I might have been killed?"

He shook his dark head. "I think not," he said, quite unperturbed. "This dart is not poisoned, nor was it intended to kill. It was more in the form of a warning."

"A warning!" I echoed blankly. "A warning against what, I'd like to know?"

Without answering he went on slowly, "There is no need for arms on Io, Cambridge. I should have thought you'd know that. There are no dangerous animals—only the underbrush bugs and rocket-birds, and they're harmless. Furthermore, I don't think it prudent that any of us should have flame guns. Suppose one of us got delusion fever? It's a not uncommon symptom of straight moon fever. Suppose Hu Ling got it, for instance? Why, he'd murder the lot of us!"

"I'm not Hu Ling, and I'm not liable to get fever," I said bitterly. "Give me a gun and quit playing around."

He took up the dart and turned it over slowly in his long, sensitive fingers.

Suddenly his eyes looked at me steadily.

"I cannot grant that request. I thought I had made that quite clear."

"Too damned clear!" I exploded. "There's something phony about this whole expedition, and you're the only person who can explain it. I insist on those guns, for the safety of the entire camp. Especially for Miss Brook. At least she oughtn't to be jeopardized—especially as she's your fiancée!" I couldn't help the bitterness I got into that last line—but his moon-white face didn't alter in the least.

"I'm quite aware of our engagement," he said softly, "but after all, Cambridge—I am the leader of this expedition. You are a little overwrought by this experience. Suppose you remain what you are—an astrogator?"

From the way he said it, I might have been an animalcule. I quivered on retorting—on demanding to know about the dart tip—then realizing that if I hit him it might lead to complications, I swallowed my fury and stalked outside. I felt his pale eyes watch me go.

III.

As I moodily returned toward my own tent I encountered Hu Ling moving silently toward me. He gave his little obeisance. "Mister Nick would converse with you," he said smoothly.

I nodded shortly and headed for our tent. Nick was sprawled on his bunk as I entered. Immediately he sat up. "Ling found you then? Where'd you go? I've been looking for you."

For a moment I hesitated, then— After all, Nick was to be completely trusted. Briefly I told him what had happened.

"I—see," he mused slowly. "Matter of fact, it was about guns that I wanted to see you. I don't feel safe being unarmed with that guy Reid around. He's the nastiest bit of work I've seen in a year of moonrises. So it seems to me that the only way to get guns is to take 'em, tonight."

"But there's never any night on Io," I reminded him.

"I know that—but Io has a forty-two-hour revolution, and that means that in roughly two more hours the Sun and Jupiter will both be out of sight. That leaves Europa and Ganymede light to worry over, and they're not very strong. Pretty low albedoes— I think I could make it across the river to the ship without being noticed."

I nodded slowly. "O.K. It's an idea. I'll keep watch while

you—"

I stopped short. Both of us twisted our heads sharply at a sudden wild shriek from the clearing outside. Immediately we were at the tent opening. Reid, Ada, and her father also came into view. The only other person in sight was Hu Ling, staring steadily toward the bushes. A jackknife glittered wickedly in his hand.

"What's all this noise about?" demanded Reid, striding toward him. "Was it you, Ling?"

The Oriental started out of his immobile posture. "The blue-skinned infidel attacked my honorable personage. I will not be defiled by the scum of this moon—"

Reid's jaws clamped shut for a moment, then turning to the jungle he shouted Kiol's name. Amidst a rustling of tickle-brush the Ionian slunk into view. Reid eyed him with a cruel stare. "You attacked Hu Ling?" he asked tonelessly.

"No agree in shelter," said the Ionian helplessly. "We not fitted to keep company—"

Reid didn't let him finish. Swinging round his fist he struck Kiol in the chest. Since Reid was a powerful man on Earth with three times normal strength on Io, the blow sent the native hurtling backward to the ground where he lay whimpering in fright.

"You'll have to learn that while you're in this company you must keep your hands to yourself. You are only an Ionian native—we are Earthlings, no matter what our color." Reid stopped, then spat out, "Get back in that shelter! Quick!"

"Just a minute!" It was Ada who moved quickly forward and placed her slim body defensively in front of Reid as the Ionian slowly rose. She went on hotly, "You've not the least right to treat Kiol like this, Lud! It doesn't matter what world he belongs to, or what creed. Quite probably Hu Ling had just as much to do with it!"

The Chinaman's slant eyes smoldered a little brighter in the moonlight, but he said nothing, The rest of us closed the circle as the girl went on talking, her voice now cutting with anger.

"At least I know now what sort of a man you are, Lud!" Deliberately she turned her back on Reid and nodded sympathetically to the Ionian. He looked at her steadily for a moment, unmistakable gratitude in his eyes, then nodded toward the jungle.

"Sleep there—more natural to me," he said briefly. "Come back in few hours."

"You'd better!" Reid ground out. "Be here with the rise of Jupiter—" He turned to the white-faced, rigid girl as the native crept away into the lofty grasses. "Most heroic of you, my dear," he murmured, smiling faintly. "Perhaps you forget that I understand natives far better than you. To allow another world native to attack an Earthling is to admit the lowering of interplanetary prestige—"

"Be hanged to your prestige!" the girl flamed back. "Kiol has feelings just as you and I—if you've got any feelings, that is! You acted like a—a brute!" She flashed him a biting glance then turned and strode back to her tent. Without a word we others broke up.

For a long time Reid stood thinking, stroking the lapel of his immaculate white coat. Then at last he returned to his tent. An hour later his gas-glow light went out.

"O.K.," I murmured to Nick. "He's doused the light. Now's your chance."

Quickly he kicked off his boots, stripped to the waist, and slid softly into the river at the clearing's edge. I watched him go, his head like a blob in that silvery ribbon, dimly saw him reach the other side and move quickly to the gray ovum of the spaceship. In fifteen minutes he was back, bitter-faced.

"No dice!" he snapped, "That damned Reid has locked up the arms cabinet. I don't like it, Dick!"

I hardly answered him. Somehow his discovery seemed to confirm my worst suspicions. I sat staring through the tent opening across the shadowed clearing, trying to imagine what possible purpose the cold-blooded Reid had in mind.

I fell asleep thinking about him.

When I awoke, Jupiter was just pushing his rim over the horizon. I looked around for Nick, but instead of finding him I discovered a note pinned to his bunk. It stated briefly that Reid had set off upriver in a motorboat with Kiol to look for the *ilution* trees, and that Nick had decided to follow him in another boat in an effort to discover what his game was.

"The damned fool!" I breathed bitterly, crushing the note in my hand. "If Reid's the man 1 think he is and sees you, you'll never get back to this camp alive. And unarmed, too!"

That was the main thing that worried me. Nick was the kind of reckless guy who'd do anything. His only source of protection was a jackknife!

Small wonder that I was jumpy through the hours that followed. I hardly answered any of the questions that Ada directed toward me after we'd finished Hu Ling's most excellent breakfast.

"It's Nick," I explained, when she finally cornered me staring anxiously up the river. "He followed Reid."

She looked surprised. "Well...is there anything wrong in that? After all, we're bound to know where the *ilution* trees are one day, and—"

I turned quickly to her. Her pretty face was puzzled in the queer light. "Listen, Ada, do you really believe we came here for rubber trees?" I asked seriously.

"Well of course! What else should we come for?"

"That's just what I'm wondering," I muttered. "The more I think of it, the more I believe that Reid planned this whole expedition as an excuse to get here. It takes plenty of money to equip a spaceship and for some reason he—" I stopped and looked round impatiently as Hu Ling appeared before us. His yellow face was troubled.

"Quickly, Miss Brook! Your honorable father is ill!"

"Ill!" she cried, startled, then we turned together and went quickly into Brook's tent. He was lying flat on his bunk, breathing noisily, his face a delicate green hue that wasn't altogether caused by the shifting lights.

"Moon fever," I said cryptically, instantly recognizing the symptoms. Turning to the anxious girl I said, "Fetch me my kit from the tent. You can go, Ling. There's nothing you can do."

For that matter, there isn't much anybody can do with moon fever. It gets you right away, lays you out flat—and you stay flat until the crisis wipes you out or you recover with startling suddenness.

I gave the magnate an injection of *galpha*, made him as comfortable as possible, and left it at that. The attack might last anywhere from a few hours to a few Earth-days.

"No use worrying, Ada," I said to her, as she stood moodily outside the tent. "He'll be all right."

She nodded despondently. Worry for her father and my own worry for Nick's safety kept up apart quite a deal, and at the end of several more hours we were a pretty morose pair. But at least we had diversion by the return of Reid from upriver, accompanied by the Ionian.

Instantly I was all anxiety, looking for Nick. There was no sign of him. Striding across the clearing I intercepted Reid as he was about to enter his tent. I noticed that he carried in his hand a container full of rubbery-smelling sap.

"Where's Nick Charteris?" I demanded stonily.

He raised an eyebrow. "Should I know?"

"You know damn well you should! He followed you upriver when you set off. He hasn't come back."

"Really?" He meditated a moment, then shrugged. "I wonder if you'd mind coming into the tent? This sap is a trifle odorous." He turned deliberately and entered, switching on the gas-glow light. Putting the pot down off the bench he lighted one of his eternal Titan-flower cigarettes.

"So Charteris followed me, did he? For what reason?"

"Because, like me, he thinks you're up to something!" I said bluntly. "Seems mighty queer you didn't see him—"

"Well, I didn't! Nor do I like these constant innuendoes!" For a moment he looked at me nastily, then smiled disarmingly. "After all, Cambridge, I am sure you are worrying yourself quite needlessly. There are no dangerous creatures in the jungles, and one has only to follow the river to get back to camp."

"You stand there and say there's nothing dangerous, and yet darts get thrown around?" I cried hotly. "That isn't very convincing, Reid. What's more, I don't believe you! What's behind all this? What have you done with Nick?"

He was still smiling cynically. "Your concern is most touching, Cambridge, but I can only repeat what I've said. And now, if you'll be so good as to leave me, I have work to do with this *ilution* sap."

He turned very definitely to the chemical bottles on the bench. I swallowed hard in my throat and longed to punch him in the jaw. Then I growled out, "Mr. Brook's ill with fever."

"At 120° F. that's not very surprising," he murmured, preparing to remove his white coat.

I stared at his back. "You mean you're not even interested enough to go over and see him?"

"Why should I? What can I—?"

It was Ada who cut him short. Her worried, frightened face appeared suddenly in the tent opening.

"Come quickly, both of you! Nick's boat is drifting downstream but there's no sign of him. I think the boat's got something heavy in it."

I was outside in a flash, vaulted the distance to the river edge in two leaps and stood staring fixedly at the stretch. Ada was right. A silent motorboat was drifting along, but weighted as few things on Io are weighted—so much so the boat's top was nearly level with the river.

Wading into midstream I grabbed it as it came floating within reach, tugged it quickly to the bank. Dazedly I stared in its bottom. Ada's breath caught quickly as she looked over my shoulder.

Nick was lying there all right, but something had happened to him. It was just as if he was a stone statue, an effigy of himself, and when I slipped my hands under his shoulders I encountered hard, brittle heaviness! Even in such slight attraction it took me all my time to raise him.

Perforce we had to call Reid and he gave us a hand to carry that unnaturally stiff body into his tent. In the gas-glow light we could see more clearly—and what we saw sent a cold chill of horror down my spine and caused Ada to gasp and back into a corner of the tent with a hand to her lips.

Nick's face was frozen into an expression of utter terror. His lips were drawn back and fixed—gray and hard. His eyes stared like frosty balls. Every part of his body was cast in the same inflexible mould. Even his teeth had turned greenish.

"Why, he's—he's turned to stone! Petrified!" I screamed huskily. "Reid, do you see? He's petrified!"

He nodded very slowly. "He must have gotten out of his boat at one of the calcium areas—probably cut himself. The stuff entering his bloodstream in such undiluted form could easily transform him into stone—"

"And then he got up, walked to the boat, and lay down?" I sneered bitterly. "Be damned to that for a tale! Somebody did this, and if any man knows anything at all, it's you!"

He looked at me icily. "You're a damned fool!" he said flatly.

"Even if you didn't actually do it, you're responsible!" I went on hotly. "You wouldn't let any of us have guns. Nick went with his life in his hands."

"That was his fault; I didn't ask him to follow me."

Reid paused a moment as Ada, evidently finding things too much for her, moved quietly out of the tent. I turned back to Reid with a glare.

"Now get this, Reid; it's time for a showdown! I'm not putting up with anything more like this. Bring out those guns and come clean on what you're up to. You're not hunting for *ilution*. You're hunting for something that only you and Kiol know about!"

He elevated an eyebrow toward the sap he'd brought in. "What would you call that, then?"

"I wouldn't know—I'm only an astrogator! Even if it is *ilution* in a natural state, it's only a cover up for something else. Come on—out with it!"

For reply the pocket of his white coat suddenly bulged ominously. I saw that his hand was thrust in it.

"Get out!" he ordered stonily.

I looked at the pocket. I could tell from the outline that it hid a small but powerful flame gun. And I could tell, too, from the brittle, snaky stare in Reid's pale eyes that he meant those two words.

There was nothing else for it. I went.

IV.

An hour later we buried poor Nick's remains in the soft, oozy ground beyond the main clearing. Reid recited a burial service that was clipped, heartless, and brief—then he went back to his tent and had a meal brought to him.

I roamed around in moody silence, listening to the moans and cries of Brook as he reached the delirium stage of his fever. Ada wandered about alone, too, avoiding all company, so heavy was the general worry on her mind.

Since Kiol was missing, I presumed that now his particular work was done, he'd slipped off into the jungle to rest. As for Hu Ling, he was only visible now and again as he came outside his cooking tent to throw away water and waste into the river.

I stood idly watching him on one of these occasions, trying to figure out some way of getting the truth out of Reid—then I suddenly stood upright. Hu Ling had uttered a gasping scream. His water pail floated from his hand and bobbed to the ground; he himself went over and over in a sudden frantic effort to remove something from his neck.

I hurled myself across the clearing, but by the time I'd reached him he was almost dead, yellow, trembling fingers clutching for the last time at a tiny barb protruding from his throat. He relaxed, became still.

Ada gave a little cry of horror and turned away, raced for her tent. Reid came up in the mixture of lights, drawn by the Oriental's last despairing cries. Our eyes met.

"What this time?" he demanded curtly.

"Ling's been murdered!" I lifted him easily in my arms and for the second time within a few hours bore a dead body into Reid's tent. He examined the body briefly then plucked out the dart with tweezers, staring at the end. He smelt it quickly.

"Cyanic acid," he announced. "Kills in about seventy seconds."

I looked at him murderously. "So it's another of your precious outfit on the job?" I breathed. "The same crowd that had a go at Ada and me—"

"Don't be absurd," he interrupted calmly. "This is only a sliver of wood, not a dart. Besides, only one person did this—Kiol. He could easily get at my supplies of cyanic acid in the tent here. Fashioning a dart and blowpipe would be nothing to him. Clearly it was revenge. He loathed the very sight of Hu Ling, as you may remember."

What was I to say? It was perfectly logical reasoning, and very probably quite true. Besides the dart was only crude; nothing like that other one—

"Listen, Reid," I said slowly, "Ling's death is perhaps explainable in the way you've said. But with regard to the other things—"

I broke off purposely, took him off guard. In one swift action, timing my leap exactly with the gravitation, I vaulted the table, grabbed him round the throat and bore him to the floor. The uppercut I slammed at him dazed him completely. By the time he'd recovered his wits, I had his gun steadily leveled.

"Now you're going to spill something!" I snapped, with a pleasant satisfaction in my heart. "And remember it would be a pleasure to kill you if you try any tricks! It looks as though one murder more wouldn't make much difference anyhow! Get up, damn you!"

He got up, his face like marble. "I really see no reason for such violence," he said irritably, fingering his jaw.

"Spill it!" I ordered inexorably. "And be quick about it!"

He seemed to hesitate, then shrugged. "All right, I'll tell you.

Probably you'd know in any case in the finish, so what's the odds? Maybe you'll see how foolish you've been. Where do you imagine the lost races of Mars went to?"

It was a surprising question, but I answered it quickly enough. "Vanished under the sand. Anybody knows that. We've examined Mars from end to end and found their buried cities—traces of their vast scientific achievements and marvelous resources. We've even found broken Martian coins—"

"Coins! There you have it!" For once his pale eyes were gleaming almost fanatically. "Like every other scientist I have examined Mars. I have broken coins amidst my souvenirs. But imagine my feelings when Kiol, a native of Io, came to Earth and brought me a couple of darts with tempered *jilian* steel tips, the halves of several coins which roughly matched my own souvenir coins, and the story of a hidden city! The coins, of course, were not identical halves, but of same type. See here."

He felt in his pocket and produced two broken halves of a coin. Indeed, they fitted roughly and were undoubtedly of Martian origin. He made to return them to his pocket, but I snatched at them quickly—too quickly. They slipped from my hand and plopped into the sticky *ilution* sap on the bench, sinking instantly.

"It doesn't matter," he said. "You can see it's true enough."

I looked at him in bewilderment. "You're not suggesting that the Martians came to Io, are you?"

"Not all of them, but some did—probably a remnant who escaped from the red planet before it finally succumbed to the devastating effects of dehydration. They chose Io because it was best fitted for their purposes. The gravitation is not entirely dissimilar to Mars. This world at that time would be rich and comfortable. Yes, they established themselves in what are now the jungles, and remains of their cities are still here. Kiol saw them—and now I have seen them."

"Then that dart—"

"A Martian dart, obviously. In the interval of the ages these migrated Martians have lost nearly all their old skill and become degenerate, have reverted to the methods of the primitive. But the primitive doesn't match up entirely when they tip their darts with *jilían* steel! That was what gave me my first clue. There they have an art that we of Earth haven't even begun to master.

"Think then for one moment of the vast buried scientific secrets in that city of theirs—secrets far greater than those on Mars itself, for the migrating people would naturally take their most valuable possessions. Today I saw that city, guarded by a handful of degenerates. Most of the place is apparently automatic and requires no brains to keep it going. A glorious scientific and mechanical heritage left from a day of supreme knowledge—

"In that city are secrets beyond our knowledge—but among them are such solved enigmas as matter projection over a distance, super-telepathy, the release of atomic force, the tempering and fashioning of incredibly hard metals—

"Now .you know what I'm trying to do. Trying to rediscover Martian science for the sake of Earth—wrest it from these degenerates who no longer need it."

"So that's it!" I said slowly, musing. "Then where does the death of Nick Charteris fit in?"

"I've already told you I don't know," he answered calmly.

Even then I didn't believe him—but I did believe the Martian migration theory. I'd seen the darts for myself.

"Then the *ilution* trees were just a gag to get here?"

He smiled twistedly. "There was no other way. I have very little money of my own. I knew Brook would never fall for the idea of a Martian migration, but something up his own alley got him right away."

"But that piece of rubber you showed us?"

"That was genuine," he said, surprisingly enough. "I have the secret of untearable *ilution* rubber. As a matter of fact, it is done by a chemical extracted from an ore which I found on Mars. I could have made plenty of money out of it, of course, but I preferred to defer it for a while and use it as a means to an end. To come here. That stuff in the pot there is ordinary *ilution* which I melted over a fire." He stopped and looked at me steadily. "Well, now you know. What are you going to do?"

1 started to say there was little I could do, but Ada interrupted me. She looked eagerly from one to the other of us; then said, "I think Dad's getting better! Come and look!"

I took her arm and we hastened across the clearing. The moment I looked at Brook, I could tell he was better. He was sitting up in his bunk, rather breathless, but the greenness of the moon fever had left him.

"What the devil's been going on?" he demanded impatiently. "I don't seem to remember—"

"You've been ill—and things have been happening," I told him seriously. I thought the two murders better be kept quiet for the moment on the off chance of a relapse.

He made a wry face. "Ill!" he snorted disgustedly. "And after all the preventatives I took! Well, ill or otherwise, I want something to eat—and quick! Something good! None of that damned canned stuff from the ship."

"I'm afraid there's nothing else," remarked Reid quietly, coming in. "Unless, of course—" He fell to thought for a moment.

"Unless what?" Brook snapped. He had the fierce impatience of the moon fever's hangover.

"Unless one of us could kill a rocket-bird. Their flesh is as tender as turkey. Unhappily, I'm not very good at game hunting." Reid looked at me suggestively. Certainly I knew more about the job than him.

"How soon do you want a meal?" I asked Brook, and he blew out his cheeks in exasperation.

"Right now, of course! I'm starving, man! And I want some coffee, too! Black!"

"I'll—I'll see to it, Dad," said Ada quickly, and went away swiftly to take Ling's place at the cooking tent.

"I'll do my best," I said. "I'll want a rifle, Reid."

We went out together, looked at each other silently.

"I hope by now we understand each other?" he asked slowly.

"Now you see why I stopped any arms. Not only from the point of view of possible fever madness, but because a chance Martian coming near this clearing might have got hurt. That might have released diabolical scientific forces upon us. See?"

I didn't, but I nodded. Handed him back his gun. "O.K.," I growled. "Maybe I was wrong at that."

"I'll get your rifle," he murmured, and went toward the river, unhooked one of the motorboats, and went over to the *Stardust*. In ten minutes he was back and handed me an ordinary rifle.

"See you later," he said, in a voice that somehow struck me as peculiar. Then he turned back to his tent to make the necessary arrangements for the burial of Hu Ling.

I looked round the clearing, listened to Ada's bustling with pots and pans, the impatient shouts of her father, the creak of the table in Reid's tent as he hauled the dead Oriental off it. Then I turned and strode into the jungle, heading to the point three miles away where there was apparently a good nesting ground of rocket-birds.

Yet as I went I was uneasy. Why, I did not know. The thought of Ada alone with Reid troubled me. Even more so when I realized that Brook would be unable to protect her. Moon fever leaves a fellow's legs like tapers for days afterward.

Besides, he was unarmed. Reid had the key to the arms cabinet.

V.

The jungle was completely silent as I moved swiftly through it, guiding my course like any other jungle expert by the position of the stars. Once you know Io's revolution and changing sky and moons, it isn't difficult.

I chose a particularly fat specimen, sighted, and fired. The din of my gun boomed in the hot silence. The shot bird's parachute membrane collapsed and it dropped lightly to the ground. In five minutes I'd scooped it up from the moving, disturbed birds, and headed back into the jungle.

But as I came within earshot of the camp once more, I could hear Brook shouting hoarsely. Shouting for me!

Immediately I doubled my efforts, vaulted the last bush, and came into the clearing. It was oddly deserted in the pale light. Dropping the bird in the cooking tent, I raced across to where Brook was hollering.

"What is it? What's the matter?" I panted, bursting in.

He gulped for breath. "It's—it's Ada! Reid went off with her a few minutes ago, along with Kiol. I saw it all from here and couldn't do a thing!" He clutched my arm. "He took her by force, Dick!" He panted. "Threw her over his shoulder, gagged her to stop her cries—but I saw them just the same. I can't understand it. They—they went upriver. Blast it, if only I wasn't so weak!" he finished in despair.

Without a word I raced out of the tent, grabbed a few tins of compressed food and a bottle of restorative, and took them in to him.

"Get these inside you!" I said curtly. "You'll have to wait for your rocket-bird. I'm going after Ada. I damn well felt something like this would happen!"

"But what does it mean? Where's he taken her?" he demanded huskily. "I never thought Reid—"

"No time to explain now," I tossed out as I left, and in flying leaps headed for the river. Then at its edge I stopped. For one thing, Reid had driven a hole through the bottom of the remaining motorboat, and it was awash. For another, I had no idea where this Martian city was situated. And even on Io a thousand miles of packed jungle is pretty impossible to search in.

The only thing to do was to repair the boat and then take a chance. I had it out of the water in five minutes. In another five I was at work with tools repairing the four-inch rip in the bottom. I worked with a desperate, feverish intensity, the thought of Ada slogging all the time into my mind.

I saw it all now. Reid had engineered it very nicely from the beginning. He'd put Kiol and Ling together and favored their antipathy until at last the Ionian had killed for revenge. Then he'd undoubtedly been back of the death of Nick Charteris. And lastly the idea that I leave camp and look for food— That had been smart! It had left him free to take Ada. But *why*? That was the thing that appalled and perplexed me.

I worked onward in a grim mood, wondering as I slammed home the rivets how I could possibly trail Reid upriver. Then a sudden movement in the bushes of the clearing to my rear brought me round with leveled rifle. To my amazement it was Kiol who burst into view, breathing hard, sweat glistening brightly on his blue skin.

For several seconds he could not speak, only gulp for breath and motion back to the jungle. Then at last he got it out.

"Miss Brook and Reid—they back in jungle. City. Woman in exchange for science. She help me one time. I escape and help her now. Come tell you. Have to hurry." He looked back over his shoulder anxiously.

My jaws snapped shut suddenly. I drove home the last rivet and pushed the boat into the river, tossing in my rifle. Racing to the cook tent, I swept up some stuff and tossed a sleep-preventative tablet into my mouth. Returning to the boat I motioned to Kiol and had him leap in beside me. I took no thought for Brook. He was safe enough anyhow. The immediate job on hand was to locate Ada—before it was too late.

I drove the motor on our little boat to the absolute limit of its capacity, sending the craft chugging in a tremendous wake along the swiftly flowing river. Naturally, with a lesser gravity, we moved at a far greater speed than would have been possible on Earth.

Kiol kept his eyes fixed on the long vista. He hardly spoke at all, and when he did it was only to urge greater speed. That couldn't be done; we were going all out.

It seemed an eternity to me. I never knew a river to stretch so far—but I found that we had actually been on the way for thirty minutes when Kiol finally signaled sharply and pointed to a lee of the bank. Immediately I pulled toward it, grabbed my rifle, and vaulted off the boat yards before it touched shore. Kiol came up beside me, pointing to a faintly defined trail in the shifting light.

"Through there—straight to city," he said quickly.

At top speed I jumped along it, vaulted the shrubs that loomed in the way, and finally burst through the screen of vines at the top of the rise. Immediately I came upon my first sight of that forgotten outpost. It stopped me involuntarily.

In the light of Jupiter and Europa it covered perhaps two miles of a natural jungle clearing, at the most barren point of which I was now standing. In every direction loomed the crumbled ramparts of once magnificent architecture—eroded columns of stone, skeletal walls, their masonry crumbled into now-smashed streets that had once been picturesque.

I began to move forward, only to stop as Kiol suddenly cried sharply and dropped in his tracks. In horrified amazement I stared down at his head. Half of it had been incinerated!

"Kiol—" I cried hoarsely, then I broke off and twisted round at a smooth voice behind me.

"I shouldn't make any moves if I were you, Cambridge. Drop your rifle!"

It was Ludwig Reid, of course, standing just in front of the nearby bushes. On either side of him were two of the queerest creatures I'd yet seen. In some vague way they looked Earthly, but only in the faces. Their bodies were those of an insect, supported on eight bowed, powerful legs.

"The degenerates," Reid explained casually. "Men of Mars, no longer masters of the mighty intelligence they once possessed." He came up slowly as I studied them, his flame gun held at the ready. "I rather fancied you'd come along when I missed Kiol!" Turning deliberately he kicked the dead Ionian in the ribs, then with a sneer turned back to me. "You don't place much value on your life, do you, Cambridge?"

That was too much for me. In that moment my accumulated hatred for the man suddenly spilled over. I hurled myself at him with clenched fists—but I never landed a blow. Instead, he anticipated the move and slid to one side, at the same time bringing the butt of his gun down with tremendous force.

Blinding fire burst soundlessly before my eyes.

* * * * * * *

As I recovered consciousness, I realized that I was lying on cold stone in the moonlit ruins of what had once no doubt been a vast hall of scientific instruments. Indeed, the instruments were still there. I could see their shadowy outlines as I slowly opened my eyes and warily looked about me.

Very carefully I turned my head and saw a dim vista of huge, incomprehensible instruments crouched in the shadows. Most of them seemed to be intact, but in design they were quite incomprehensible. My main impression was that of titanic electromagnets, tubes, generators, vacuum globes, and other generalized material, all of which seemed to be linked by heavy cables to a huge switchboard at the far end of the place.

I turned a little farther, then the movement was arrested as an insect Martian merged out of the shadows bearing in his tentacled 'hand' a cup of beautifully wrought *jilian* steel. In his other hand was one of his deadly darts, poised ready for an instant drive into my heart if I refused his advances.

There was only one chance, and I took it. I raised the cup toward nay lips, then paused suddenly and gave a hoarse shout, pointing at the same time to the distant shadowy masses of machinery. As I'd hoped, the guards twisted round briefly, and in that second I hurled the cup's contents over my left shoulder. By the time they looked at me again I was simulating all the actions of drinking.

I 'drained' the cup, handed it back, and waited tensely. I wondered whether I was supposed to drop dead or throw a couple of handsprings. It was Reid who supplied the answer. He came softly from some adjoining part of the hall and looked at me in grim amusement in the moonlight.

"Well, you begin to feel the hardening effects?" he asked

pleasantly. "In case you're not aware of it, you have just drunk a liquid containing inert calcium. In that condition it is odorless, but the moment it starts to mix with the hemoglobin of the bloodstream it becomes an active element and changes your entire body to stone, in the space of perhaps an hour. Pleasant, isn't it?" He looked at me in unholy satisfaction.

"So it was you who killed Nick!" I breathed murderously.

"What else did you think, you fool? It was sheer mischance that Ada happened to see the boat containing his body. I rather hoped it would be carried unnoticed down the river and end up over the Sawback Rapids. Much better than leaving the body here for these Martians to examine."

"And now?" I whispered, at the same time carefully feeling the weight of the stone slab on which I sat.

"Now you will watch these dumb heads give up their secrets. They know a little English—enough for that, anyhow. Here in this hall they have all the machines I've dreamed of. The actual knowledge is long since gone from their minds, but they still remember how to use the major switches, which set the machinery in action. Here we have the source of *jilian* steel tempering, matter projection over a distance, and a hundred and one other things. The matter projection is particularly interesting, but to demonstrate it, it is necessary, of course, to have a living subject. I could find only one—Ada!"

I sat still. If I simulated growing paralysis I might get somewhere. "You had no need to take her!" I grated back. "Anything would have done! Even a rocket-bird."

He shook his untidy head. "A rocket-bird is not ordinary flesh and blood. The effect wouldn't have been the same."

"You mean you would deliberately kill Ada, change her into atoms, in order to learn one of several blasted secrets that we're bound to discover on Earth in due time?"

"Ah, but when?" he asked doubtfully.

"If I get the secrets first, it will give me an enormous advantage. I told you once that I was short of money. I'm taking care of that from now on!"

He turned aside quickly and uttered a command. A distant door of the great hall opened and two more Martians appeared, carrying the unconscious form of Ada between them. In perfect silence, save for the scrape of their insect feet along the floor, they bore her to a device that closely resembled a giant vacuum tube. I saw a great semicircle of glass glint momentarily as it rose upward, then it clamped into place again with the girl inside it. In growing anxiety I noticed the anode and cathode poles at either end of the tube.

Still I sat tight and glanced anxiously toward the guards. They were by the wall now, watching me intently. Reid had turned away from me, his whole attention given to the scientific experiment he intended to note down. The other two Martians were moving toward the switchboard preparatory to closing the switches that, I presumed, would bring hidden energies to work and actuate the machinery.

I had two things only in my favor—the gravity, and the fact that I was supposed to be in the first stages of paralysis. From the rigid way I'd been sitting I think I fooled them into believing it. But with that gravity I had in consequence three times as much strength as on Earth. The only thing to do was to utilize it immediately. And I did, with a plan in mind beforehand.

Suddenly I sprang upward to my feet, clutching to the stone on which I'd been sitting. It was heavy in my hands. On Earth I couldn't have raised it. In one mighty sweep I lifted it over my head and hurled it forward with shattering force. The effect was just as I'd hoped. The two Martian guards, taken utterly by surprise, had not the time to dodge. The hurtling slab carved into their brittle, insectile bodies, snapped them in two and plastered them messily against the frowning wall behind.

With a cry of alarm Reid swung round and ripped out his flame gun, leveling it to fire—but I'd been expecting that. I dove into a flying tackle, bracing my plunge with my heels hard against the floor. The terrific thrust sent me hurtling into him and we both went flying six or seven yards, his gun sailing out of his hand.

Keeping my head, I clung to my original plans, leapt to my feet, and vaulted clean over Reid's sprawling body. In an instant I'd seized his gun, swung it round and pressed the button. The tremendous blast roared across the hall and immediately incinerated the two remaining Martians at the switchboard.

Reid seized his chance to hurl himself upon me, snatched at the gun—snatched too hard and it went sailing away across the shadows. His fist came up and jolted me from head to foot. I floated backward with a spinning brain, contacted the wall, and automatically thrust my feet against it.

I had a vision of him racing toward Ada, probably with some plan in his mind to try and complete the experiment—but he didn't make it. The force of my thrust hurled me upon him again, and this time I was ready for him. I clutched him with my left hand, jerked him upright, then with the full power of my right arm drove my fist into his face.

He shot backward as though fired from a gun, his face shining sticky red with the force of that three-times Earth punch. He steadied himself suddenly and whipped out that dagger-like knife of his from his pocket. Menacingly he came toward me as I measured him narrowly from the shadows.

He was an unlovely picture. The blow I'd dealt him had smashed his nose, I think. I crouched, waiting for him to spring—and at last he did. But in that split second I stepped aside and brought up a terrific uppercut that made his jawbone soggy under my knuckles. The knife dropped from his hand. He came reeling drunkenly down from the lofty ceiling and, braced against one of the vast instruments, I slammed him again. The blow hurled him floorward.

Still unsatisfied I hauled him to his feet and drew back my arm for a final blow—but it wasn't necessary. That last blow on the jaw, driven with pile-driving effect, had snapped his neck. He sank down in a limp heap to the floor.

For just a moment I stood looking down at him, breathing hard. Then I turned swiftly and smashed open the tube in which the senseless Ada was imprisoned. In a moment I had her over my shoulder, weighing no heavier than a child.

Stooping, I picked up the ray gun and turned away to run swiftly outside into the jungle, fearful that other Martians hidden somewhere in the city's depths might start a pursuit.

But none did. I can only assume that those four were the last of their race. I reached the river half an hour later and pushed off hastily into midstream....

Of course, old Brook was disgusted about his *ilution* trees, until I made a surprising discovery. As we packed up for departure to Earth, I came across that *ilution* sap in Reid's tent. To my surprise it had set to complete hardness, nor could I make any impression on it! I tipped it out of its pot and it stood in a solid block, perfectly transparent, but—

Suddenly I remembered those two halves of Martian coin that I'd accidentally dropped into it. By rights they should be visible—but they weren't! They had chemically amalgamated with the *ilution*. Immediately I called Brook and Ada and told them what had happened.

"But—but what does it mean?" Brook asked in astonishment.

"It can only mean one thing," I answered slowly. "Reid said he had a hardening chemical extracted from Martian ore. It can only mean that these coins are made from that self-same ore and chemically assimilate with *ilution*. The thing's simple in that case. On Mars there are countless tons of the same metal from which these coins are made. It can be bought cheap—though but for this accident we might have searched for years to discover Reid's secret. Obviously, he didn't know the coins were the same ore, otherwise he'd not have been so casual about my dropping them in the *ilution*."

"You're right—dead right!" Brook breathed wonderingly.

THE MISTY WILDERNESS
BY JOHN RUSSELL FEARN

From *Modern Wonder* #78, 1938,
and *Startling Stories*, September 1939

In 1937 the giant Odhams Press in the UK launched *Modern Wonder*, a very attractive juvenile boys' weekly, tabloid size, but printed in glossy photogravure. It contained mainly science fact articles, and features on modern transport, engineering, etc.—but also had a small but significant amount of science fiction. Alerted by Gillings, Fearn was quickly on the case, and he soon crashed the magazine with a very clever series of articles, tailor-made for the magazine: "The Chronicles of a Space Voyager." This was a series of speculative/factual articles on each planet of the solar system, strictly based on modern astronomical knowledge, but leavened with a science-fictional framing device of the planets described from the viewpoint of the crew of an exploratory spaceship.

Having got his foot in the editorial door, Fearn sent the editor the synopses of a number of science fiction short stories, some of them based on earlier unsold stories. Fearn was then commissioned to produce three short stories as quickly as possible.

For the first story, "Death at the Observatory", he created a modern-day scientific detective, Marlo, called in to investigate an "impossible" murder at an observatory. Appearing first in *Modern Wonder* No. 76 (1938), it was reprinted in the U.S. in *Captain Future* in September 1940, and reprinted as a classic ten years later in the first issue of the same publisher's reprint magazine, *Fantastic Story Magazine*. It has since been anthologised.

His third story was "The Misty Wilderness", which had been quickly rewritten from one of Fearn's Weinbaum-flavour Thornton Ayre stories that had been rejected by *Astounding* at the beginning of the year. In the original, Fearn's villain, Eboni, had been a woman (based on Weinbaum's "The Red Peri"). Fearn changed the character to a man (in accordance with the requirements of a boys' magazine). The story, an interplanetary detective yarn, duly sold, and appeared in *Modern Wonder* No. 78 (1938). Like the others, it was not an ostensibly juvenile story, as was proven by its being reprinted by *Startling Stories* in September 1939.

This story's quality was further attested by its being translated and published—along with his second *Modern Wonder* story (from No. 77), "The Weather Machine"—in a French newspaper, *Ric et Rac*, on the 6th and 20th of December, 1939. With the Second World War having already broken out, this was a truly astonishing coup for an English author, as well as being the first translated science fiction short stories to ever appear in a French newspaper!

"The Misty Wilderness" was later translated into Italian in 1982, and along with "The Weather Machine" it was again translated and published in the French magazine *Le Rocambole* in 2002.

THE MISTY WILDERNESS

Selton of the Spaceways dares Uranus' trackless trails to hunt down Eboni. The Planetary Buccaneer.

Dudley Selton closed the switches that gave the power to the forward under-jets. His space machine instantly slowed in its onrush through the dense upper-level mists of Uranus and quickly nosed upward. He corrected that reaction, brought the ship back to a diving angle.

As he dropped he studied the infra-red screens, intently watching that small ship not more than two miles ahead which was likewise dropping to the spongy, unstable magma that constituted the ground of the Uranian unexplored belt.

"Thought you'd get away from me, eh?" Selton murmured, as the ship settled. "No black-haired pirate can get away from the Space Way Service—and from me last of all! I may be new to the game, but I always get my man."

Ahead of him, invisible to the eye but still impressed on the screens, the little ship gently landed. Selton eased his own machine along to within a hundred yards of it, cut the jets. Then, strapping a flame-gun belt round his waist, he opened the airlock and took a deep breath of the green world's warm, enervating atmosphere.

Warm because Uranus still possessed vast internal heat reserves, constantly seeping out on the dayside in the form of terrific geysers and mud eruptions. The air, mainly inert argon, but with a thirty percent oxygen content, was breathable enough to an Earthling.

Selton stepped outside his vessel on to the spongy black soil and glanced at the upper-level clouds—whirling, dense to London fog consistency, kept incessantly on the move by the eternal higher winds sweeping in from the nightward hemisphere. Down here at ground level the air was hazy, overhung by that low, shifting ceiling.

He moved along slowly, then paused as the other ship's airlock swung open, casting forth a long diffused fan of light.

The powerful figure of the man he had followed came slowly into view, attired in the customary leather jacket and breeches, gun holsters at his sides. The instant he saw Selton his hand flew to them—but Selton was quicker.

He strode up, gun leveled. "Take it easy! One false move and I'll wing you."

The man raised his arms as Selton relieved him of his guns.

Selton looked into cold blue eyes set in a brown masterful face. The chin was square, the lips half curved in a contemptuous smile. But the hair—that was enough! Absolutely as black as space.

"What have I done?" the prisoner inquired coolly.

Selton stared at him. "Done! You steal all the cargoes of the freighter ships on the Jupiter-Mercury run, then ask what you've done? You're an outlaw, running around in a private ship so you won't be detected. I've followed you all the way from the Jovian moon area."

He paused and studied the man's coal black hair. "Whoever called you Eboni was right," he murmured.

"Do you mind if I put my hands down?" Eboni asked politely. "Now that you have disarmed me?"

"Sure—sure; you can lower your hands."

Eboni did so, but so rapidly that he took Selton right off his guard. In one tricky movement that remotely resembled ju-jitsu Selton found his gun flying out of his hand.

A stabbing pain shot the length of his arm and he found himself sitting flat on the wet ground staring up into that resolute face and his own leveled gun.

"All right—get up!" Eboni snapped. "Quick."

Selton rose slowly, muttering under his breath. Still covering him, the outlaw plucked out the Space Service man's remaining gun and threw it into the mist. He retrieved his own weapon before discarding the second

"Now, listen," he breathed. "I know you followed me all the way from Callisto, so you could stop right with me. Your idea is to waltz me back to Earth, but you've got more ideas coming. I'm heading for the north of the unexplored belt, and if you know anything about this planet, you'll know that that'll take us to Equator Peaks."

Selton started. "But you can't do that, Eboni! That means going across unknown territory. Besides, the seasonal change—"

"Shut up!" Eboni eyed him grimly. "What's your name?"

"Dud Selton—Space Way Service V Detachment."

"Cub sleuth, eh?"

"What of it?"

"Oh, nothing. Anyway, your mother had the right idea when she gave you that first name. Now let's go!"

The outlaw leaned inside the airlock of his vessel and switched off the lights. Selton regarded him doubtfully, then tried again.

"Look here, Eboni, be sensible! How do you expect to get back here? You ought to know that the Uranian pole has no magnetic properties, and therefore a compass is useless—"

Eboni thrust out his powerful arm and revealed a small object like a watch upon his wrist. "This is a magnetic indicator, Dud—" He grinned again at the abbreviation.

"The needle swings to a magnetic plate in my machine. I can't fail to find my way back. Since you won't be coming back with me, what are you worrying about? Now get going."

Their feet made no sound in the sodden wilderness as they began to move. The broad soles of their boots sank half an inch into the ground at every step. Had the gravity been compatible with the 31,000-mile diameter of Uranus, it would have been an utter quagmire; but with a density of only .27, effort was almost similar to that demanded on Earth, and therefore saved them sinking any deeper.

After a while Selton asked: "What's the idea of heading for Equator Peaks? Hideout or something?"

Eboni did not answer immediately. His powerful face was still curiously amused in the faint light sifting through the upper-level clouds—a light cast by a sun with only one-three hundred and sixtieth of the power on earth.

"Can you think of a better place?" he asked presently. "A world wrapped in fogs, a vast expanse of crazy, slipping landscape, a veritable deathtrap to the uninitiated. Where better to have a hideout than in the foothills of Equator Peaks?"

Selton's face hardened a little. "Well, thanks for telling me that much, anyhow. I can use it in my evidence against you."

The outlaw said nothing, and they went on silently. When they were some distance from the ships, alone in the dim, misting twilight, he lowered his guns and slipped them into their holsters.

"We're far enough from the ship by now for you to lose your way if you try to escape," he explained calmly. "While, if you attack me and gain possession of this compass, it won't do you any good because it will only work on my wrist. It's tuned to my particular electrical wavelength and anybody else's would only jam the thing. Anyway, I'm quick on the draw—as you may have heard."

"Don't worry—I shan't attack you." Selton smiled coldly. "I want to find the location of this hideout of yours before I try running you in. The only point I don't understand is how you find your way to the Equator Peaks in a landscape like this."

Eboni glanced upward. "Try using your brains," he sneered. "The upper-level clouds move in a direct line from the Equator Peaks because of the colder winds sweeping in from the night-ward side. By following their line of movement it's a cinch. They're not very far from here; I know that."

Selton pondered over that. Uranus with its queer axial tilt, had forty-two years of night and forty-two years of day. The heat of the sun affected the atmosphere but little, but it was sufficient to raise the temperature on the sunward side some fifteen degrees.

This warmth, in contrast to the colder winds from the night-ward hemisphere, produced the upper-level clouds and eternal moisture drifts.

In Hemisphere Chasm, indeed, central passageway through the Equator Peaks to the night side, there were perpetual electrical storms, moving left to right for forty-two years, then right to left for another forty-two.

"You certainly picked a great planet for a base," Selton grunted as they squelched along. "How do you know that your hideout will even be there? The Uranian surface is always changing and sliding and—"

"Wait!" Eboni interrupted him sharply, halting. "I hear something!"

They both peered into the ghostly expanses. Selton, too, heard it now—a soft hissing noise like water on the verge of boiling. Abruptly he jerked his head up and stared at a rapidly swelling bubble in the ground not two hundred feet away.

Eboni frowned. "Never saw anything like that before. Looks like a bubble of sorts." He stopped short as the bubble suddenly reached maximum size and burst with a sharp *pop*. The air instantly became filled with warm, showering mud—mud that fell to the ground and wriggled. Eboni took a step back, staring down in disgust on scores of four-inch objects writhing in the ooze.

"What the deuce are they?" he growled aloud.

"Organisms, of sorts," Selton said as he looked at them closely. "Too big for animalcules, I'd say—unless everything's big on this world. Low-form organisms, evidently spawned in the boiling water below surface. Looks as though life here likes things hot."

"That bubble erupted them, then?"

"Apparently so—maybe a natural way of starting them off in life on the surface." Selton stopped and looked at Eboni sharply: "Say, what's the idea of asking me all these questions? You ought to know Uranus even better than I do!"

"Why? You don't think I spend my vacation here, do you? I only know the outstanding geographical facts; the local fauna's as big a mystery to me as to you."

Eboni broke off and glanced at the fast-growing disk-like things in the mud. "Better move before they get really big," he finished anxiously. "Come on."

Another mile's progress brought little change in the landscape—if a sloppy black magma with normal and treacherous surfaces lying entirely undistinguished could be called landscape. Time and again weird bubbles rose, swelled and popped, hurled their disgusting life through the dank air.

"Dud, I don't like this!" Eboni's voice was serious for a change. "I never struck things like this before on Uranus. Look at that one! Nearest thing to an umbrella I ever saw!"

He was right in that. An almost full-grown specimen resembled an open umbrella without the stick, the rib ends corresponding to viciously clawed hooks.

The whole thing was principally a gigantic flying object, membranous, and already quivering for flight. Even as the two stood watching, it suddenly took off from the wet ground and went sailing into the mists.

"Towards the Equator Peaks," murmured Selton, glancing up at the cloud rifts. "I wonder why?"

Eboni reflected. "Is it possible, I wonder, that Uranus life is migratory? Surely it will be with a forty-two-year day and night. We've about arrived at the change-over. Night is coming down here and day is on the other side. Suppose these creatures are the spawn left in the ground from the last migration, and that now—by some natural process—they are born and vomited out of the mud to make their way to the daylight side?"

"It's an idea," Selton said, pondering. "In any case, I don't see it matters much. Our main concern—or yours, is to reach this hideout. Then I'm going to run you in."

"You think so?" Eboni smiled twistedly. "You'll never do that. Later on you'll find out just why."

As they moved on again, the evidences of the great planet's ponderous changings from light to dark became more evident. The drenching vapor-drifts from the distant Equator Peaks began to thicken; the upper-level clouds no longer moved definitely from the nightward side.

Instead they were crisscrossing each other in dirty, smudgy bands, blurred with fantastic green lights as the far distant sun cast not direct, but oblique rays, gradually deepening to twilight as the clouds piled thicker.

"If we don't find this precious place of yours before night, we're going to be in a lovely mess," Selton remarked presently.

"Real night won't drop for eighteen months yet."

"At this rate it will take that long," Selton growled. "Then in a sour voice he demanded, "Why didn't you fly there in the first place and save all this trouble?"

"Because I had a reason. Besides—"

Eboni broke off and stopped walking, swung around as a sudden tremendous whirring sound came from the mists to the rear. With demoniac speed an umbrella organism came hurtling into view, flying close to the ground.

It was sheer luck that the outlaw happened to be in its way. Immediately its frightful claws spread defensively, hooked themselves more by chance than design in his tough leather jacket. He was jerked into the air, struggling desperately. Then he dropped again to the accompaniment of a sudden tearing. He reeled to his feet with his jacket in shreds.

"Hurt?" Selton demanded, stumbling forward through the reek.

"No, not much." Eboni seemed unconcerned for his own well being; his eyes were staring at his wrist. In dead silence Selton stared, too. The wrist compass had been smashed by Eboni's fall to the ground.

"Lost!" Eboni breathed at last, dragging his tattered jacket together. "Lost in this wilderness—we can never find the ship again. The only hope now is that we can get to the hideout. I've a radio there; we can call scout vessels on the main service ways. It'll mean giving myself up—but I guess I know when I'm licked," he finished.

He turned slowly, started moving a little ahead. Then without the least warning he was suddenly thrown violently into the mud by a terrific vibration of the ground.

Selton stared after him uncomprehendingly. Then he noticed that the entire area around the outlaw was shifting and sliding madly, convulsed within itself.

"Quick! Jump for it!" he yelled. "It's a mud eruption!"

He dashed forward, dragged Eboni to his feet, but by that time it was too late. The square on which they were standing was separated from the mainland by several yards, was floating like hard scum on the swift-moving surface of a ground displacement.

Uranus, with its warm interior, particularly on the day side, together with an insubstantial crust, was continually breaking up in much the same way as Earthly ice floes at the spring thaw, the hardened mud floating on the surface of a sudden new-born liquid mud current below.

So the two, outlaw and spatial policeman, now found themselves clinging to each other for dear life, swept along on their muddy raft through the dull, lowering haze.

"Why the blazes didn't you jump?" Selton demanded, glaring. "Heaven knows where we'll go now! If we get thrown into one of the boiling water areas, you know what that means!"

"I couldn't jump because I was stuck," Eboni growled. "See!" He pulled his right foot with an effort out of the cloying mud to demonstrate. "We'd better keep our feet moving if we don't want to sink through this overgrown mud pie."

Selton kneaded his feet up and down. It felt like tramping on a giant sponge. Still holding unsteadily on to each other they stared anxiously ahead into the curving wreaths. The upper-level mists now almost touched the ground.

"It's the seasonal change, all right," Selton muttered. "The mists show it. For one thing the upper-levels are slowly veering round in the opposite direction. That means they're starting on their right-to-left forty-two-year movement through Hemisphere Chasm. The lower mists are, of course, caused by the cooler air sweeping in and condensing with the warm ground—"

"You're telling me!" Eboni interrupted him bitterly. "I've lost my sense of direction being carried around like this. Since the upper drifts are changing, too, we don't know where we are."

"If we stick on this raft we may drift to better regions. Maybe towards the Equator Peaks."

"How do you make that out?"

Selton answered calmly.

"Observation," he said. "I've noticed that everything is drifting one way—upper-level mists, mud drifts, the fog, and this mud raft. It means that the blocked-up areas on the night side are thawing out. Formerly impassable barriers have opened up, and the whole surface is moving in that direction. Probably

Hemisphere Chasm will be a torrent of disgorging mud, animalcules, giant organisms, umbrellas, and so forth."

"Maybe you're right." Eboni pondered a moment and gave a shrug. "Not that it helps much in any case. We'll perhaps escape this thing only to die of starvation. This planet hasn't got a single edible thing on its whole surface—unless there's some food stored at the hideout."

"Why, don't you know?" Selton demanded in amazement.

"No." The outlaw said nothing more, looked anxiously round him.

The mud raft seemed to drift for an interminable time. Now and again the two could feel it sag as some portion of its underside gave way, but in the main it held firm, bobbing along the surgings of the great mud river down which they were being carried.

Occasionally the clinging reek lifted slightly and enabled them to see barren stretches of the great drift, moving like a dark brown edition of an Arctic thaw, traveling with ever-increasing speed towards the Equator Peaks which, so far as the stranded two could judge, could not now be very far distant.

Occasionally a huge umbrella organism would sweep down and fly on ahead in the direction of the drift. It could only mean that Selton's guess was right. At the Uranian seasonal change everything changed places; in particular, the spawn of the previous season was ejected and grew swiftly to enable it to move to the summer region.

"Dud, do you hear anything?" Eboni asked at length, easing his strained body a little to turn. "Sort of bumping and roaring?"

They were both silent for a moment, listening to the slowly growing concussions and thunderings booming through the murk. As the raft floated onwards there were distinct signs of flashings through the fog at remote heights.

"It's the Equator Peaks!" Eboni shouted hoarsely. "The lightning's over Hemisphere Chasm!"

"You're right," Selton breathed. He turned suddenly. "In that case, this is where we'd better part company with this sponge.

Point is, how?"

"Jump," Eboni said laconically. "No other way—here goes."

He drew himself together, eased his feet from the disk, then leaped outward with all his strength, landed in the midst of the filth. Selton only hesitated a moment, then followed his example. He sailed through the air, crashed heavily into soft, slimy ooze.

Dazed, his mouth full of mud, he got up. He sank to his knees in the stuff, but touched bottom. The main mudflow was some ten yards distant, a vast sweeping wall of brown pouring into Hemisphere Chasm. The mud raft was already out of sight in that mad cataract.

Staggering forward, Selton helped Eboni to get to his feet. He spluttered disgustedly.

"If mud improves beauty, I'll take the world's prize after this," he gasped out. "Good job we fell in it, though—broke our fall."

They moved forward out of the slopping ooze and came to the firmer ground at the immediate base of those vast ramparts. As the mist ahead of them thinned slightly they caught their first glimpse of something shining like dull silver—something long and graceful, delicately pointed at both ends.

"It's—it's a space ship!" Selton cried hoarsely. "Eboni, a space ship—here! How do you account for—"

He broke off. Eboni had pulled out his guns and was examining their muddy mechanisms. Finally he nodded to himself and Selton waited grimly. The Space Service man's emotions changed to surprise as Eboni turned toward the opening of a cave outside of which the space machine was lying.

Slowly the outlaw moved into the cave, his feet echoing in the hugeness. Within, everything was black and dark. Selton fumbled in his saturated kit and finally pulled forth his electrode lamp.

To his satisfaction it worked the instant he pressed the button, casting forth a brilliant fan of light round the cave's great area. Upon every side of it, stacked to the lofty ceiling, were all manner of materials, most of them recognizable as crates and goods stolen from the space freighters.

He lowered the beam to turn to Eboni, then he stopped in amazement as he beheld a figure sprawling on the floor—the figure of a man, his coal black hair covered in dirt, his arms grotesquely outflung.

"What the—" Selton stared at him in bewilderment, then dropped to one knee and made a quick examination.

"He's dead," he proclaimed briefly. "Venusian fever by the looks of it. Been dead several Earth days. But who in blazes is he?"

"Eboni," said his companion quietly. "A pity he ended up so tamely. I knew he had Venusian fever, but I hardly thought it would kill him so soon."

"Eboni? Then—who are you?" Selton gasped, leaping up.

"Me?" The powerful, mud-splashed face broke into a grin. "Well, you came up to me when we landed and accusing me of being Eboni on account of my black hair, so I let it go at that. I could see you were new to the job and very eager, so I let you have it.

"Thought it might be a good idea to teach you a lesson. I'm an old hand. Bruce Anderson's the name—Space Way Service, W detachment. Next to yours."

WORLD WITHOUT CHANCE
BY POLTON CROSS

FROM *THRILLING WONDER STORIES*, FEBRUARY 1939

In the June 1939 *Thrilling Wonder Stories* letter column, reader Frederik Pohl wrote of this story:

> "In the February Issue, 'World Without Chance' was great, a better story than any other in any science fiction magazine for the past year. It was based on a theme which has been insufficiently exploited for fictional purposes: that of entropy, the most basic of functions. Author Cross deserves a permanent niche in the SF Hall of Fame, and I want to be the first to propose 'World Without Chance' for reprinting in 1949."

William F. Temple's letters to Fearn give an interesting evaluation of many of his stories of the period. In the early forties, it was extremely difficult to obtain copies of the U.S. SF magazines in this country, and Fearn used to loan his to Temple, inviting comment:

> "'World Without Chance' had one big fault. No narrative interest. No real plot. But what ideas! Fascinating. Best chunk of pseudo-science I've read in ages. That wanted some thinking out. Honestly, Jack, you've got a remarkable ability for invention—imaginative

invention. Think you might have been someone in scientific research and theory if you had been brought up in a lab or scientific atmosphere. 'Fraid you haven't the patience for it now, even if it paid. But it's a pity that such a fertile brain as yours is running to waste (if you look at it in the larger sense) in the American pulps."

At least Fearn did not let the "fascinating ideas" in this story go to waste. He would later reuse them, suitably adapted, in his later Golden Amazon novels *Parasite Planet* and *Standstill Planet* (both forthcoming from Borgo Press)!

WORLD WITHOUT CHANCE

Wanderers of the void roam the uncharted galaxies and find the Zero Planet!

A great experiment shackles a race of Supermen for over twenty million years!

CHAPTER I
Mystery Planet

When Archer Lakington had set forth from Earth in August, 2136, to search for new worlds or planetoids worthy of future prospecting by the American Interplanetary Corporation, he had certainly not expected to roam through the deeps of space for six years.

Perhaps it was the uncanny fascination inseparable from the void that had driven him on. Perhaps it was the thought that he and his wife Joyce, bounded by the circumscribed limits of their space machine, were in a world all their own and unfettered by the idiocies and problems of a gigantic modern world.

Whatever the cause, neither he nor his young wife were

yet weary of their trip. During the six years they had sped far beyond Pluto into the outermost edges of the Milky Way galaxy, were speeding now at the rate of 160,000 miles a second—the maximum rate that hovered on the very borders of dissolution by reason of the limiting power of the Fitzgerald Contraction.

Inside the ship neither of them was aware of movement. They could only perceive it by their relation to the slowly moving points of the blazing stars. With floor gravitators to overcome the weightlessness of constant velocity, they were able to move about in comfort in this little sphere that seemed destined to travel onwards for evermore.

"Six years and not a world worth bothering about," Lakingtpn murmured, as he lounged at the outlook port. "Little worlds, big worlds—some with atmosphere like smelling salts and others as void as a vacuum trap."

He shrugged and smiled faintly. The rugged outlines of his face, seeming much older than his actual thirty years, were painted by the starshine. His broad, muscular shoulders loomed in silhouette against those dimensionless blazing points.

"So Archer Lakington will have to go back with a tale of failure!" he mused regretfully. "The guy who discovered the *mulacite* mines of Venus, the *ravdon* trees of Pluto, the—"

"Arch! Come here a minute!" The voice of his wife suddenly interrupted his soliloquy.

He straightened up from his lounging position and moved over to the girl's stooping form. Her shock of honey-colored hair tumbled around her head as she peered fixedly into the spatial detector. From the very tenseness of her slender, lightly-clad body he could sense that something unusual was absorbing her.

"You rang, madam?" he questioned lightly, as she remained rigid save for the movements of her capable fingers as they twirled the milled edge of the focusing wheel.

"Take a look," she ordered, standing erect. "Unless I'm going simple-minded through being locked up with you too long, I think there's a planet right ahead of us. Quite a respectable-looking planet too!"

"Planet?" He laughed indulgently as he saw the eagerness in her blue eyes. "A miracle like that hasn't happened in six years, so you decide to create one!"

He bent to the instrument to escape the wrath manifesting on her lovely face. Immediately the ultra powerful lenses of the detector revealed something that made him start in surprise— something that was beyond normal telescopic range and only impressed on the detector by the stepping up of faint light waves from immense distances.

Fixedly he studied a gray globe with belts of what were apparently clouds lying in ringed formation across it. It reminded him of a small-sized Uranus. He went on staring until his eyes ached, shifting the instrument gently until it was centrally fixed over the lined, transparent graph inside the lenses.

Finally he straightened up.

"Darned if you're not right!" he exclaimed in amazement. "Sorry, Joyce. It's a queer sort of planet, though—doesn't budge an eighth of an inch on the scale lines. There ought to be some kind of apparent motion—"

He broke off as he realized with some indignation that his wife was not listening. She had gone over to the untidy desk in the corner and was figuring laboriously.

"It's—er—roughly one thousand five hundred million miles distant," she proclaimed, waving her paper triumphantly. "Take us about two hours and a half to get there."

"Yeah—to find an atmosphere that even a Venusian squid fish wouldn't live in, I'll bet," he growled back. "For that matter, we don't even know if it has an atmosphere. Those line formations may be surface markings and not clouds at all."

"I don't care what they are, we're going to look," she returned flatly. "It's a mystery world and that adds spice to the whole thing. Think of it! A planet that doesn't revolve, that hasn't even the slight apparent libration of Venus or Mercury. Nor is it because tidal drag has brought it to the end of its turning days because it has those clouds. Besides that, it has a young and vigorous Sun."

Lakington nodded slowly, and stroked his chin. "Guess you're right," he admitted. "It is a bit odd at that. Okay, we'll head that way."

He turned actively to the control board and changed the vessel's aimless hurtling into a direct course for the unknown world. Then he settled down to wait.

Outside, as the ship tore onward through the growing minutes, blazed the incomprehensible sentinels of the galaxy. Stars and Suns, perhaps even worlds beyond visibility, planetoids, cosmic dust—the whole vast agglomeration of infinity drawn on a scale calculated to stagger the mind.

Archer Lakington and his young wife gave less attention to spatial wonders now. Their attention was devoted to an analysis of the unknown world as it grew visibly in size in the instruments. Both of them felt their bewilderment deepen as the passing time revealed no change in its appearance.

It had not revolved in the slightest since the first observation, nor was it pursuing any orbit round its Sun—a typical G-type of dwarf star, from which it was distant approximately 100,000,000 miles. It seemed to be just one world alone, devoid even of neighboring planets.

"It's like trying to make equations without any knowledge of figures," Lakington growled, after making futile efforts to arrive at mathematical postulations. "Only thing to do is to wait until we get there."

"Such genius!" Joyce murmured. She had forsaken the instruments and was lounging on the wall bed. "I could have told you that an hour ago, only I like to watch you work for a change."

She locked her hands behind her yellow head and smiled. Finally she laughed aloud.

"Ha-ha," Lakington mimicked sourly. "What's so funny, Mrs. Lakington?"

"That planet!" she drawled. "Just suppose it's a spatial mirage? We've encountered them before, remember. It may be a phantom reassembly of light waves that departed into Einstein's unbounded space millions of ages ago. Our instrument may merely have intersected the convergence of the light images."

"In that case it wouldn't be a world with clouds," he returned with a little asperity. "It would be a mere hulk, the reflection of a dead world that cracked up—according to Eddington's figures—nearly six thousand six hundred million years ago. And anyhow such a supposition isn't so funny."

"But it would be if you returned to Earth and handed old President Bentley a bunch of nothing to colonize! I can just picture his face."

"Never mind his face. It gives me a pain anyway. Quit lounging about and check up our distance. How much further have we to go?"

She slid dutifully from the bed and checked up.

"Be there in about another sixty-four minutes. Then you can stick a flag right in the middle of emptiness."

"Seriously, Joyce, you don't think we are chasing a myth, do you?" he asked anxiously, and she shrugged.

"How should I know? I've done plenty of speculating, though, and I can't see what else that planet can be. Every planet must conform to certain known laws, and this one doesn't obey one of them! I don't have to tell you that mighty queer things can happen in space. Not only can we have mirages by light wave quirks, but we can also have delusions by reason of unknown thought waves affecting our brains from sources unknown."

"Granting the presence of brains," he murmured acidly. "Truth is you want an excuse to run away. Just plain scared now we're getting near."

"Scared!" she flared. "Why, you—" Then she stopped and relaxed as he suddenly reached over and his arms went about her tightly.

"Like all women in space your brain is about as empty," he murmured, kissing her. "Still, I guess I can stand you at that.... Now stop making love to me, will you? Don't you know there's work to do?"

He released her slender body and turned back to the control board, fingering the switches purposefully. From that moment onward both he and his wife became mechanized units in a plan of action, all irrelevancies thrust aside in the management of the ship as it came at last within measurable distance of the strange planet.

It hung directly ahead now. Level cloud belts gathered round it, bathed in the sulphur-yellow light of the Sun.

Lakington studied it for a moment through the window, then gave full power to the softly humming engines that had been guiding the course. Immediately the rocket tubes flared violently and began to slow the vessel down in tremendous jolts and thrusts, bringing the two passengers into direct acquaintance with the sickening laws of inertia.

"That's no myth!" Lakington muttered, his gray eyes fixed on the queer world. "It's as solid as this ship. Give your left forward tube a bit more power, Joyce.... That's it!"

CHAPTER II
Trees Turn to Ash

Rocket discharges spurting powerfully, the ship curved round in a gigantic arc and went sweeping downward to the vast gray concavity directly below. Down and down, slackening and dragging with the flying seconds, clean into the midst of the clouds.

The instant that happened, Archer Lakington's expression changed from satisfaction to alarm. Usually he relied upon atmosphere to help cushion the ship's fall, but this time he met no resistance whatever! The air was as resistless as the void itself.

Swearing fervently, he gave the forward rocket tubes the limit. The ship flattened out under terrific strain, just in time to skim the needle summits of a high mountain range.

"Gosh!" Joyce whispered, drawing a long breath and dabbing at her damp brow. "What are you trying to do? Endanger my life?"

"Why not?" he asked, and grinned at her maliciously. Then

he studied his meters and gauges.

"Something screwy around here.... Well, what do you know about that?" he finished blankly, staring through the window as the ship finally burst free of the clouds and began to drop gently to the landscape below.

Joyce gazed with him, a vaguely bewildered expression on her cameolike features. She, too, could detect something peculiarly different about this world—a curiously immovable appearance as though it were a still life photograph given the advantage of a third dimension.

"No wind—no movement—no anything," she almost whispered, as the vessel came gently to rest on a long undulating plain of substance resembling earthly moss. "Just one big immovable landscape."

Lakington rose from his control chair and stood with lips compressed, looking over her shoulder. His gray eyes took in the moss plain and, bordering it, an immense and motionless jungle that somehow reminded him of Earth's Carboniferous age. Beyond the jungle reared the tremendous mountain chain with which he had nearly collided.

In the opposite direction the moss plain extended to horizon limit—vast and empty. Overhead were the unmoving clouds, as frozen into inactivity as though they were indeed part of a photograph.

"Are we wrong or is the landscape?" Joyce finally questioned, turning. "Did you ever see a planet so nicely ready for somebody to walk into?" She finished dubiously: "Or out of?"

Lakington looked at his external registers and gave a low whistle of amazement.

"Is everything screwy around here?" he asked helplessly. "Temperature, air pressure, humidity—all of them register zero! That just can't be! The clouds alone prove water vapor and atmosphere. The moss proves life. What sort of a planet is this?"

Struck with a sudden thought, Joyce reached out her hand and broke the current for the floor gravitating plates. The fact that she had done so was hardly noticeable.

"There you are!" she exclaimed. "The gravitation is okay, anyhow—about the same as Earth's. In fact the entire planet isn't altogether unlike Earth at that.... We're going outside!"

She gave her ultimatum with decision, and headed for the closet where the spacesuits were kept.

Handing one to her puzzled husband, she began to scramble into her own, and screwed her helmet in place. Automatically the air cylinder on her back began to function. Then she disappeared into the storeroom and returned with a space-proof haversack of tabloid food and drink slung over her shoulder.

"Ready?" Her voice came clearly through the helmet phones.

Lakington nodded, fingering his atomic energy gun. Turning to the airlock, he twisted the massive screws and swung the immensely thick cover inward.

"Looks all right," was his comment, as he contemplated the landscape through his face glass.

"Appearances may be deceptive," Joyce reminded him. "Even though things look all set for a garden party, we're safer inside spacesuits to begin with. Let's get going."

She set the example by stepping onto the moss-like ground with her thick boots. Almost immediately she stopped and stood looking down in bewilderment at the ashen gray prints she left behind. It was as though she had walked in powdered snow.

"Looks as though the moss is crystallized or something," she said in a tone of wonder. "Any suggestions, mastermind?"

"None yet," her husband replied, straightening up from studying the phenomenon. "We'll keep on going for a bit. Incidentally, if I'm not too curious, where are we heading?"

"The jungle, of course." She waved a bloated arm toward it. "Unless you prefer to hitchhike across the moss plain instead. It's up to you."

He ignored her sarcasm and plodded along in silence beside her, trying to form some sane line of reasoning in his mind. Beyond all doubt this world was literally standing still. It had no axial revolution and no orbital revolution nor, according to the instruments, had it any air pressure. That point, at least, was visibly disproved by the banked clouds; either the instruments were cockeyed or else—

He shook his head inside his helmet in exasperated perplexity, and followed Joyce as she gained the first outpost of the jungle.

After proceeding for a few yards within it, she suddenly stopped and looked closely at one specimen of the towering trees around them. Jerking an instrument like a voltmeter from her belt, she started to jab the needle-pointed end into the trunk. To her consternation, the entire tree collapsed in a cloud of fine ash and smothered her completely.

She emerged from the midst of the setting fog to find her husband doubled up in suppressed mirth.

"Great!" he gasped. "Absolutely great, Joyce! Do it again. I didn't get a good look the first time."

"Never mind the cracks," she returned sourly. "Suppose you bring your supercharged brain to bear on the problem of why an entire tree should collapse like that? I was going to test its temperature. I only just touched it, and—"

"I know," he said, becoming serious again, "but even if you could have taken its temperature, you'd have found your instrument as haywire as those in the ship. Nothing here registers one way or the other. Seems to be in a state of flat in-between."

His head bent back inside the glass helmet as his eyes looked up the length of the neighboring trees with their lacy but oddly stiff-looking foliage. Broad spatulate leaves graced all the branches, but they were totally without motion. That in itself was almost unbelievable, for there must certainly be air to produce clouds, and even the stillest air has some slight vibration. Everything seemed to be one vast contradiction.

The undergrowth was the same when he came to look at it, except where he and Joyce had trodden. There he found a zigzag path of ash gray where roots and twisted creepers had fallen to infinitesimal pieces as though they had been saturated in liquid air and then dropped.

"Crystallization?" he asked, in a harassed voice. "No, that couldn't happen. Frost? Hardly, with sunshine behind those clouds I'm damned if I know! Push on a bit further, Joyce."

They resumed their steady progress, pushing their way through growing density that snapped into inconceivably fine powder at their clumsy approach. At least there was no necessity for them to blaze a trail. It stretched in a line of crumbled ruin to their rear.

"Do you think it possible that elements here might have evolved in a totally different fashion to anything we understand?" Joyce asked presently, thinking hard. "Isn't it possible that if they pursued an evolutionary line—"

"No evolutionary line can explain a planet that doesn't revolve and has motionless clouds," Lakington returned irritably. "If only we could find some sign of people, or—"

"Oh, Arch! Look!" Joyce stopped so suddenly that he bumped into her.

Instantly he followed the line of her pointing glove and stared in amazement at a veritable monstrosity. In an uncritical mood he might have called the thing a toad, magnified about fifty times. It was squatting in gigantic immobility in the very midst of a heap of brittle grass, a thing of stone gray with its wide saucer eyes staring unseeingly.

"Life!" Lakington breathed, his eyes gleaming. "Pretty tough-looking sort of brute, but life just the same."

"Life, my eye!" Joyce said acidly. "The thing's as crystallized as the rest of the stuff. Look!"

She reached forth her hand and touched it. Instantly it was gray dust.

"You yellow-headed dimwit!" Lakington yelped exasperatedly. "I was going to take that back to the ship as a specimen. How do you expect us to start an analysis if you break everything up around here?"

"Hasn't it occurred to you that you couldn't carry a thing like that for two miles?" she challenged hotly. "Even a touch finished it. Besides, I've better things to do than watch you do an egg and spoon race back to the ship."

She swung round and stalked off indignantly. With a grin,

Archer Lakington followed her. For a long time they twined in and out of the peculiar loveliness, all the time with fast deepening bewilderment. The span of an hour brought them to a clearer space, leading upward to a small hill where the jungle entirely disappeared.

"Keep going," Lakington counseled, answering his wife's inquiring look. "If there's nothing there, we'll turn back."

He began to follow her, then gave a grunt of irritation as he stumbled over a piece of rising ground. The slip dislodged his atomic gun from his hand. Mechanically he stooped to pick it up, but long before the action was complete the gun flew back into his open hand with perfect precision! Mechanically his fingers closed over it.

"What the—?" he began dazedly. Then he swung round and charged after the girl before their interconnecting helmet phone wires were snapped by distance.

"Hey, Joyce! Joyce! Wait a minute? Look here!"

CHAPTER III
RANDOM ELEMENT

Lakington flung down the gun as he ran. It hit the ground in a puff of ash and rebounded back in a line, dead centered on his palm.

"Now what?" she asked tartly, halting. "Nothing better to do than play ball?"

"This is my gun!" he shouted, drawing level with her so she could see it. "If I throw it down it rebounds to the point of origin with exactly the same speed as the throw. The ground isn't resilient, either. Anything but."

"But—but that's impossible!" she protested.

"I know that, but it happens all the same. What does it imply? Quick! Help me think."

Joyce did think—and quickly. "It proves that the gun retains both the energy and organization of energy of the original fall," she swiftly decided. "Normally the kinetic energy of the gun should have been converted into heat-energy. Its molecules would move downward with equal and parallel velocities until it struck the ground, when they would be completely disorganized."

"And they weren't!" he cried excitedly. "They weren't! There was no disorganization. Somehow the gun must have got hold of an extraneous energy which lifted it back to the same place—"

"Or else there was actually perfect organization all the time!" Joyce put in quickly. She fell to thinking again, then laid her gloved hand on his arm. "Listen, Arch, it looks as though we've blundered into a whole lot of mystery. Suppose by some incredible freak this planet has achieved a perfect organization? It would mean no progress or retrogression, because Time would be a zero quantity where organization is at a complete equilibrium. The possible shuffling of molecules and atoms is at maximum efficiency. There is no random element!"

"No random element," he repeated slowly. "That means that nothing can ever happen. But why? How the Sam Hill did the planet get that way anyhow? What about gravitation?"

"Gravitation is something we don't know much about—nor does anybody else either," she reminded him. "It might be a warp or a force, all depending on the way one views it. It's quite possible that it would be a thing apart from organized equilibrium."

"And the sunlight behind those clouds? That involves the action of light waves?"

"Unless they are the same light waves that were in existence when this world got this way. In that case they, too, would be incapable of exhaustion, and also incapable of increase. The result is just—well, plain daylight. The more I think of it, Arch, the more sure I am that we've struck the most amazing planet in creation. One where there actually is no random element."

"We'll figure this out on the ship," he decided promptly. "We'll see if there's anything over the hill, then head back."

They resumed the climb and gained the hilltop in the space of a few minutes. Once there they stood gazing down on the amazing sight of a deserted city, stone gray as was everything else, but conveying the suggestion of once having reached inconceivable scientific attainment.

Its area was probably nearly forty square miles, reaching clear to the horizon on all sides. In appearance it was almost like that of Earth, save that it was far in advance of even the colossal futurist cities of Earth, 2136. The main impression seemed to be one of square towers reaching to the unmoving clouds; towers that were studded with windows and braced by slender bridges. The streets were canyons, laid out in perfect order and symmetry, groups of four running into a broad and cleverly planned square poised over what were obviously far-reaching subway systems.

"Dead—quite dead!" Lakington muttered at last, drawing a deep breath from his air cylinder. "Science down there far beyond anything we ever knew, I expect, and we had to come too late!"

"Suppose you stop being dramatic and come with me and find out if you're right?" Joyce suggested crisply. "We might find a clue if nothing else. How about it?"

"Of course. If you're not tired?"

"Active bodies never get tired," she returned in a tone of mocking challenge.

She set off boldly down the brittle moss defile, slipping ever and again, until caution against the possibility of ripping her spacesuit forced her into a crawl. Her husband was right beside her.

Only once on the descent did they stop to consume a few of their food and water tabloids, thrusting them through the special vacuum traps in helmets and haversack. Then again they were on their way. Two hours more, and they gained the first broad street of the strange metropolis and stood regarding its enormity in perplexity.

"This is going to present some difficulty," Lakington murmured, nodding back to the roadway. "Wherever we touch anything, we leave this ashy deposit. Look at the apparently solid stone behind us." He pointed to the trail of footmarks. "If we go inside a building it might come down on top of us! Like your tree."

"But that idea's not so good," Joyce observed thoughtfully. "No reason why a complete building should come down unless we deliberately push it. Walking along its floor should be fairly safe." She hesitated a moment. "There's something else I've been considering, too," she said slowly. "If we are actually on a planet that's achieved organization, doesn't it occur to you that we represent a random element ourselves. Maybe that's why we make such a mess everywhere we go."

"Maybe you're right." He shrugged. "Still, we've no time to worry over that now. We've started this thing, and we may as well finish it. Watch your step when we get right into the city."

They advanced again, leaving that long trail of ashy substance in their wake. At length they gained the central square with its bordering edifices.

Curiously enough, many of the great doors were wide open, but there seemed to be no trace of inhabitants. Only the empty vista of streets leading beyond the square; only the stationary clouds bunched overhead.

Archer Lakington stopped before a promising-looking building and stared into the interior at a dimly visible mass of machinery.

"We'll chance going in," he announced, and with Joyce by his side began to ascend the steps. The imprints of crumbling dust still followed them.

Once within the enormity of hall, they stood looking around. There was no trace of dust. The daylight was bright through the mighty floor-length windows, revealing a wilderness of incomprehensible machines of the stone-gray color. In rapt attention, Archer Lakington left his wife and began to wander round, taking good care to keep his distance from the machines in case the slightest tremor from him should send them crumbling into ruin.

"Whoever put these together sure knew all the answers," he

said thoughtfully, as Joyce caught up with him. "I can't figure out a third of it. Transformers are here, condensers and armatures of an advanced design, but the rest of the stuff has got me licked. I should imagine—"

He stopped abruptly as they came around the corner of a gigantic engine that looked like an overgrown dynamo. He felt Joyce's gloved hand tighten on his arm as she, too, saw what was focusing his gaze—a motionless, fantastic figure seated before a control board in the very heart of the machinery.

"Take it easy this time," he cautioned. "Leave your meddling for less interesting things."

Joyce was too absorbed to think of a retort. With careful footsteps, they moved to within two feet of the creature and stood perplexedly regarding it.

It had little parallel to anything they knew, unless it was perhaps an upright alligator with greatly extended forepaws. The back was scaly and the belly smooth. Legs were only brief and ended in appendages remarkably like sea flippers. Similar curious extremities rested gently on the multiple banks of switches comprising the control board.

Leaning farther sideward, it was just possible for the pair to see the face—almost fishlike, with large eyes, no nose, and a tight, set scar that was probably a mouth. The eyes were the most remarkable, faceted like diamonds, and uncannily inhuman.

"Nice little playmate," Joyce muttered, with a shudder, after a breathless space. "Wonder if it was ever intelligent?"

He snorted expressively.

"What do you mean, intelligent? Of course it was intelligent! How else could it understand a switchboard like that? Probably had far more brains than you and I put together." He groaned helplessly. "Hell, if only it could speak! This is like being stuck in a wax museum."

"You'll be making me homesick next," she retorted tartly, "and here are we stuck amongst a lot of junk that doesn't make sense, with a frost-bound alligator seated one day at the organ. I'm getting fed up with this!"

"Not so fed up as tired, probably." Lakington smiled inside his glass, "Tell you what we'll do! We'll have one more nose around the other buildings and then come back here and have a rest—if you can rest in a place like this. How's that?"

"Check."

She nodded, and they retraced their crumbled footprints to the exterior and started another investigation.

CHAPTER IV
The Experiment

In the time they allotted themselves, they only managed to add to their perplexity. They found further infinities of machinery, obviously all remotely controlled from the first edifice they had entered. Other buildings were apparently offices and domiciles, equipped with all manner of odd furniture to suit the queer inhabitants.

Most remarkable of all was one gigantic place filled from wall to wall with thousands of beings, like the one they had seen in the control room, all frozen into one solid mass in various postures, their unseeing, faceted eyes gazing at a solitary alligator at the far end of the hall. Since it was impossible to reach him without smashing the jammed beings to dust, the two investigators reluctantly turned away and went back to the first edifice. They squatted down on the floor near that main switchboard, fervently wishing it were possible to remove their hot and cumbersome spacesuits.

"It looks to me as though some experiment brought about this mess," Archer Lakington murmured presently, his abstracted eyes traveling once again to the motionless machine controller. "Maybe some experiment in matter that brought about the elimination of a random element. It's a hard fact to credit that a world might exist without it, without entropy, where everything is, and never becomes. Yet in cold fact it is just as possible as a world where the random element does exist."

"Like the pack of cards from the maker which you shuffle

once and can only shuffle into the primary order by a coincidence?" Joyce questioned with a yawn. "Gosh, I'm sleepy!"

"Like that, yes. The more you shuffle, the worse the disorganization; and the more things you shuffle, the greater the disorganization. Only a complete state cannot be shuffled. It is free of the random element. If we suppose that these alligator gentlemen found a way to weld their entire planet and all it contained into one absolute state, it would destroy the random element. It would be like taking the king of spades out of the card pack and trying to shuffle it alone."

Joyce's weary face brightened momentarily behind the shield of *sonium* glass.

"After all, that isn't so impossible as it sounds!" she exclaimed. "The quantum laws admit of the emission of certain kinds and quantities of light from an atom, and they also admit of absorption of the same kinds and quantities, the undoing of the emission. That very process defies a random element, but in losing the random element it gains something far more complex—the loss of future and past time, because a certain sequence of events running from past to future is the *doing* of an event, and the same sequence running from future to past is the *undoing* of it.

"That infers there is no time at all. The laws of Nature are indifferent as to the doing or undoing of an event, so they must be just as indifferent as to a direction of time from past to future."

"Mathematically correct," Lakington admiringly confirmed. "Left is minus x, right is plus x; past is minus t, future is plus t. What more do you want? And it holds good for all single units, but is at once destroyed when one achieves a composite."

He fell silent, brooding, his eyes on the incomprehensible machinery.

"Yes, I think we've hit it," he averred after a while. "The behavior of my gun, the absolute timelessness of this world. Perfect organization has been achieved, either by accident or design. I don't suppose we'll ever know. Say, has it ever occurred to you that absolute organization of molecules can be shown in poetry? Listen:

> "The famous Duke of York
> With twenty thousand men,
> He marched them up to the top of the hill
> And marched them down again."

"So what?" Joyce questioned sleepily, curling up in the ashy hole her body had made in the floor. "I'm going to take a nap. You can recite poetry. Why not try Humpty Dumpty? He was the exact opposite of the Duke of York. Disorganization plus! Remember the stuff about all the king's horses and all the king's men that couldn't put him together again? Random element entered into Humpty—and how!"

She was asleep before she could answer him. He smiled down at her, then with a sigh at his own peculiar lassitude, he lay down beside her, allowing his drowsy mind to play over the incredible things they had discovered together.

But long before he could formulate a reason for the organized planet, he had fallen dead asleep.

To be conscious of the fact that he had fallen asleep was something Lakington could not understand. Where he should have encountered oblivion or hazy indeterminate dreams, he found instead that he was in a profoundly complex condition of sleeping wakefulness.

His brain was remarkably alert and keen, yet it was no longer controlling his body. An inner conviction assured him that he was fast asleep, or else in a curious state wherein his bodily reactions had no power. He vaguely wondered if Joyce was undergoing the same experience. He could not see her—could, in fact, see only a blank wall of darkness. Nor could any effort of will break it down. His body was no longer under control.

"Have no fear. You will not be harmed."

His brain jolted at the sudden inception of that sentence. It was not spoken, for his ears were useless by reason of the all-enclosing helmet. Neither was it Joyce who had spoken. Vaguely he realized that it must be the pure essence of thought, in sympathy with his own mentality.

"I am the being at the switchboard," the communicator suddenly resumed. "By some indeterminate chance you and your mate have come out of the cosmos to this world to release us from a bondage of our own foolish making. You have not gone to sleep in the fashion you call sleep; rather you have succumbed to my stronger mentality, which has temporarily deprived you of the use of your bodies. Only in that state, with your minds dissociated from the mastery of your physical selves, am I able to communicate with you."

There was silence for a space and Lakington yearned, with a helpless desperation, to ask the questions surging into his mind. Then suddenly the being resumed.

"My name is Ixal, so far as I can transcribe it into your language. Before this experiment I was the leading scientist of our people. We numbered five hundred thousand, all of us the last of our race that had formerly occupied other planets in this system. Those other planets have died away. Even the Sun they possessed has ceased to be, and another one has come into being.

"The course of our experiments took us into the study of entropy, probability of electrons, and disorganization. We reasoned that by a process of molecular selection we could force our world and all it contained into a state of perfect organization, thereby defeating the primary and secondary laws of Nature and bringing into being a state of perfect thermodynamic equilibrium.

"We achieved this state by working from the basis that energy is not infinitely divisible, or at least not infinitely divided in the process of shuffling. This involved a completely new science of physics, including what you term the quantum laws, which admit of the reversibility of varied radiations from an atom back to the point of origin.

"We began to study the major stars of our galaxy and determined that their interiors were in a condition of perfect thermo-dynamic equilibrium. The energy within them was shuffled as it was radiated from matter into ether and back again, so that the possibility of shuffling soon attained maximum limit.

"Every change had been made and perfect organization achieved—but there were certain laws that governed that process, laws relating to atoms and molecules which are the prime basis of all disorganization. If there were not such laws, perfect balance could never be achieved.

"The same laws that produce disorganization can be reversed to produce the opposite effect. A flying object striking another object can, by the government of electro-dynamic laws, be made to retain its original kinetic energy and return to its starting point without conversion into heat energy. This fact we proved for ourselves with the instruments we constructed. Thus we built up our science of molecular and atomic organization—a science basically implying that one law can be made to govern another and eliminate the random element from matter and energy.

"Unfortunately, however, though our experiments were perfect, though our machines definitely brought into being the electrical laws governing the organization of energy, we omitted to reckon in our eagerness that perfect organization cancels the law of Time. This will be clear to you, because increase of a random element indicates the future; more organization indicates the past—but perfect organization without increase or decrease achieves the state of balanced non-entropy, no time."

Ixal's thoughts saddened a trifle as he went on.

"We were all eager to test out the idea on a large scale. We became the slaves of a scientific obsession, built larger and larger machines capable of bringing organization to bear on all parts of our planet. We arranged a day when the machine should be loosed. My fellows congregated in the main hall of science to listen to our ruler's preliminary speech. I took up my position at the master control board here and waited for the signal. When it came I released the engines.

"Since then, millions of years ago, I have never moved. Nor

have my fellows. In that instant we came to a dead standstill, neither living nor dying, in a state of perfect timeless equilibrium. Our minds have lived on because mind is not a thing of molecules and atoms, but one sector of an inconceivable pattern of mentality in space.

"Our world could not crumble, could not change, could not revolve; could not do anything but stay exactly as we placed it in that instant of organization. Only by the coming of a random element could we find release.

"You, my friends, have brought us that release. You have introduced the first random element in nearly twenty millions of years. With every second the shuffling will increase. It started from the instant your space machine entered our atmosphere. Time will catch up with itself and our world and all it contains will cease to be. Be warned of that fact. Leave it immediately!"

CHAPTER V
Return of Chance

Archer Lakington stirred with sudden uneasiness and jolted his eyes open in abrupt bewilderment to survey the great mass of the machine hall. As he sat up in the deepening hole where his body lay, his mind was still swirling with vivid memories of the things he had been told.

"Did I hear that, or dream it?" he muttered, regarding the motionless alligator man in deep perplexity.

"You don't imagine a limited mind like yours could dream a technical thing like that, do you?"

He twisted round to find Joyce looking at him. Her heated face behind its glass helmet was half serious and half amused. She slowly began to nod.

"We both heard it," she confirmed. "The alligator talked to me as well as to you." She went on reflectively. "Funny, isn't it? Two boneheads like us from an incredibly far-off world drop in here and provide the key to a prison that's had these infinitely brilliant people locked up for twenty million years!"

"Which reminds me!" Lakington interrupted, scrambling to his feet. "He told us to get out of here in double-quick time. Let's get moving."

They cast one last envious, half perplexed look at the vast machinery, tribute to a science that had defeated its own end, and then crept silently out into the ashy street.

The moment they reached the top of the steps they stood transfixed in consternation, overwhelmed at the sight that met their eyes. Something had happened—something that unimaginably changed the outlook.

In all directions the gigantic buildings were crumbling and collapsing in clouds of ashen gray, like objects flawlessly patterned in dust suddenly blown by a mighty wind. Overhead the clouds were no longer motionless, but writhing and boiling as strange hurricane drafts tore through them and gave glimpses of the blazing Sun beyond.

"Arch, what—what's happened?" Joyce faltered nervously, and that second all her self-sufficiency collapsed. She was a pale, frightened girl clinging to the rubbered arm of her equally perplexed husband.

"It looks like an earthquake, but it isn't," he answered her grimly. "It's something we can't understand—that damned random element old Ixal was talking about. What fools we were not to turn back when we had our theory all doped out, instead of coming on here! It's our own intrusion that's caused it. Our breaking through the forest, our footsteps on the ground— everything. We started a process that leads right to extinction." He grasped her arm tightly.

"We've got to step on it, Joyce if we're to reach the ship. Come on!"

They went down the steps three at a time, steps that crumbled and rotted away into impalpable powder as they trod them. The buildings around them slewed and shifted crazily, fell into absurd and unbelievable nothing as their long inert state was shattered utterly by the return of the law of chance.

The farther the two went, panting hard for breath in the

restricted area of their space suits, the more they realized the desperate struggle ahead of them. Even as they ran they dropped knee deep in ground that was no longer ground but a whirling, spreading enigma of emptiness fast losing all relation to material law.

Solidity and organization had gone forever. The crazy, timeless world was catching up on itself with ever-increasing speed as the random element became eternally faster by very reason of the growing variety of atomic shufflings.

Beyond the end of the road they slid to a baffled, horrified halt. The little hill they had come down was no longer there! It had collapsed to form what was now a crumbling, level plain in the midst of which there frothed and boiled and flew the dusty phantasmal creations that had formerly been trees and undergrowth.

"The ship!" Joyce panted hysterically, "Arch, the ship! We can't possibly reach it. It's several miles away. What in Heaven's name are we going to do?"

"How should I know?" He looked around helplessly, then staggered forward as the ground underneath him suddenly began to collapse. Instantly his young wife grabbed him and drew him back, stumbled forward again with him.

"Have to keep going," he gasped. "Either we'll give in or else the planet will! We've got to take the chance!"

Arms locked round one another, they blundered onward, buffeted now by an insensate hurricane that suddenly sprang from nowhere as the molecules of the atmosphere underwent mad and inexplicable transformations, flew into new paths. Cyclone, rain, raging tumult battered and hammered them with overwhelming force, forced them to stagger blindly forward, hardly able to see through the drenching cataracts streaming down their glass helmets.

"A—a swell planet this would be to colonize!" Lakington choked, floundering waist-deep in the midst of rolling water and mud. "Hell! It's worse than a Venusian backdraft!"

"Unless I miss my guess we check out here," Joyce whimpered weakly. "We can't make the ship, Arch, and you know it!"

She swooshed from the midst of the water and halted momentarily on the crumbling ground, bracing herself against the raging wind. When Lakington looked at her, her face was hardly visible through the dirt and ashy substance plastered to the glass of her helmet.

"What do you—?" she began, then ended with a wild, desperate cry as the trembling ground under her feet parted abruptly into a yawning, gaping abyss.

She did not stand a chance. One minute she was swaying and trying to speak; the next, she vanished utterly in the boiling smother of the chasm. With the sudden tug on the helmet communication cord Archer Lakington found himself slammed forcibly down on the chasm edge. The cord parted with a snap and left him staring in dumb, blank misery at copper wire swaying wildly in the half-light.

"Joyce!" he screamed frantically, and his voice dinned inside his helmet. "Joyce! Oh, my God!"

Sweat poured down his face in the agony of those seconds. He lay staring down into the frightful gulf, at the tottering walls of it beyond. Everything was swinging and twisting insanely. Joyce had gone! That was the only thought in his tortured brain—his wife was gone beyond recall!

"Joyce!" he choked, trying to form some kind of rescue plan in his stunned mind.

Then even as he lay there the ground, under his sprawling form, ceased to be and he was pitched helplessly forward into the depths. For breathless seconds he fell with sickening speed, heart and brain struggling madly to cope with the frightful drop. Then to his surprise his speed began to slacken. The misty vaporings that had been remote chasm sides receded and puffed into nothing.

The wet and dirt on his face shield cleared somewhat, the former turning into visible frost and then vanishing entirely as water vapor expired. He was dimly aware that he was slowly revolving, blinded by the light of a mighty Sun below him.

Shielding his tortured eyes as best he could he stared in bewilderment at his surroundings. He was in space! Slowly drifting toward the immensely powerful gravitational field of that blazing star. All traces of the strange, timeless world had disappeared. Nothing was left but the void and stars.

The thought of Joyce stabbed back into his aching mind. He tried to twist around but only succeeded in drifting crazily and without direction. But in the action he did glimpse the bloated figure of his young wife drifting in the emptiness, and further beyond her the space machine itself gleaming brightly in the sunshine.

The sudden desperation of the predicament forced itself upon him. Joyce, separated from him by a good mile of void, was not making the slightest movement. For all he knew to the contrary she might be dead. The ship was easily three miles away, moving with swifter speed toward the Sun's gravitational field by reason of its greater mass.

Lakington did not need to realize that there is no foothold in space. His helpless efforts to reach Joyce only sent him turning in circles and parabolas, left him staring through half-closed eyes at the writhing prominences curling from the insufferable globe below.

Desperate with anxiety, he clutched himself tightly in readiness to try again. Then he paused in the action as his gloved hand smote upon the hard outline of his atomic gun in its belt holster. For a moment he fingered it, a thought turning over in his mind. Then he snatched it out and leveled it at his feet, taking care that the beam did not actually strike him.

Savagely he pressed the release button and, as he had wildly hoped, the stunt worked. The terrific backward recoil hurled him with the exact equivalent of energy in the opposite direction, straight toward his wife. Again he pressed—and again. He cannoned into her softly floating form and flung an arm around her belted waist.

Fear began to grip him again at the smallness of the leaps under the added mass of her body, yet he dared not release her and work alone as yet, because of the fast-increasing power of the Sun. He had three miles to cover and twelve more charges left in the gun.

Setting his teeth, he fired again and again, correcting his course each time. The eleventh charge found him within two hundred feet of the vessel drifting toward the Sun. There was nothing for it but to finish solo. Instantly he cast Joyce adrift and fired for the last time, catapulted forward just far enough to grip the edges of the manhole opening.

Within moments he was inside the vessel and had leaped to the control board, set the rockets blazing fiercely in a pull against the Sun.

The rest was easy. In a few minutes he had dragged Joyce inside and closed the airlock, switched on the gravitators, and got the air plant to work....

"I thought I'd managed to get rid of my yellow-headed distraction for good," he told her briefly, when they were seated together an hour later, eating a much-needed meal. "Evidently the fall into the chasm did you no more harm than it did me. Pretty obvious that that world just cracked up into nothing and reverted to where it should have been ages ago. You and I and the space ship were the only solid things left."

"I'll never get over being childish enough to faint," Joyce mourned in self-condemnation. "Must have been the shock. That atomic gun idea was pretty smart, though."

"Thanks!" He leaned over and kissed her, then went on eating. When he looked up again it was to find her staring out over the eternal void.

"Where next?" she asked, catching his glance.

He shrugged unconcernedly.

"No idea. There must be something somewhere worth colonizing. Guess we'll keep on cruising until we find it."

She did not answer, but instead began to laugh, finally ended up with a delighted scream of merriment.

"Why the hysteria?" he questioned gruffly.

"Just think!" she cried breathlessly. "I was right in what I said. You could go right back to President Bentley and hand him a ball of nothing! That's all that world turned out to be!"

"As empty as your yellow head," he agreed calmly. "Maybe next time we'll find one just as dense as—"

He broke off with a widening grin, then ducked as Joyce whisked a cushion from the wall bed and hurled it at him with deadly accuracy.

CHAMELEON PLANET
BY POLTON CROSS

FROM *ASTONISHING STORIES*, FEBRUARY 1940

Whilst the editor of *Thrilling Wonder Stories*, Mort Weisinger, remained receptive to Weinbaum imitations, he was finding himself bombarded with this type of story as a result of Campbell's decision not to run them. Weisinger rejected "Chameleon Planet", although it was a sequel to the previous story he had accepted, this time on the grounds that they were overstocked with this type of story. Several authors, particularly Henry Kuttner, Arthur K. Barnes, and Eando Binder, had been selling them Weinbaum-style stories, and they were not to publish "World Without Chance" until February 1939.

Because the characters were also due to appear in the first story in a rival magazine, Fearn's agent did not deem it expedient to offer "Chameleon Planet" elsewhere until Frederik Pohl launched his two new magazines, *Astonishing Stories* and *Super Science Stories*. The astute Julius Schwartz remembered Pohl's letter that had appeared in the June 1939 *Thrilling Wonder Stories* praising the original story.

Schwartz had guessed correctly that Pohl would be receptive to running this sequel to the story he had liked so much. It was sold to him in early December 1939, and quickly assigned for the cover and lead spot in the first issue of *Astonishing Stories* (February 1940). Oddly, Pohl changed the heroine's name from Joyce to Elsie! For this reprinting, with the stories appearing consecutively, I have restored it to Joyce.

Artist Jack Binder painted a splendid illustrative cover, and also executed two fine interior illustrations. "Chameleon Planet" was an excellent story, fully as good as the first one. The story's novel theme of 'telescoped accelerated evolution' (which had been beaten into print by 'ideas man' Edmond Hamilton in his 1938 story The Ephemerae") was quite influential in science fiction—amongst the authors reprising Fearn's ideas would be no less than Ray Bradbury (in "The Creatures That Time Forgot", appearing in *Planet Stories* for Fall 1946). Much less notably, I myself incorporated the story into my continuation of Fearn's Golden Amazon series in *Chameleon Planet* (2005). Whilst Fearn's rationale for the telescoped evolution remained fairly mysterious in his original story, it was strongly hinted at: "A mad, silly little world obviously under the pull of gigantic gravitational fields—perhaps dead stars lurking unseen in the vast void." To me, this suggested that the planet might be very well orbiting a black hole, and modern science postulates that all kinds of odd time distortions might occur in the vicinity of a black hole. So I rewrote the story accordingly. In this collection, however, the story is reprinted exactly as Fearn wrote it in 1937, when, of course, the existence of black holes was unknown. In passing, however, I would remark that Fearn would later write a story that actually *did* postulate the possibility of black holes, *and even named them as such*! This was in "Space Trap" as by Polton Cross, in the Summer 1945 *Thrilling Wonder Stories*. I suspect that this was the very earliest usage of the phrase 'black hole'—at least in science fiction. Unfortunately, whilst the idea itself was inspired, "Space Trap" was one of Fearn's *worst-ever* stories, being tailored to the juvenile slam-bang action formula then being briefly favoured by the magazine. As such it will likely never be reprinted! Meantime, we can at least enjoy this earlier, much better story, and whilst you read it, you might care to think of a black hole as a rationale for the events in the story—as I did!

Following the story's publication in 1940, William F. Temple commented on the story to Fearn thusly:

> "'Chameleon. Planet' is the goods. Another of your original notions like 'The Man Who Stopped the Dust,' and not a borrow from a film. I know it isn't too hard to scratch up original ideas now and again, but you never seem at a loss for one. Do you keep a notebook and jot them down as they cross your mind? I gather that you derived the idea from studying the progress of the foetus in the womb. Now what were you up to, to be so interested in that? Natural curiosity?
>
> "Two things are a bit hard to swallow in the yarn: you say this planet is about the size of the Earth, and working from the 2-hour day, it revolves on its axis six times as fast. Surely the visitors wouldn't be able to walk naturally, as they did, against that terrific centrifugal force? Or did it possess a more powerful gravitation to counter balance that effect? I guess you'll say it did! Again, if evolution was proceeding in the caveman's mind at millions of years per minute, Arch and his wife's movements would be so slow in comparison that the caveman wouldn't be able to detect them. And certainly he wouldn't be able to speak slowly enough to converse with them. His very slowest speech would be somewhere up in the supersonics. But, there, I know what you think about these technical quibbles. The story's the thing, and I derived pleasure from it, so what?"

To which Fearn cheerfully replied: "Yes, I guess I made mistakes in 'Chameleon Planet'—but I wrote it long ago, so please forgive. The process of birth was from Forneir D'Arbes *Man the Animal* (Blackpool Public Library). Wise guy, huh?"

CHAMELEON PLANET

*Life was speeded up on Chameleon Planet—where an
ape could become a Superman between meals!*

CHAPTER ONE
THE FLYING WORLD

Spaceship 17 of the American Interplanetary Corporation
moved at the cruising velocity of 90,000 miles a second through
the barren endlessness of the eastern limb of the Milky Way
Galaxy, pursuing its journey in search of new worlds to be colo-
nized or claimed in the name of the Corporation.

In. the vessel's compact control room, ace colonizer Archer
Lakington stood moodily gazing out into the void, gray eyes
mirroring the abstract nature of his thoughts. His broad but
hunched shoulders gave the clue to his boredom. Speeding
through infinity without a trace of excitement or interest was
anathema to his adventurous soul. This had been going on now
for eight weeks....

At length he turned aside and surveyed his instruments.
The long-range detector needle was rigidly fixed on zero. The
moment any possible world came within range, even though
invisible to the eye, an alarm would ring by the actuation of a
highly sensitive photo-electric cell. The detector, responding,
would immediately fix the position of the disturbance.

"The more I see of space the more I think I'm a mug to be
cruising around in it," he growled at last, hands in the pockets
of his leather cardigan. "I'm getting a sort of yen to be back
amongst the smells of New York, seeing familiar faces, telling
tales of conquest over a glass of viska water."

"While you're seeing familiar faces, don't forget President
Bentley's," a dry feminine voice reminded him.

He twisted round and surveyed the bush of yellow hair just
visible over the top of the wall couch. Joyce, his wife—his sole
partner in this endless journeying—was pursuing her usual

occupation when things got monotonous; simply lying down with her hands locked behind her head. She turned a pair of level cool blue eyes toward him as she felt the strength of his gaze.

"You don't have to remind me about Bentley," he said gruffly. "If he wasn't President of the Corporation, I'd head back right now for New York!"

"You mean you're scared?"

"Scared nothing!" he snapped. "I mean I'm—"

He broke off and twirled round with delighted eyes as the detector alarm abruptly clanged into noisy action. In an instant he was squatting before the instruments, keenly studying their reactions. He scarcely noticed that, true to duty, the girl was crouched beside him, her slender fingers twirling the calibrated knobs and controls.

Without a word to each other they began to check and calculate carefully. The lenses of the detector came into use and visually picked up the cause of the distant alarm. When they had both gazed long and earnestly, they looked blankly at each other.

"Gosh!" Joyce exclaimed, startled. "That's the fastest planet I ever saw! Did you see it, Arch? Flying round its sun like a bullet?"

He puzzled silently for a moment, then stooped down and again sighted the strange distant world in the powerful sights. Clear and distinct it was, a planet perhaps only slightly smaller than Earth, but behaving as no self-respecting planet should. Alone in its glory, apparently sheathed in ice, it was pursuing a highly eccentric orbit round its quite normal dwarf type sun.

Starting from a close perihelion point, it went sweeping out in a wild curve, zigzagged sharply at one place on its route with a force that looked strong enough to tear it clean out of its path—then it pulled back again and went sailing at terrific speed to remote aphelion almost beyond visual range. A mad, silly little world obviously under the pull of gigantic gravitational fields—perhaps dead stars lurking unseen in the vast void. And as it went its surface coloring changed weirdly.

"Some world!" Arch commented, as he straightened up. "We ought to be near it in about two hours if we step on it. Not that it will be much good though. The darn thing's frozen solid—"

"If you were more of a scientist and less of a fathead we might do some useful work," Joyce remarked tartly, herself now peering through the lenses. "That world is only ice-sheathed at aphelion limit but becomes all green and gold at perihelion," she went on. "Sort—sort of chameleon planet," she finished hazily, looking up.

"Spectrum warp, probably in the lenses," said Arch wisely; but she gave an unwomanly snort.

"Spectrum warp my eye! Don't try and avoid the issue! That's a planet that may have something worthwhile on it, even if it does hold the cosmic speed record. You wanted relief from monotony—and you've got it! Grab yourself a control panel and restore my faith in husbands."

Arch gave a mock salute and squatted down. Giving the power to the silent rocket tubes, he increased the smoothly perpetual cruising speed of the vessel to the maximum 160,000 miles a second, sent it plunging like a silver bullet through the cosmos while the girl, rigid over the instruments, rapped out instructions in her terse, half cynical voice.

True to calculation, the vessel came within close range of the flying world 120 minutes later, keeping pace with it in its hurtling journey.

Puzzled, the two looked down on its surface and watched the strange spreads of color that suffused it at varied points of its orbit. The nearer it came to the sun the grayer it became, seemed to actually cover itself with clouds—then it moved on again at top speed, merging from gray to green, to blue, fading down into red, then white, and resolving at aphelion into primary black only barely distinguishable against the utter platinum-dust dark of space.

"Chameleon planet is right!" Arch breathed, fascinated. "I still don't see though how we can colonize it. It's just a haywire rocket."

"Never mind talking about fireworks—descend and have a look at it!" the girl counselled. "It may have valuable ores or some kind of salvage worth collecting. Wait until it gets nearest the sun and then drop down. At the rate it's going that will be at any moment...." Her eyes followed it speculatively as it raced away into space.

Arch bent more closely over his controls, easing the vessel sideways from the planet's gravitational pull. With tensed muscles he waited. His gaze, along with the girl's, followed every movement of that hurtling globe as it suddenly began its return trip.

He gripped the major control switches tightly and began to jockey the vessel round, twisting it in a great arc and then flattening out as the racehorse planet tore past.

His judgment was superb—the machine leveled out at 1,000 feet above the gray turbulent surface. Working dexterously he drove the nose downwards, plunged into the midst of the gray, and found to his satisfaction that it was cloud, cushioning atmosphere that broke the terrific down rush of the ship and eased her gently to a surface that was spongy and steaming with amazing warmth.

The vessel dropped softly at last in the center of a small clearing, surrounded by immense trees. They rose on every hand in fantastic array, their lower boles as smooth as billiard balls and bluish gray in color. Beyond this shiny, bald space they sprouted into circular tiers of similar hue, oddly like hundreds of umbrellas piled on top of each other.

Even as the startled two looked at them through the window, they visibly grew and added fresh veined vegetational domes to their height, quivered in the mystic ecstasy of some inner life. Nor were they isolated in their queerness.... In the midst of the lushy soil, vines of vivid green twirled their roots and tendrils in and out of stolid-looking, bellying bushes like gargantuan mushrooms. Everywhere, in every direction, was a swelling, tangling wilderness of stubbed, crazy shapes—here bulging, there elongating, like the irrelevant, frightening illusions of a nightmare.

"Life—gone mad!" murmured Arch soberly, then he turned away and glanced at the external meters. He felt vaguely satisfied at finding an atmosphere compatible with Earth's, a gravity almost identical, but a temperature and humidity equalling that of the Carboniferous Age.

"Breathable, but as hot as hell," Joyce said expressively, gazing over his shoulder. "We could go outside without helmets. The sun's clouded, so I guess pith hats will do."

Arch glanced again at the fantastical, swaying life.

"It's a risk," he said dubiously. "I don't mean the air—the form of life."

"What do explorers usually do? Get cold feet?" Joyce demanded. "If you won't go, I will. That's flat!"

Arch caught the challenge in her bright blue eyes. He nodded a trifle reluctantly. "O.K., we'll chance it, if only to grab a few specimens. We'll take full precautions, though. Fit up our packs with complete spacesuits as well as provisions. Use the space-bags; they'll stand any conditions. I'll look after the portable tent and flame guns."

"Check!" she nodded eagerly, and went blithely singing into the adjoining storage closet.

CHAPTER TWO
Dinosaurs and Umbrella Trees

Five minutes later, surrounded by surging waves of sickly greenhouse warmth, they were standing together just outside the ship, the airlock securely fastened behind them. Their backs were loaded with full packs, Arch bearing the larger accoutrement in the form of a strong but collapsible *vulsanite* metal tent.

In silent dubiousness they looked around them on the umbrella trees and tangled shooting life that sprouted with insane fervor on every hand. Despite the heavy, drifting clouds they could feel the intense heat of the sun beating down through the protection of their pith helmets, its ultraviolet radiations tingling the skin of their bare arms. They began to perspire freely.

"Well, bright eyes, what's your suggestion?" Arch asked querulously. "Looks to me as if wandering in this tangle will make us perform a complete vanishing trick."

"We're explorers, not magicians," the girl answered briefly. "Obviously, the planet's no good for colonization, but we can at least grab a few of these plants for specimens. Let's go!"

She stepped forward boldly, flame pistol firmly gripped in her hand.

Arch looked after her slim figure for a moment, then with a resigned shrug prepared to follow her. Mentally he decided that the whole excursion was only fit for lunatics.... He moved, like the girl, with studied care, glancing around and below him at the twisting vines and sprouting shave-grass. Here and there in the patches of damp loam there frothed areas infested with minute, scuttling life, and, for every step he took, he had to dodge aside to avoid a wickedly spired, carmine-hued stem as it rose like a livid bayonet from alluvial soil.

So intent was he in guarding himself, indeed—in surveying the ground, he momentarily forgot the girl, until a sudden wild shout from ahead caused him to look up with a start.

Horrified and amazed, he came to an abrupt halt. Joyce was rising upwards into the air in front of the nearest umbrella tree, the carmine stem of a bayonet-bamboo thrust through the tough leather belt about her waist! Struggling wildly, she reared up to a height of thirty feet, striving frantically to free herself and calling in hysterical fright.

The ludicrous figure she cut set Arch laughing for a moment—then with a single slash from his flame gun he cut the plant in two and broke the girl's fall as she came toppling down breathlessly into his arms.

"We've no time to play at acrobats," he reproved her drily, as she straightened her rumpled clothing. "You ought to know better, Mrs. Lakington."

"Could I help it if the thing grew while I was studying an umbrella tree?" she demanded wrathfully. "This place is so darned swift you need a time machine to keep up with it! I'm going back to the ship before worse things happen!"

She broke off as she half turned. Dismay settled on her pretty face at the sight of spreading, spiraling masses of incredible growth. In the few brief minutes occupied in her bayonet-stem adventure, the clearing had changed utterly.

Wild, rampant growth had sprouted up soundlessly on all sides, had already hidden the ship from view. Colors, weird and flamboyant, provided a crisscrossing maze of bewildering inter-lacings. Umbrella trees, bayonet-bamboos, bile-green vines, swelling objects like puffballs—they were all there, creaking in the hot, heavy air with the very speed of their growth, providing a blur of vivid colors that was eye-aching.

Arch did not need to be told that the ship was fast being smothered. The girl's sudden startled silence was sufficient. For a moment he was nonplussed, then gripping her by the arm he plunged forward towards the tangled mass with flame gun spouting in a vicious arc, but even before he had the chance of seeing what happened, an intense, saturating darkness flooded down.

"Now what?" he yelped, in exasperated alarm. "Have I darn well gone blind or—"

"No, Arch; it's night!" The girl's voice quavered a trifle as her hand gripped his arm. "At the terrific speed this planet rotates and moves the day's already exhausted! We'll have to try— Ouch!"

She broke off and staggered in the darkness as a vicious unseen thorn stabbed the bare flesh of her arm. Arch drew her more tightly to him and switched on his belt torch. The clear beam revealed the solid, impregnable mass on every side.

Bewildered, they stumbled round, all sense of direction confused. Razor-edged masses were springing up now, merci-lessly sharp, leaving slashes on their tough leather gum boots.... Gripping each other they moved onwards, literally forced to do so to escape the mad life twirling insanely around them.

Twice they blundered into an umbrella tree, reeling aside

only just in time to escape the sudden sharp closing of its upper folds. It seemed to be more a mystic reflex action than actual carnivorous strain.

At last the girl halted as they came into a slightly quieter region.

"Look here, Arch, what are we going to do?" she panted. "In case you don't know it, we're completely lost!"

He stared at her torch-illumined face. "I'm open to suggestions. We can't find the ship again in this stuff, that's a certainty. We have provisions to last a month, and in that time—"

"A month!" she echoed, moving quickly as she felt an avid vine shooting over her feet.

"How do you figure we're going to survive a month in this hole? We'll be stabbed or strangled long before that!"

"Wonder what causes it? The growth speed, I mean." Arch's voice came musingly, out of the dark. "Incredibly fast plant mutations must have some cause behind them. Maybe something to do with the planet's orbital speed. Even time seems different here. From space this world looked to be revolving like a humming top, yet now we're on it, night and day seem to arrive normally—"

He stopped short as at that identical moment the stifling, terrible dark suddenly vanished and gave place to daylight again. The glare of the cloud-shielded sun flooded down on the wild growth, which, in the case of the umbrella trees at least, had already achieved cloud-scraping proportions.

"Normal, huh?" the girl questioned laconically, but she was obviously relieved.

"Well, if not normal, it at least resembles day and night," Arch amended. "I expected something so swift that we'd encounter a sort of winking effect."

Joyce said nothing to that; her eyes were traveling anxiously round the confusion. The thought of the vanished spaceship, the absolute craziness of everything, was obsessing her mind.

"Only thing to do is to keep on going," Arch decided at length. "Maybe we'll find a place to pitch camp and lay further plans."

"I wish I shared your optimism," the girl sighed enviously, then easing the burden of her pack she prepared to follow him....

Forced to keep moving by reason of circumstances, the two blasted their way with flame guns through the crazy rampancy ahead of them. Confused, bewildered, they found themselves constantly confronted with things defying understanding.

One particularly vicious type of plant, which they nicknamed the 'bellow bulb', caused them a good deal of trouble. Lying in the soupy soil like a bladder, it released a powerful lethal gas when trodden on. More than once they found themselves tottering away from these things on the verge of unconsciousness.

But at last they became thankfully aware of the fact that the insane growth of the jungle was ceasing. The vast agglomeration of trees and plants seemed to have reached maximum size: there was no longer danger from slicing barbs, blades, and thorns.... Once they realized a passive state had been achieved, they sank down gratefully on one of the ground-level vines and took their first nourishment.

"Wish I could figure it out!" Arch muttered worriedly, twirling a tabloid round his tongue.

"Looks to me as though this is a sort of swamp age," the girl muttered, thinking. "The plants have stopped growing: by all normal laws they ought to start collapsing to form future coal—Oh, but what am I saying!" she exclaimed hopelessly.

"It isn't possible for that to happen. That's the work of ages."

"On a normal world it is—but here we have a world opposed to normal," Arch pointed out. "Since orbital speed is so swift, it is possible that evolution might be the same way. Remember that the space plants scattered in the crater floors of the moon pass through their whole existence in the span of a lunar month; On earth a similar occurrence would demand ages. On this chameleon-like planet anything might happen...."

"Might!" the girl echoed. "It *does*!"

Arch fell silent, vaguely perplexed, then he aroused himself to speak again.

"Guess we might as well pitch camp here for the time being," he said briefly.

"We need rest before we think out the return trip—granting there'll ever be any! Give me a hand."

The girl came willingly to his assistance as he slid the portable shelter from his back. In the space of a few minutes the ultra-modern contrivance with its hinges, brackets, and angles was snapped into position, its slotted little beds sliding into fixtures as the four walls were clamped.

Grateful for the protection from the fierce ultra violet radiations of the clouded sun, the two scrambled inside and pulled off their provision packs; then for a while they sat together on the edge of the beds, gazing through the open doorway...until Arch stiffened abruptly as his keen gray eyes detected a slight movement in the nearby undergrowth. Instantly his hand went to the flame pistol in his belt.

"What—what is it?" breathed Joyce in amazement, gazing with him as there emerged into view a remarkable object like a monstrous earwig, two bone encrusted eyes watching from the midst of a rattish face.

"Outsize insect," Arch said quickly. "Harmless, I guess."

He lowered his gun and waited tensely, in increasing amazement, as between shave-grass and creeping-plants huge salamanders pulled themselves into sight, their queer, three-eyed, crescent-shaped skulls giving the effect of Satanic grimace. Scorpions came next, armed with viciously poisoned needles that quivered like daggers on protruding whip-like tails. Insects began to flit about—titanophasmes, as big as eagles. Above the tops of the lower lying liana dragonflies with yard-wide wings streaked swiftly.... Nor was that all. There were immense grasshoppers, millipedes as big as pumpkins, nauseous spiders dangling on ropy threads.... A hideous and incredible vision.

The two sat for perhaps fifteen minutes anxiously studying the creatures, when light fell again with its former startling suddenness. Day had lasted exactly two hours!

Arch gently closed the door and switched on his torch.

Joyce's face was strained—her efforts to conceal fear were pretty futile.

"Two hours day; two hours night," she said nervously. "This place is crazy, Arch! And those horrible things outside! You're not suggesting we stop here with them around, are you?"

"What do you propose?" he asked quietly. "We daren't go outside—we'd be worse off than ever. No; the only thing to do is to stick it and hope for the best, hard though it is."

The girl shuddered a little. "Guess you're right, but it's not going to be easy."

She relapsed into silence. After a time Arch opened the door again and risked using his flashlight to see exactly what vas transpiring outside. To the utter surprise of both of them the jungle was collapsing! The entire mad growth was breaking up into dried sticks and dust....

And the insects! They scuttled round in the confusion, yet not for a moment did they look the same. By lightning changes they increased in size, lost their insectile appearance, and became sheathed in scaly armor. The stupendous dragonfly creatures whizzing overhead grew larger with the moments, also achieved a protective covering that pointed beyond doubt to a reptilian strain.

Until finally, by the time daylight arrived once more, a new metamorphosis was complete. The two gazed out n awe on a scene magically different—evolution had slid by in a brief two-hour light! Another jungle was rising, but of a more delicate, refined nature, from the ruins of the old. Ferns of considerable size had sprouted in the clearing—behind them in fast-growing banks were gently waving masses bearing strong resemblance to earthly cycads and conifers.

But nowhere was there a flower: only the fantastically colored vegetation held back from crazy growth by some new muta-tional law in the planet's inexplicable chemistry.

"If we set back for the spaceship now we might find it," Joyce remarked anxiously. "The going would be simpler, anyhow."

"So far as the jungle is concerned, yes," Arch agreed; "but there are other perils. Look over there!"

He nodded his head to the opposite side of the clearing and the girl recoiled a little as she beheld a vast head of gray, the face imbecilic in expression, waving up and down on the end of a long neck. Flexible, rubbery lips writhed in avid satisfaction as the extraordinary beast lazily ate the soft, fast-growing leaves of the smaller trees. Once, as the wind parted the vegetation for a moment, there was a vision of vast body and tail.

"Why, it's—it's an iguanodon!" she cried in horror, but Arch shook his head.

"Not exactly it, but very much like it. Herbivorous, of course.... You know, it's just beginning to dawn on me what's wrong with this planet—why life on it is so crazy."

"Well, although I'm glad to hear the brain has finally started to function, I'm still anxious to get back to the ship," the girl said worriedly. "We can risk the monsters. That herb-eater is harmless enough, anyhow."

"But it won't be the only type," Arch reminded her grimly. "There'll be all kinds of things abroad—perhaps as frightful as our own one-time diplodocus and allosaurus."

"You mean we stop here?" Joyce's eyes were on the gray head. The swarming plant life had now almost hidden it.

"Until man comes, anyhow," Arch said reflectively.

At that the girl twisted round from the doorway and stared at him amazedly.

"Until man comes!" she echoed. "Now I know you're crazy! If you think I'm going to sit here while these playboys grow up through millions of years you're mistaken! I'm heading back right now for the ship!"

"In what direction?" Arch asked sweetly, and she pursed her lips.

"I'll find it!" Her tone was defiant. "I've got a wrist compass just the same as you have!"

Arch shrugged and leaned more comfortably against the doorway. For a while he heard the determined little bustling movements of the girl behind him—then her activity slowed down a little. At length he found her beside him.

"Maybe you're right," she admitted, with a rueful pout. "But at least you might tell me what you're getting at."

"It's simple enough. Evolution on this world is straightforward, fast though it is. The only way it differs is in that it passes through its mutations all at one sweep of existence instead of dying and being born again, in a more adaptive style. The giant creatures of this moment are the very same insects and millipedes we saw last night—same minds, only changed outwardly by an amazing mutational process. Since this planet has such a weird orbit, it probably accounts for it. Its close approach to the sun at perihelion produces Carboniferous Age conditions: as it recedes further away, the condition will cool to normal, finally reaching a frozen glacial state compatible only with Earth's last days. What I'm wondering is, what will happen when we reach that zigzag part in this planet's orbit. May be trouble."

The girl puzzled for a moment. "Oddly enough, Arch, I believe your mutational idea is dead right, though how you figured it out all by yourself is beyond me, What became of the First Glacial Epoch, though? That should have appeared between the insect and mammalian stages."

"Because it happened on Earth doesn't say it must happen here. In fact, it's wholly unlikely. Life here will simply progress from warmth to cold, and during that period we'll have a pretty good simile of the lines Earthly evolution will take. This planet being practically the same in mass and atmosphere, it isn't unusual that similar life to Earth's should evolve."

Joyce looked out over the changing forest, her brows knitted. For an instant her gaze caught the gray hurtling form of a monstrous archaeopteryx—a natural helicopter.

"Evolution like that seems so, impossible," she muttered.

"Why?" Arch objected. "On the contrary, it's very sensible. Death, and thereby a possible break in the continuity of knowledge, is done away with. Besides, there is a biological parallel to bear it all out."

"Meaning what?"

"Meaning that a human embryo before it is born undergoes in nine months all the primeval states. The fertilized egg form from which the human biped develops is in the first instance, a primeval amoeba. In the nine months of its genesis it performs, unseen except by X-ray, the very incredible fast evolution we see here in actual fact. First the amoebical cell, the clustered cells like a mulberry—a globular animalcule. It then moves on to the first stage and shows visible gills: it traverses the scale of the lower invertebrates. Fishes, amphibians, reptiles, lower mammals, semi-apes, human apes, and lastly *Homo sapiens* are all passed through. Then the child is born. If it can happen invisibly to a human embryo, why not here in the form we behold? Maybe it is the only way Nature can operate. Being pressed for time, as it were."

"You think then that man will appear in, say, two days?" the girl questioned thoughtfully.

"Not quite so soon, perhaps, but certainly before very long. It may represent inconceivably long generations to this life, but we measure time by the hours on our watches. The ship won't hurt in the interval. It's safely locked anyhow. When this forest dies down to give place to new forms, we'll be able to find it easily enough."

She nodded agreement and settled herself down again to await developments.

CHAPTER THREE
The Storm

The day was uneventful save for occasional showers of amazing rapidity, and a certain cooling of the air that could only be explained by the amazing planet's rapid orbital recession from the Sun.

During the brief two hours there were multi-alterations, and when the night fell again, it was alive with change.

The two listened fearfully to a myriad unfamiliar noises—

the screech of unknown birds as they flew close over the camp; the monstrous, avid bellowing of forty-ton beasts—the ground-shaking concussions of their colossal feet. Somewhere something chattered with the hysterical abandon of a hyena.

At brief intervals the two slept from sheer strain and fatigue, until near the time for dawn when they were aroused by a sudden deep bass rumbling in the ground.

"Whatever is it?" Joyce gasped in alarm, leaping up. "Sounds like an explosion...."

She jumped to the door and wrenched it open. Outside, rain was descending in hissing, blinding sheets.

"More like an earthquake," came Arch's sober voice from the gloom. "Here—grab the provisions and pack in case we have to make a dash for it!"

He snatched at the girl's baggage and thrust it on her shoulders, but almost before he had slipped into his own equipment they were both flung off their feet by a terrific earth tremor.

"It's that zigzag deviation in this planet's orbit!" Arch gasped, scrambling up again. "We must have reached it. Let's get out of here quick, before the whole camp comes down on top of us!"

"But where do we go?" the girl asked helplessly. "It's raining a deluge outside—"

"Can't help that!" he returned briefly, and hugging her to him they plunged out into the raging dark.

Lucky it was that his foresight had guided him, for they had hardly gained the clearing's center before another tremendous convulsion of the earth overthrew them. A visible ripple raced along the ground in the dawn light, ploughed down swaying trees and shelter in one all-inclusive sweep.

Raging, cyclonic wind gripped them as they staggered helplessly towards the rain-lashed jungle. Clutching each other, soaked to the skin, they were whirled along in the midst of crashing trees and ripping, tearing plants. The whole planet seemed to have suddenly gone insane.

Simmering volcanic forces had abruptly come into life, undoubtedly created by that orbit deviation swinging the globe out of normalcy.

Panting and drenched, they halted finally in the jungle's depths, crouching down in the rain-flattened bushes as a herd of crazed animals thundered past. Mighty brutes, overpowering in their mad hugeness. It was a vast parade of armored plates, horns, laniary teeth, beaks and claws—the stampeded herd of an incredible saurian age on the verge of yet another weird metamorphosis.

"What do we do next?" Joyce panted, as the earth heaved violently beneath them.

"Only stop as we are until we get a break!" Arch looked worriedly at the sky. Not only was it thick with lowering rain clouds, but there also drifted across it the thick acrid smoke columns of volcanic eruption. Somewhere a crater had burst into being.

He turned back to the girl with a remark, but at that exact moment there came a roaring and crashing from the jungle to the rear. He was just in time to, see a vast wall of water plowing forward, bearing everything before it in a towering deluge of driftwood and tumbling vegetation—then he and the girl, clinging frantically to each other, were lifted on high and hurled wildly into the foaming chaos.

They went deep, locked tightly in each others' embrace, rose up again gasping and struggling for air, threshing wildly in the driftwood as the weight of their packs pulled upon them. In the half-light it was difficult to distinguish anything. On every hand there was din and confusion; the piercing shrieks of drowning monsters split the screaming air.

"O.K.?" Arch yelled, clutching the girl to him, and she nodded her plastered head quickly.

"Sure—but I could think of better places to play water polo—What's that ahead? Land?" She stared through the smother.

"Of sorts," Arch threw back—and in three minutes they struck shelving ground from which all traces of forest had been blasted by earthquake and tempest.

For a space they could do nothing but lie flat on their backs and gasp for breath, staring at the clearing sky—then little by little it came home to them that the earthquake and tidal wave were spent.

The heaving and trembling had ceased; the mad little world was itself again. For the first time sunshine filtered down through the densely packed clouds, gathering strength and intensity until the wet ground was steaming with the intense heat.

Joyce sat up at last and thankfully lowered the pack from her back.

"Well, thank Heaven neither water nor space can get through these," she remarked gratefully. "We can still survive a bit longer, though I certainly have a lurking suspicion that it isn't going to be easy to find the old spaceship after this! Incidentally, Arch, doesn't it seem to you that it almost matches up—in a shorter version—with the Deluge and terrific repatterning Earth underwent in the early stages?"

He nodded rather gloomily, staring out over the newly formed ocean.

"Very like it," he admitted. "Nature's law operating in a slightly different way—eliminating vast numbers of the giant beasts and permitting only a few to remain. Since they possess the powers of adaptation without death or heredity, they will presumably pattern themselves on a smaller scale now. Everything large will probably have passed away—those things that resembled the dinosaurs, ichthyosauri, and pteranodonyes of Earth.

The girl made a wry face. "Boy, can you sling jaw-crackers around!" she murmured, scrambling to her feet. "Still, I guess you're right. Seems to me we'd better move before some sort of sun fever gets a hold on us, though at the rate this place moves, I hardly think it's possible to get ill— Well, what do you know about that!" she finished in astonishment, and pointed to the flat plain behind them.

Arch rose beside her and stood gazing in amazement. The plain was no longer a barren mass, but was already thickly wooded in the glare of sunshine, backed at the rear by a newly risen mountain range. They stood looking on foliage that was vaguely familiar, almost earth-like—which, considering the planet's resemblance to the home world wasn't very surprising.

Dark plane trees, waving oaks, beeches—they were all sprouting and growing upwards rapidly. Amidst the branches there flitted the first signs of birds, the first visible feathered things. A steady humming presently proceeded from the forest—the low and ordered note of bees, dragonflies, moths, butterflies; and here and there as they watched a stinging specimen of the anthropoid genus came into mystic being, chirped loudly, and sped swiftly away into the sunny silences.

"Do things move on this planet!" Arch whistled at length, tentatively fingering his gun. "An hour or two ago they were giant monsters; now they've changed again and resolved into the smaller classes— And look at that!" he finished, in a yell of amazement.

Joyce hardly needed his directions. Her eyes were already fixed in astonishment upon a profusion of scampering but nonetheless recognizable creatures. There were marsupials, waddling armadillos, changing even as they were watched, with incredible swiftness, into rodents and hoofed animals. The birds too, as they flew. merged astoundingly into new specimens, slipped swiftly by wild mutations into bats and insect-eaters.

"Pretty little playmates!" Joyce murmured at last. "I guess we might take a closer look. We're literally between the devil and the deep sea, so what about it?"

Arch nodded. The Sun was already curving down swiftly towards the horizon. Very soon it would be night. The forest, for all its wild and peculiar life, was a safer and more understandable proposition. Anything might emerge out of the ocean at the coming of nightfall.

They turned and strode forward purposefully. When they reached the forest, it seemed to have already attained maximum limit. Yet despite its dense profusion, only blasted clear by the flame guns, it was nowhere near the solid impregnability of the earlier jungles—was more natural, more beautiful, subtropical.

Darkness fell with its usual blanketing suddenness. Afraid to pause, the two went on steadily, beheld things they could not have thought possible. Rats of astounding size occasionally flitted across their vision: some attempted to attack until they were shattered to dust with the guns. In other directions unclassifiable monstrosities lurked in the twisted grass, stared out with great diamond-like eyes or scuttled away into the friendly blackness. The whole place was infested with weird life, some very earthly, some very alien.

Once, as the flashlight circled a wall of vegetation ahead, the two caught a vision of a ridiculous thing like an ostrich running away from them in sudden fright, its bushy tail standing up like an earthly cauliflower.

"A dinoris, or something very like it," Arch commented. "A forerunner of a future ostrich. Like—"

He stopped dead, muscles tensed and hand tightening on his flame gun as a pair of fiendishly malevolent green eyes blazed suddenly ahead. A body of brilliant stripes moved through the quivering changing-grass.

"Saber-tooth tiger—a genuine pip!" he whispered, clutching the frightened Elsie to him. "No time to take chances. Here goes!"

He fired his gun mercilessly at the very instant of the magnificent creature's spring. It never ended its leap; simply puffed into ash in mid-air.

"I hate to think what would happen if the guns gave out," the girl breathed shakily. "This is sure no place for a picnic."

She fell silent again as they resumed the advance. By the time they had passed through the thick of the jungle and reached the base of the mountain range beyond, the dawn had come again. But it was colder, much colder, and the sun seemed smaller....

For a time they wandered through the midst of loose rocks, finally singling out a cave opening in the sheer wall of towering cliff. Weary and exhausted they crawled within and flung themselves down in relief, gazing back through the opening towards the rioting confusion of jungle a mile away, and, further away still, the ocean born of the tidal wave.

"Before very long all this will pass away and maybe we'll glimpse something of modernity—something that thinks, something that will explain why this planet behaves so queerly," Arch said musingly. "All the same, I think my own ideas are pretty correct."

Joyce yawned widely. "Well, theory or no theory, I'm going to take a rest. This place is too much for me!"

They both pulled off their packs and squatted down, Arch with flame pistol ready as instant protection—but before very long fatigue got the better of his good intentions and, like the girl, he slept soundly.

CHAPTER FOUR
THE FIRST MAN

When they awoke again, it was to the knowledge that, according to their watches, two nights and two days had slid by. The cave was unchanged. Once they had refreshed and eaten, they crept to the opening and stared out onto the jungle.

It was different once again—still more refined but still primeval. Here and there first new life forms were moving: bullet-like hairy beings shot from tree to tree with terrific speed. The ape evolution had been gained, was speeding onwards up the scale in absolute unison with the chameleon planet's gradual withdrawal from the Sun.

"If this evolutionary scale is similar to Earth's, we ought to get another Glacial Epoch around here," Joyce murmured musingly. "It's a good job we brought spacesuits with us. It's getting pretty cold even as it is."

"There won't be a Glacial period," Arch said with certainty. "Earth's ice age was responsible for the final extinction of the saurians, but here they require no extinction: they simply merge into something fresh like a tadpole metamorphosing into a frog. Those distant apes we can see will be men before we can hardly realize it. Remember that by normal evolution millions of years passed in between states of change—but the speed of ascent from ape to man could be measured in mere thousands of years. That's why it should also go quicker here."

"In the meantime, we stop right here then?"

"Sure—it's a safe spot. Why shouldn't we?"

"I was thinking of the spaceship."

Arch laughed forlornly. "Swell thought that is! Probably it went west in the earthquake. Even if it did, there will soon be life on this amazing world quite capable of building us a new one. You can count on that."

Joyce became silent, staring moodily through the cave opening—then she suddenly stiffened and cried sharply.

"Look down there. Arch! A couple of apes fighting it out to the death! And the smaller one's getting the worst of it, too!"

He joined her in gazing, studied the mighty hairy forms that had emerged from the forest and were battling savagely with bare hands and fighting fangs for the possession of a piece of quivering animal flesh. The speed they fought at made them mere blurs of motion. And even as they fought they were changing swiftly. The heads were broadening out; the teeth and prognathous jaws projecting less.

Finally, the smaller of the two fell backwards, to be immediately pounced upon by the larger. At that Arch jumped to his feet, flame pistol tightly gripped in his hand.

"What's the idea?" Joyce asked in a startled voice.

"A thought's just struck me. We could do with a companion from this world to tell us what it's all about. I'm going to rescue the smaller ape, if I can. Before long he'll be a man. Stay here or come with me. Please yourself."

She scrambled to her feet at that and followed him through the cave opening. Running swiftly together over the loose rubble they gained the fighting pair at last and paused, momentarily appalled by the overpowering fury and speed of the brutes. Beyond doubt it was a fight to the death. The forest behind was echoing with the gibbering of apes, subhumans, and queerly fashioned things that had no discernible origin, scuttling wildly through the fastness.

Arch hesitated for a moment, maneuvering for a good position—then as the giant aggressor abruptly stood upright for a final plunge, Arch released his flame gun. Vivid streaking energy struck the brute clean in the stomach, blasted his great hairy body into fragments amidst a passing stench of singeing hair and flesh.

"Nice going!" Joyce breathed in delight, then swung round nervously as the other ape got painfully to its feet.

By the time it had fully stood up, it was miraculously healed of its injuries and had become less apelike in form, less shaggy. Instead it had all the evidences of an Earthly Heidelberg man— huge, hairy, and terrible.

Arch backed away gently, flame gun ready, calling to the biped coaxingly.

"We're friends. Want to help," he said anxiously. "Don't try and start anything or I'll let you have it!"

A momentary silence fell. Even the forest went quieter— changing and sliding strangely into new and complex patterns, whirling in the sea of mutations.

The rescued apeman stood in puzzled bewilderment, grinning diabolically. Joyce drew tightly into Arch's arm at the sight of that receding forehead, protruding eyebrows, iron hard jaws, and sharply pointed ears.

"Couldn't—couldn't you have chosen a better-looking pupil?" she ventured, voice trembling. "He's giving me the jitters."

"As long as I've got this flame gun, we're safe enough...."

Arch held out his hand slowly, then snatched it back as the brute's huge teeth bared in petulant anger.... Then suddenly it raised a hand to its little forehead and seemed to give the slightest of shudders. When it lowered the hand the facial appearance had changed again into that of a near-Neanderthal man.

Arch tired of the mutual scrutiny at last, tired of guessing at the workings in the creature's little brain. He turned, pointed towards the cliff cave, and headed back towards it, glancing ever and again over his shoulder.

"Maybe he'll follow," he murmured, and the girl sniffed.

"I don't fancy being bottled up in a cave with that brute," she grumbled. "Apart from the fact that he isn't handsome, he might make the place smell."

"Will you get it through your thick head that he'll one day be a man of supreme and far-reaching intelligence?" Arch snapped. "At the rate he changes at, he'll be equal with you and me at the end of a few days. Besides, he'll be darned helpful to us. He owes us a debt, don't forget. We saved his life."

She glanced back nervously, "Well, he's following us anyhow," she said worriedly. "Suppose—suppose we stop outside the cave? Maybe it'll be safer."

Arch nodded assent and once they gained the cave he stood ready and waiting until the brute came up. There was something incredible and baffling about the mad evolution of the creature. The subhuman effect had changed again: the creature had lost the power of operating the nodules of its simian-pointed ears. At terrific speed he was developing into an intelligent man.

Finally he came level, looking in almost childlike wonderment at his outspread fingers. Between them reposed the vestigial remains of his saurian origin. In thirty seconds they had become natural fingers, but thickly stubbed.

"We're trying to help you," Arch said presently, making dumb motions. "We want you for a friend."

The brute looked up; a faint flash of wisdom crossed his apish face and then disappeared. His only response was a deep, chesty grunt, then he sat down heavily right across the cave entrance as though to wait.

"No dice," Arch growled. "He would choose that place to squat. Guess we'll have to wait until he gets more intelligent."

Joyce, her fears abating somewhat at the evidence of the creature's docility, relinquished her hold and squatted down too. Within a few minutes the Sun westered over the fantastic forest and sank at lightning speed.

The brute slept during the two-hour night, watched ceaselessly by the chilled and wondering Earthlings.... When the Sun rose again, the creature was no longer an ape but a naked man quite on a par with a modern earth being.

The moment he woke up and beheld the two shiveringly watching him he leapt lithely to his feet and sped at a terrific speed into the distance—not towards a forest, but towards an area now sprouting with rudely designed huts and abodes.

The age of the wild had passed.

"Pity he dashed off like that," was Joyce's comment, as she rose stiffly and rubbed her chilled bare arms. "Maybe he got self-conscious at finding himself a nudist. If he was as cold as I am, I'm not surprised."

"The cold is our growing distance from the Sun," Arch said. "As to our friend, you've said something a darn sight more accurate than most of your observations. The need for clothing, in his now advanced mind, will be a strong urge. Bet you a dollar he turns up again!"

"Check!" the girl said, and after diving into the cave for the provision bag, she settled herself to eat and wait again, grateful for the sun, smaller though it undoubtedly was.

For an hour there was no sign of the ape-*cum*-man. The only changes lay in the queer city. With every passing moment it changed indescribably. Illusory flutterings constantly rippled over it. In fifteen minutes the crude dwellings were normal edifices; the first ramifications of a city were coming into being.

"Do you think that city builds itself or is it actually erected by the labor of unseen creatures?" Joyce asked at last, her blue eyes utterly perplexed. "It isn't even reasonable to suppose that any beings could work at such a frantic rate and with progression of ideas."

"Don't forget that this planet is in top gear," Arch murmured. "Think back on the terrific speed at which everything has moved—or at least it's looked that way to our senses. Remember the speed. of the earlier metamorphoses, the whirling rate of that ape fight—the way our naked friend streaked off like lightning with the lid off. Because Earthly evolution and movement is so slow, it doesn't imply that the same thing must exist everywhere else. This chameleon planet has to cash in on the fruits of an entire existence in the equivalent of a mere earthly fortnight. That means that the inhabitants work in like ratio—don't even waste time on dying. Just grow right up from beginning to end. Their buildings appear like blurs because of the rate they move at. The further on evolution and intelligence travel, the faster everything will go, I expect. Increasing knowledge and modernity makes for increasing speed. What really interests me is where it is all going to end. Maybe Almega will be able to tell us if he comes back."

"Almega?" Joyce asked in surprise, frowning.

"Sure—Alpha and Omega cut short. Suits him, don't you think?"

"Not bad—for you," she admitted slyly; then before she could speak further, there came a streak of dust from tumult of the city.

Out of the sunshine there suddenly merged the figure of Almega himself, half smiling, now a complete man of an ultramodern age.

A one-piece garment, blue in color and elastic in texture—specially designed to accommodate the constant changes of his figure—covered him from heels to neck.

Arch jumped in surprise.

"We're friends," he began again. "I tried to tell you—"

"I know, when I was in primordial form," Almega interjected briefly. "My brain was not then developed to its present stage."

Arch gazed in amazement. "Say, how come you talk my language?"

"Thought waves," said Almega briefly. "I have not much time to speak. I am so fast and you are so slow. Listen to me. I speak under effort. Forced to go slow. Very slow."

"Shoot!" Arch invited.

Almega hesitated for a moment, then said, "Our evolution is

very rapid. Soon I shall be a superman. Then on to other states. Come to thank you for saving me. My brain was then only 430 grams. Now it is 1,350 grams. Soon it will be 2,000 grams...."

He stopped again, visibly changing. His forehead, already massive, was commencing to bulge strangely. His body changed form swiftly, becoming thinner and smaller than before.

"Your spaceship was not destroyed. Lies in a straight line that way, some distance off." He pointed the exact direction and Arch checked it minutely on his wrist compass. "Reach it as soon as you can. This world will pass shortly to remote aphelion. Cold will completely destroy you but we shall adapt ourselves."

"Am I right in believing that time is far swifter here than it is to us?" Arch questioned eagerly.

The swelling head nodded swiftly. "Quite right. Our evolution is encompassed in one circling of the Sun—we go from beginning to end without dying and leave cellular spores at the end of our course, to start again at perihelion. Our climate too pursues the same changes, though of course it is an inactive state. Rain and sun here are so swift to you, you will hardly see the difference, save in the long disaster at the erratic point of this planet's orbit, which you have already experienced. We look like you because of similar conditions."

"When you've run this course of mankind, then, your world will be empty?" Joyce asked interestedly.

"No; man's stage only represents one dominion. Be same on your world in the future. My brain is better now. I see your world is very far away. No matter. Man on any planet is only one form of dominion. Before that stage we were the masters in other forms. Just as there have been former types, so there will be later types. Incessant change. Shortly I shall lose sense of smell and develop spectroscopic eyes and ears. I shall read the light-symphonies of Nature; I shall hear the pulsations of the universe. My teeth will disappear, so will my hair. My eyes' visual range will change as this world speeds further away from the sun and becomes embraced in twilight. As the dark deepens I shall see in that, too."

"Then?" Arch asked, thinking of a possible Earthly parallel.

"Ears will disappear," said Almega dispassionately. "We shall conquer all things as Man—so swiftly you will not see it. We shall conquer space and the universe. To you a mere blur. Evolution will go on."

He changed again. His eyes glistened queerly: his body went even thinner. But with hardly an alteration in his clipped voice he went on:

"I can think better now. We shall become insects. So it will happen with your world. Already your insects are adapted for future control. Particularly your cephenomia fly. It is the fastest flier on your planet. So will we be. We shall war with termites, gain brief mastery, and change again. By then—to you mere days—our planet will have moved very far from the sun. It will be cold. We shall change into wormlike beings—echinodermata, as you call them. We shall go further than that; move into the state from which we came—a single cell. In that wise, still intelligent, we shall live through into the ultimate night of our world at aphelion. The cell will remain, to be born again at perihelion and repeat the life-cycle."

"A single cell!" cried Arch in amazement.

"Yes," Almega said, changing again into something that was all head and penetrating, thought-battering eyes. "You had a similar thing on your world in the alluvian epoch. You called it *Caulerpa*. It looked like green algae, had a fernish body, and grew to four feet in height. All in one cell."

"He's right there!" Joyce exclaimed. "I've heard of it."

"And the purpose behind this astounding evolution of yours?" Arch demanded. "You live through all your stages and work back to a single cell, then you do it all again. Why?"

"Why is anything?" Almega asked surprisingly. "My race and I will not come again. When our intelligence passes at the planet's aphelion, we shall go elsewhere, leaving behind only a cell, which, at perihelion, will sprout again. But with another mind. Where our own minds go we do not know. Like you, we do not understand the riddle of death."

He turned with sudden swiftness and glanced at the westering sun. "An epoch has gone!" he said anxiously. "You go—keep safe. Thank you...."

And the space where he stood was suddenly empty. Only a line of settling dust sweeping down to the crazy, changing city revealed the magically fast path he had taken.

"Can that guy move!" Arch whistled. "He could play badminton with himself and sleep between serves...." Then he sobered a little and glanced at the girl. "Well, you heard what he said. Guess we'd better be moving, Mrs. Lakington."

"It is a bit chilly at that," she agreed. "Now we know all about it from our sentence-stilted friend, we might as well go."

They shouldered their packs again, cast a last look at .the cave, then as they moved away from it darkness returned to chameleon planet.

That night of all others was painted with sights unique in their experience of planet exploration. As they moved sharply in the direction Almega had indicated—apparently due south by Arch's wrist compass—they beheld the transformation of the city in all its weird, incredible glory.

The scene presented was that of a blur of lights as buildings supplanted buildings, as the air machines of a now far-reaching science streaked the blackness. Sound, deep-pitched and vibrant, floated across the intervening space like the droning of a super beehive. It was hard to imagine that in that enormity of power and mutation a race was passing literal epochs.

The two only stopped twice during the night to rest. When the dawn came, the city was behind them, momentarily still in its wild up-building. The chill wind of that dawn, the paling light of the increasingly distant sun, both embraced a city that had come to a stop, the ingenuity of architecture evidently at last played out. A row of tall, slender buildings reaching to the sky, atop which there stood complicated towers and the various devices of a far advanced science, stood in mute testimony to the slow passing of a race that had reached its mightiest thoughts— in man form at least—in two short hours of apparent night!

"Don't you think it's time we wrapped ourselves up a bit?" Joyce asked at length, rubbing her arms vigorously. "It's getting freezing cold. The air's thinning a bit, too. No telling yet how far we may have to go."

The night shut down like a breath from the void, sending them stumbling onwards with a slowly rising terror—the monstrous fear of unknown forces' reaching out of that great and ebon dark. Afraid to stop, they kept on going.

The dawn was the strangest they had seen. The sun was as red and cold as a super-Arctic, so vast was his distance. Its long, slanting red wavelengths fell upon a forest directly ahead.

"Is—is it a forest?" asked Joyce uncertainly through the helmet phones, stopping wearily. "I thought all life had gone for good:"

They moved more slowly now, both from fatigue and the cumbersome folds of their spacesuits. In five minutes they gained the forest and passed into its slowly changing midst. It was so far the slowest and yet the most astounding place they had witnessed. A woodland of gray, frosty shapes, sheerly beautiful, deeply red lit. The life that tenanted it, harmless apparently, moved with a certain slowness...but what life!

Enormous reeds were gliding along through the thinning air like decapitated serpents, twisting and writhing, unutterably grotesque. In another direction bristling gray footballs were rolling swiftly along in search of hidden prey, propelled after the manner of an earthly polypus by whip-like tentacles.

As the Earthlings passed wonderingly through their midst, staring incredulously at the infinitely diversified forms, one or other of the strange objects burst suddenly apart and became two—bipartition of cells.

"Unicellular life of the nth degree," Arch breathed, fascinated.

"I'd sooner see a spaceship than a whole lot of cells." Joyce sighed. "How much further, I wonder?"

They went on slowly through the very midst of the balls and rods, through the thickest part of the lacy, cellular trees, until at length they were through it. Behind them, the forest began to disappear.... Gigantic bacteria, the toughest, most adaptable things in life, were beginning the final dominion before the utter extinction of death itself.

Ahead there stretched a desert of ice. Nothing was stirring in that redly lit bitterness: no new form of life was manifesting under the sheathed armor of what had once been land and water. Chameleon Planet was on the verge of death.

Joyce stopped suddenly and gripped Arch's inflated arm.

"Suppose we never find the ship?" she asked almost hysterically. "Do you realize what it means? This world is finished— and so will we be if something doesn't—"

She broke off. The Sun, slanting swiftly down to the horizon, suddenly set something gleaming brightly not half a mile distant—a pointed spire in the ice field. She jerked forward so quickly that she nearly broke the helmet phone cord.

"What the hell—!" Arch gasped, then he pulled up short on the ice as he saw the reason for her wild lunge.

It was the ship! Half of it projecting sharply out of the ice; the rest of it was buried in the frozen tomb. Quick as a flash he whipped out his flame gun.

"Still a chance!" he panted. "The door's shut, so the inside will be unharmed. It won't be crushed, either—the plates are plenty strong enough to resist ice pack. Get busy!"

Without further words they both set to work with their twin flame guns.

Tearing off his pack, Arch dived, perfectly protected by his space suit. He used his flame gun constantly to keep the ice from reforming and crushing him to death.... To spin the external screws of the airlock was a matter of moments. His shout of triumph traveled into the girl's helmet phones as she too came floating through the narrow tunnel.

By degrees, working like divers, they shut the three safety compartment doors one after the other and finally gained the grateful interior of the control room.

Still space-suited, Arch gave the power to the rocket tubes.

The exhaust blasted ice and water in a vast shower.

Half an hour later the two looked out into the void—but Chameleon Planet was out of sight.

ACKNOWLEDGMENTS

"Penal World" by "Thornton Ayre" was originally published in *Astounding Stories*, September 1937. Copyright © 1937 by John Russell Fearn; Copyright © 2013 by Philip Harbottle.

"Whispering Satellite" by "Thornton Ayre" was originally published in *Astounding Stories*, January 1938. Copyright © 1938 by John Russell Fearn; Copyright © 2013 by Philip Harbottle.

"Domain of Zero" by "Thornton Ayre" was originally published in *Planet Stories*, Fall 1940. Copyright © 1940 by John Russell Fearn; Copyright © 2013 by Philip Harbottle.

"The Degenerates" by "Polton Cross" was originally published in *Astounding Stories*, February 1938. Copyright © 1938 by John Russell Fearn; Copyright © 2013 by Philip Harbottle.

"The Misty Wilderness" was originally published in *Modern Wonder* #77, November 12, 1938, and in *Startling Stories*, September 1939. Copyright © 1938, 1939 by John Russell Fearn; Copyright © 2013 by Philip Harbottle.

"World Without Chance" by "Polton Cross" was originally published in *Thrilling Wonder Stories*, February 1939. Copyright © 1939 by John Russell Fearn; Copyright © 2013 by Philip Harbottle.

"Chameleon Planet" by "Polton Cross" was originally published in *Astonishing Stories*, February 1940. Copyright © 1940 by John Russell Fearn; Copyright © 2013 by Philip Harbottle.

ABOUT THE AUTHOR

British writer JOHN RUSSELL FEARN was born near Manchester, England, in 1908. As a child he devoured the science fiction of Wells and Verne, and was a voracious reader of the Boys' Story Papers. He was also fascinated by the cinema, and first broke into print in 1931 with a series of articles in *Film Weekly*.

He then quickly sold his first novel, *The Intelligence Gigantic*, to the American magazine, *Amazing Stories*. Over the next fifteen years, writing under several pseudonyms, Fearn became one of the most prolific contributors to all of the leading US science fiction pulps, including such legendary publications as *Astounding Stories, Startling Stories, Thrilling Wonder Stories*, and *Weird Tales*.

During the late 1940s he diversified into writing novels for the UK market, and also created his famous superwoman character, The Golden Amazon, for the prestigious Canadian magazine, the Toronto *Star Weekly*. In the early 1950s in the UK, his fifty-two novels as "Vargo Statten" were bestsellers, most notably his novelization of the film, *Creature from the Black Lagoon*.

Apart from science fiction, he had equal success with westerns, romances, and detective fiction, writing an amazing total of 180 novels—most of them in a period of just ten years—before his early death in 1960. His work has been translated into nine languages, and continues to be reprinted and read worldwide.

www.ingramcontent.com/pod-product-compliance
Lightning Source LLC
Chambersburg PA
CBHW031420250626
47155CB00004B/1558

* 9 781479 400515 *